The Return of the Ancients
The Aliens Book One

Sherry Derr-Wille

ISBN: 978-1-62420-413-5

Credits

Cover Artist: Designs by Ms G
Edited by Amanda Armstrong

Dedication

To the producers of the Ancient Aliens TV presentation and all the contributors and researchers.

Prologue

"Our people have traveled among the stars since the beginning of recorded history. It was many millennia ago when we learned how to use the time warps and travel to other planets. We did this in our quest for knowledge and allegiance with others like ourselves. In our travels, we came upon the third planet from the sun, or at least that is what the people on this planet called the star they worshiped.

"They called us Gods and were amazed when we built many landing pads for our crafts as well as many fortifications and buildings. We had a good relationship with these people. They worshipped us and in return we taught them many of the skills we'd perfected. These skills were medicine, mathematics, and language, both written and spoken."

Nina looked up from the words of the history book the university had uploaded to her e-reader. "If we taught them so much, why did we have to leave?"

Her father, Dragger, smiled, as he usually did before answering her questions. "There was a war being fought here on Plantas, our home planet, and those who were sent to what the natives called Earth were required to return to fight in the war. We felt we left them well prepared to populate their planet and grow in their knowledge."

"If they have been growing all these years, why are we going back now?"

"Because my darling daughter, we have been sending scouts back over the years to check on their progress. From what they have told us, the people on Earth have reached a point where they are ready for us to return."

Nina felt the cold fingers of fear clutch her heart. "Are you telling me you will be leaving here to go to some unknown planet? Who all is going? Will I ever see you again?"

"Never fear, daughter, the journey is a safe one, much safer than when our ancestors took to the heavens. We have the technology that will make a journey of many light-years in a matter of months by using the time warps. That brings me to the reason I asked you to study the history of the ancients. You are one of our top-ranking accredited scientists. You will be of the utmost importance to our mission. Once we land, we will need someone of your beauty and intelligence to communicate with these people. Through you and the others of our party we will let them know of our peaceful mission."

Nina took a deep breath. "What if I do not want to embark on such a journey?"

Her mother, Moorea, joined the conversation. "I know it is a lot to ask of you, but this is for science, for the continuance of our people and..." Moorea started to cry as she said the words.

"What your mother is trying to say is that many of our people will be making this journey with us. The star that controls our planet is dying out. We've known this for many generations, but our people have not wanted to admit it. Now there is no denying what will eventually happen. Our people will be returning to the planets we worked with in the past and build a future for ourselves. Since we have been to these planets before, we know their atmosphere is compatible with us and we hope we will be welcomed."

Nina watched as her parents left her alone in the study, to return to reading the ancient history of her people. She thought about what her father said about their sun dying out. Throughout her lifetime she'd been told there was a return to the ice age that she read about in the history books. Now she realized it was because the source of their warmth was dying.

She continued to contemplate her future. *Will the people on Earth welcome us or see us as enemies?*

Rather than continue her studies, she dressed to go out. She needed to meet with her friends at the club and see if they knew what her parents were talking about.

~ * ~

As soon as Nina entered the club, she saw Ragnar waiting for her. With all her heart, she prayed he would tell her whatever her father said was untrue. They would not be leaving Plantar and their lives could go on as they had been in the past.

"I assume you have heard of the evacuation of our planet. I have been told to prepare for a journey to Seros," Ragnar greeted her.

Nina's heart sank. Instead of reassurance, Ragnar was confirming what her father and mother told her earlier in the day.

"Seros? Father said we are going to Earth. Can it possibly be true we could be going to separate planets in the Galaxy?"

"I'm afraid so, Nina. Father told me a third of our people are going to Seros, a third to Nalo, and the remaining third to Earth. No matter how many light-years separate us, I will never forget you. Did your father tell you when you will be leaving?"

Nina shook her head, tears forming in her violet eyes. "He told me I should study the history of the ancients. When I questioned him about it, he told me we would be going to Earth. Now you tell me not everyone is going to the same place. This is an outrage. What if I refuse to go with my parents and go with you?"

Ragnar got to his feet and pulled her into his loving embrace. She wanted this security to last forever. To her dismay, he broke their embrace and held her at arm's length. Even though she knew what he was going to say, she wished it could be something else.

"That, my dear, is impossible. My parents are going to the planet where our people started their civilizations. I have to go to Seros just as you have to go to Earth. Your ancestors were the ones to first work with the people there. It is only fitting you would be the people to return and see how the work of your ancestors have progressed."

"Is it true we have sent people to these planets to monitor their progress?"

Ragnar smiled at her question. "It is very true. My brother just returned from a mission to Seros. He told me wonderful stories about the planet. I'm sure you will find you have family who have also traveled to Earth. Your father has sheltered you too much for your own good. He should have told you about these plans years ago. Face it, Nina, you will be embarking on the adventure of your life. I'm looking forward to seeing a new planet and meeting new people."

"I don't want to leave here, leave you. I always thought..."

"You thought wrong. It's not that I don't love you, Nina, but I want adventure in my life. Besides, we're much too young to be committed to one another."

"Men," Nina declared as she stormed out of the club.

~ * ~

Watching her leave tore at Ragnar's heart. He wanted to follow her and tell her how much he loved her, but the die had been cast. Unfortunately, neither of them would be able to change it.

His destiny was at one end of the Galaxy and hers at the other. Last evening he'd told his father about his feelings for Nina. His father was adamant. Their family belonged on Seros, while Nina's family belonged on Earth. It was only right. Nothing either of them could say or do would change the inevitable.

If only I could tell you how I feel about you, Nina. Once we leave this planet, we will not be able see each other again. I swear I will never forget you or the love I feel for you. If I could I would go to Earth with you, but it is impossible. For now, it must be good-bye.

Chapter One

"I think you've lost your mind, Rand Jacobson," Cynthia Adams screamed. "I'm sure you've been watching too many of those Ancient Aliens shows on TV. Why in the hell do you think you need to run off to Peru? If you do, don't expect me to be waiting for you when you get back. I have better things to do than to wait for you to go gallivanting off to South America and play archeologist."

Rand listened to Cyn's rant long enough. "Look, Cyn, you know I'm studying archeology and this is an important project. I'm honored to be asked to go to Peru, especially since I don't have my doctorate yet. As for you waiting for me, I know I'm only your boyfriend of the month. I've been told you are getting cozy with Jack Pearson. I doubt you'll be crying about me leaving for too long. From what I hear Jack will be graduating and going into his father's law practice. He'll be more than happy to take care of you."

"Why you...you bastard. How dare you accuse me of something like looking for a new boyfriend while I'm dating you? Well, since you won't be around I'll need someone who is more stable than you are. I hope you get sunstroke or poisoning from the water at that god-awful dig. Have a nice life, Rand. I'm certain I will."

Before he could stop her, she raised her hand and slapped him hard on the cheek. Rand knew she had a temper, but he didn't expect her to slap him in the face. After she landed her slap to his cheek, she stormed out of his apartment, slamming the door in her wake.

"That didn't go too well, did it?" Rand's roommate, Paul Mathews, said, coming out of the bedroom.

"I didn't expect it to."

"Did you have to throw Jack in her face?"

"Why not? It was Jack who told me she was planning to break things off with me. I just beat her to the punch, is all. As far as I can see

Jack can have Cyn. I hope he can handle her. I thought I'd found heaven on earth when we first got together. It didn't take long to hear all the rumors about her. She's high-maintenance and I can't afford someone like her in my life."

"So, have you heard when we'll be leaving for Peru?"

"I was going to tell you when Cyn showed up. I got the letter today. It says we're going to be leaving a week from Saturday. Do you think you can be ready that soon?"

Paul smiled.

They'd met when they were freshmen in college and formed an immediate friendship. Rand knew he and Paul were going to be roommates as soon as they were able to leave the dorms and live off campus in their junior year. After graduation, they'd both applied to the master's program with the university to pursue their degrees in archaeology. Being able to go on this dig in Peru was a dream come true for both of them.

"If we're leaving in a little over a week, we both have a lot to do," Paul said. "I guess I'll be going out to see my folks this weekend and break the news to them. What about you?"

Rand thought for a moment. He wished he could say he had parents to bid farewell to, but they'd never been in the picture. He'd been taken away from them as a young boy and put in the system. Over the years, he'd been shuffled from family to family until at last he landed in the home of Bridget and Matt Scott. At the time, he was thirteen and very rebellious. Matt was strict, but he was also the one who instilled a love of archaeology in Rand. Even though Matt didn't have a degree, he and Bridget spent two weeks every summer on a dig somewhere in the United States.

Although Bridget and Matt wanted to adopt him, the foster program told them he was too old to give up the surname of his birth parents. They even insinuated it was possible they would, maybe someday, decide they wanted to reconnect with him and wouldn't be able to do so if he no longer carried their name.

The first summer, Rand had been reluctant to go with his new foster parents, but in the end, he fell in love with their summer excursions. Matt awakened a love in Rand he never thought would be possible. With his foster father's guidance, he'd excelled in school. Unfortunately, while he was still in college, Matt contracted pancreatic cancer and passed away within months of the diagnosis. Six months later Bridget passed away. Although the doctors said she had a massive heart attack, Rand knew she died of a broken heart.

I wish I could come home and tell you all about the plans I have for the next few months. I know this dig is one you would love to come on with me. I'm doing this for both of you.

"Earth to Rand. Earth to Rand. Are you here or somewhere off in lala land? You didn't answer my question. What are you planning to do?"

"Sorry about that, Buddy. I think I might go along with you. I don't have anyone to say goodbye to. Hopefully your folks will welcome me with open arms."

"You know they will. Haven't you ever thought about looking up your birth parents?"

Paul's question took him off guard. "You know my background. As far as I'm concerned, Matt and Bridget were my parents. They were the ones who paid for my college and post-grad education. They also left me their entire estate when they died. To be truthful, I wish they were here so I could tell them about this opportunity. They'd love to go on this trip with me. I like to think they're watching over me."

You know we are, Rand. We will be with you all the way on this trip. Something tells me you will get more out of this trip to Peru than you ever expected.

Rand shook his head. He was unsure if he actually heard Matt talking to him within the confines of his mind. He'd heard people talk about hearing from their loved ones once they passed away, but he honestly didn't believe it would ever happen to him.

After hearing Matt's unexpected voice, Rand thought about the people who had given him life. Was it possible they might try to find him someday? If they did, how would he react to them stepping back into his life? He didn't remember his father and barely remembered the mother who had been declared unfit to raise a child. If they did reappear, would he find he had brothers and sisters? The thought of family other than Bridget and Matt was intriguing and at the same time frightening.

"You know the folks will enjoy having you come with me. What are we waiting for? We're done with our classes for the semester, so that means we're free as the birds. You don't have anything holding you here. Cyn is out and adventure is in. I'm more than ready to blow this pop stand. Our lease is up at the end of the month, so why wait to move out?"

"I agree. Since the furniture came with this place, we only have our personal belongings to move out. Hopefully the landlord will give us back our security deposit."

Paul laughed at Rand's suggestion. "He will if we get this place cleaned up. It's not like we have been having tons of wild parties. I think we can have everything cleaned up and packed by the weekend. I'll give Mom a call and let her know to expect us on Sunday."

~ * ~

By Saturday afternoon they were waiting for the landlord to make his inspection. With everything packed in Paul's Jeep they were ready to leave as soon as they got the final approval of the work they'd done.

While Paul would be able to store his vehicle with his parents, Rand didn't have the same option. He'd been relieved when he was able to sell his VW with an ad he'd placed on the bulletin board at the student union. As much as he hated to see his car go to a new owner, he was relieved not to have to pay storage fees for the time they'd be gone.

"I didn't think you'd really go through with this craziness," Cyn called as she came into the apartment.

"I didn't expect to see you today," Rand said, trying to keep the surprise out of his voice. Even though he knew she was ready to dump him, he still harbored feelings for her.

"You don't know how much you hurt me when you decided to take on this crazy project. I was hoping you'd say you'd changed your mind and wanted to be back with me again."

Paul rolled his eyes and Rand knew exactly what he was thinking. Through the grapevine they'd heard how Cyn left their apartment and went directly to Jack's townhouse only to find him there with another girl. It was evident Cyn didn't want to be without a man in her life for any length of time.

"Our plans are made and we're just waiting for the landlord to come over to sign off on our clean up and return our security. You have to understand Cyn, it was over even before I told you about our plans. You'll do fine. I'm sure you and Jack will be very happy."

As though on cue, Cyn broke down and cried. "I went to Jack's place to tell him we could be together and he...he was in bed with another woman. How could he do this to me?"

She threw her arms around Rand's neck and buried her face against his shirt, wetting it with her tears.

Rather than embrace Cyn, as he was certain she wanted, he held up his hands in surrender. "Your dramatics aren't going to change my mind, Cyn. As soon as we're cleared on this place, we're leaving to spend the next week with Paul's parents before we leave for Peru."

Gently, he disentangled himself from her unwanted embrace. He steeled himself for the slap he knew would be coming. Instead, she turned off her tears as though they were controlled with a faucet and hurried to her car. "Have a good life, Randsom Jacobson. I'm sure I will. You don't know what you're giving up. Just don't look for me to be waiting for you when you get back from your little adventure."

She squealed her tires as she pulled out of the parking lot of their apartment building.

The car no more than turned the corner when the landlord pulled in. "A friend of yours?" he asked.

"Not anymore," Rand replied.

It took only a few minutes for the walk through with the landlord. Within the hour, they were on the road driving toward Paul's parents' ranch, their security deposit in hand.

The adventure of their lifetimes had begun.

~ * ~

The plane touched down at the small airport not far from the dig. They were met by Dr. Irvin Clark who told them to call him Irv.

It didn't take them long to make the trip from the airport to the dig and to get settled in. The real work wouldn't begin until Monday morning, so they had time to acquaint themselves with the people they'd be working with for the next several months.

"How far are we from the Nazca Plains?" Rand asked.

"I'm glad you asked. I was hoping to take the two of you up there to see them next weekend. It will give you time to get acclimated to the area. We aren't far from there and it's something you should see. You do understand this is a teaching dig. We have been working it for a long time and the two of you have come highly recommended from the University. Part of the education is taking you to some of the better-known locations in the area. This is something we do with the new arrivals on their first weekend. Who knows, one of these weekends we could get lucky and be contacted by aliens." Irv winked mischievously.

"You're kidding, right?" Rand said, his mind reeling with the possibilities.

"I wish I was. I've seen lots of strange lights in the sky. Some people say there has been a lot of UFO activity in the area over the last couple of years. One never knows what could be happening to us."

Rand was certain it was all something Irv told each new group of students who came to work at the dig. Even so, he wondered if any of it could be true.

It would be a dream come true if it did happen. Matt would be thrilled to hear about anything supernatural happing during my stay here.

These are exciting times, Rand. You will be seeing the beginning of a new age and you will be on the cutting edge of everything. I always knew you were destined for great things. Now the fates have confirmed it. How I wish I could be there with you, but of course my spirit is always by your side. You know Bridget and I have always loved you as our own. Make us proud.

The sound of Matt's voice was comforting as well as confusing. What could he know from beyond the grave about what the future held?

Chapter Two

The day of departure came faster than any of them hoped. Nina was saddened by the fact Ragnar would be going to Seros while she was destined to go to Earth. Even worse, her best friend, Tarena, as well as the man she was to marry, Gardo, were destined to go to Nalo.

"How can we all be going in different directions?" Tarena questioned as they gathered at the launching pad. "I'll never see either of you again."

"Don't think about it that way," Ragnar said consolingly. "Think of all the new people you'll be meeting. This is an adventure and that's how we have to look at it. We're all young and when we get ready to go out on our own, we'll find partners other than the ones we thought we'd be with during our youth. The same goes for friendships. None of us will ever forget about the others, but eventually we would have gone our separate ways. I've seen it happen with my siblings and it's inevitable."

"I know you're right," Nina agreed. "It's just hard to say goodbye to my lifelong friends."

Tarena continued to cry uncontrollably until her parents finally came to coax her to get into the ship that would be launched into the unknown. "Oh, Daddy, I don't want to leave Nina and Ragnar behind."

"We've been over this before, Daughter. This is not your decision to make. The elders have told us who will go where, and you will follow their decree."

Tarena's sobs subsided as she embraced first Ragnar before turning to Nina. "We've been best friends forever and I'll never forget either of you. Thank the One God that Grato will be going to Nalo with me, even if he won't be on the same ship."

"You know we won't forget you. It doesn't matter how many light-years separate us, we will never be further away from each other than our memories."

Nina wished she meant the words she spoke. She'd done her crying in the privacy of her room in her parents' home. Last night she promised herself she wouldn't make a spectacle of herself on the day of departure.

She and Ragnar waved to Tarena as she got into the ship her family would be using on their journey. The rockets fired and the ships destined to leave from this destination took off into space. She knew other ships were being launched from launching pads around the planet for Nalo.

"One down," Ragnar declared, as he pulled Nina into a tight embrace. "I know we'll both miss Tarena, but she's starting out on an adventure of a lifetime, just like we are."

Nina bit her lip to keep the tears at bay. "She will be with the man she wants to marry once they land on Nalo. You and I will be separated for the remainder of our lives. How can you be so accepting of this? I don't know if I'll ever be as certain about our journey as you are. There is a possibility none of us could ever make it to where we are going. What happens if we are met with hostilities or something goes wrong during the flight?"

"You can't think that way, Nina. I told you my brother has traveled to Seros in the past and it was perfectly safe. Didn't your father tell you the same things about the expeditions we've sent to Earth?"

"He did, but Nalo is the unknown. I haven't heard of any flights going there. Have you?"

Ragnar shook his head. "I asked my father about that and he knows nothing about Nalo either. I think the people in Tarena's group are very close-mouthed about everything. It could be Nalo is as much a paradise as either Seros or Earth. I've tried to ask others these same questions and no one wants to talk about it. I worry about that part of the exploratory group going to Nalo, but I can't dwell on it. I'm excited and you should be too."

Nina nodded. "I am starting to get excited about the trip we're about to make. I just hate leaving our home as well as my friends, but the unknown does intrigue me."

Before Ragnar could answer, his father called him to board the ship that would be taking him far away from her. With a quick but loving kiss, he turned from her and went to join his family on the second ship to be launched into the unknown.

The sound of the rockets firing off was deafening, but once the ships carrying Ragnar and his family disappeared into the stratosphere, Nina looked around her world. It suddenly seemed terribly empty and dead. Knowing the eventual fate of the world in which she'd lived her entire life made her anxious to find the ship where her parents and other members of their party were already waiting for her.

~ * ~

Nina looked up from the navigational computer. Just yesterday she'd seen planet Earth appear on the screen. At the beginning of the journey, she'd been heartbroken at the thought of leaving Ragnar, the man she always hoped she'd marry, as well as her best friend, Tarena, behind. The very thought of them going to the other ends of the Galaxy was devastating, but messages Ragnar continued to send through their communications officers told her he was excited about the journey. Yesterday morning she'd received a message they were about to arrive on Seros. He was certain his family and the remainder of his party would be welcomed and revered.

It bothered her to know there had been no communication from the first delegation to leave their planet. It was entirely possible Tarena and all the people with her had not survived the journey to get to Nalo.

Nina prayed Earth would bring the same results for them as Ragnar expected to find on Seros. Even the translators her father insisted be implanted didn't mean their arrival would be heralded in the same way. She had apprehensions about the inhabitants of Earth.

In the histories of the ancients, she'd read about the backward peoples who populated the planet. Her ancestors educated them at various places around the globe. The modern names seemed alien to her. Egypt, Turkey, England, Europe, Thailand, China and their destination of Peru.

On the day she left with her family and other people from their planet for Peru, six other ships departed for the various places where they once brought the people the knowledge of medicine, language, architecture and mathematics. They'd traveled through the time warp together and now were getting ready to descend to the face of the planet en masse.

"You look worried, Daughter," Dragger said.

He placed his hand on her shoulder and studied the navigational screen.

"What if we are not considered Gods when we arrive on Earth? What if we are seen as enemies rather than friends? I read in the more recent histories of how a ship from another planet landed in a place the Earthlings called New Mexico and the occupants were killed. What if the people we meet want to kill us in the same manner?"

"The time was not right. These people have become more enlightened. They are expecting our return. We will not be seen as Gods as were our ancestors, but with this new generation, they will be accepting us as we are. We are but mortal men and women with advanced intelligence who helped to shape their world thousands of years ago. You will see, the times have changed and so have the humans we helped to mold into what they are today. We will be revered and accepted into their society. I saw the communication you received from Ragnar. We too will be as warmly received by the people of Earth as his family will be on Seros."

"What about the people who went to Nalo? We've heard nothing from them."

"That worries me as well. It is possible there was problem with the time warp. I tried to talk to some of the people headed there, but none of them wanted to talk about it. I have a feeling their explorations to Nalo haven't gone as well as those we've launched to Earth and Seros. I fear they knew they were leaving our home for their ultimate deaths. I grieve for them, but the die was cast by not only us but also by the elders."

~ * ~

Ragnar stared at the sterile white interior of the hospital room where he had been taken to be studied like a lab animal.

The adulation they'd received when they first arrived soon ended. As he was enjoying the acceptance, when the people of Seros turned on them and treated them as hostiles. As a result, he'd watched as his parents as well as his siblings were murdered. In the fight, only he survived from this portion of the mission. He prayed the missions sent to other areas of the planet fared better than they did.

Thinking of the other missions brought thoughts of Nina. He thanked the One God for separating them. He couldn't have stood watching her die as he had his family. He prayed Earth would be more accepting of her arrival than Seros had been of theirs.

Coming to Seros was a mistake. He shouldn't have ever agreed to make this planet his home. He prayed the other landing parties were more successful and hopefully his people would be able to survive. He knew survival on his home planet would be impossible, but he doubted it would happen here.

While he continued to contemplate the future of his people, two more scientists entered the room.

"What do you want of us?" the first scientist asked.

As he had before he assessed the man who now approached him, he knew if he were able to stand up they could be able to look each other in the eye. In a fight they would be equals. With him immobilized on the table, he was at a disadvantage.

"You ask me the same question every time you come in and the answers are always the same. Our planet is dying. Since our ancestors established your civilization, we have returned as the ancestors promised many thousands of years ago. We have studied your people. We thought you were advanced enough to accept our people and allow us to assimilate into your society. We have not come to make war. Instead we come in peace to see for ourselves how well you have fared since our departure."

A young woman wearing a lab coat entered the room. It was the first time he'd seen her and for a moment he thought she looked like Nina.

"Leave us alone," she demanded of the two scientists. "I want to talk to this man without any of you here. I also turned off the microphones so don't think you will be able listen to what we are talking about."

Once the scientists left the room, she walked to the gurney where he'd been strapped down for over a day. "I am so sorry you have received such despicable treatment."

He watched as she undid the bindings holding him flat on the cart.

"I've just been told about you and ordered everyone to leave us alone. I also know of the fate of your companions. Believe me, this is unacceptable behavior and I apologize. I've brought you some clothes and we will be moving to more comfortable accommodations."

"There were other ships that landed with us. Do you know their fates?"

The woman smiled and looked sincere. "I am pleased to tell you they were greeted more hospitably than your party. They have been welcomed and treated with all respect. When I learned of your arrival I came as quickly as I could. My name is Geni, for now that is all you need to know. What should I call you?"

"I'm called Ragnar. My family name is too difficult to pronounce so for now Ragnar is enough. I came here with my parents as well as my brothers. They along with the other members of my crew were murdered by your people. I am the only survivor and have been treated like a lab animal. I am a human being, not a science project."

The woman handed him clothes but did not give him the privacy he craved to get dressed. He decided she'd already seen his naked body, as had everyone else who came into the room, so embarrassment was nothing he should worry about.

Although the matter of dress was alien to him, he found each piece of clothing fit as though it had been made especially for him. "These clothes are very comfortable, but what happened to the garments I was wearing when they brought me here?"

"I'm afraid these idiots confiscated your clothing and took them for testing. In the process, they were destroyed. I assure you whatever things you brought with you on your ship haven't been disturbed. It's only because the people here were afraid to enter it. My associates have taken over. Everything you brought with you has been inventoried and taken into protective custody for you."

"Where are you taking me?"

Geni smiled. "You will be coming with me to my estate. There you will meet with the top men and women in the field of our space program. Your input will be most welcomed. Next month we will be traveling to a world counsel that will be meeting to discuss how you can help us to understand the worlds beyond this one. As for your companions, you were not the only survivor. I have already rescued the other members of your party. Some have extensive injuries, so I have brought in the best medical personnel we have at our disposal to care for them."

"How can they still be alive when I saw my entire family murdered by the soldiers who greeted us? Why would you be taking me to a world counsel? My expertise is not in space navigation. I was merely a passenger on the flight. I am afraid I would have nothing to contribute."

"The peacekeepers responsible for this atrocity have been arrested. Those you thought were murdered have been brought back to life. We have an exceptional medical team who have had great success in resurrecting the dead. Your loved ones are receiving the best medical care available on this planet. When I speak of the world counsel, I mean all of your entire party will be going."

Although Ragnar was unsure about going with Geni, he had no other options. For the first time since his capture he wasn't restrained, nor was he naked. He decided trust was better than being examined and being asked the same questions with no one believing his answers.

As they left the hospital room, he saw the look of disbelief on the faces of the scientists who had been coming into his room for the past day. He knew they disapproved of Geni taking him from their care with no restraints whatsoever.

Outside, the air was fresh and not filtered as it had been in the hospital. Rather than the pollution he'd become used to on Plantas, it was scented with the soft aroma of flowers and freshly mowed grass. The vehicle she brought him to was a hovercar much like the one he owned before leaving his home.

They sped through the streets, passing other vehicles before leaving the city and venturing out into the countryside. Although Ragnar still had reservations about where he was being taken, this was the only option open to him. He had to trust Geni even if the thought of it frightened him.

After an hour of travel, they arrived at her estate. The building she called home was magnificent. It rivaled the palace where the ruling class resided on his home planet.

"You must be a member of the ruling class."

Geni laughed at his statement. "Hardly. This estate belonged to my grandparents. They were very wealthy but it didn't come down to me. I inherited the property, but I work for my living. I'm a government employee making a little-above-average wage."

Ragnar thought of his position at home. From what she said, it was much like what Geni did on this planet. It was possible they could become friends, but only time would tell if he would be accepted by these people.

Chapter Three

"Do you see that, Nina?" Dragger asked, as he pointed to the navigational screen.

Nina stared at the screen. The flat plane below them was strewn with pictographs of animals as well as geometric drawings.

"This is where our ancestors landed when they first came to this planet. This is where we are meant to return. For now, you must prepare for our landing. All of the readings say the air is safe for us to breathe. We are home at last."

~ * ~

Rand loved the tedious work at the dig. After the first week, he'd learned more than he ever did when going on digs with Matt and Bridget. He could tell Paul was less enthusiastic about the digging and sifting as his area of expertise was in the scientific experiments such as carbon dating.

"Are you boys ready to go on an excursion?" Irv asked when he joined them in the mess hall for breakfast on Saturday morning.

"If you're talking about going to the Nazca Plains, I'm all for it," Rand replied. "I was wondering, am I the only one who saw those strange lights in the sky last night?"

"No, you're not. It's the main reason I want to get up there today. One of the townspeople said they saw a strange craft land last night, but they were afraid to go up there and investigate."

"Are you afraid to investigate?" Paul asked.

"In a way I guess I am, but this is something that has been predicted for many years. I'm more excited than frightened. Of course, if you're not up to this..."

Rand and Paul exchanged glances. Rand could tell Paul was apprehensive, but the words he heard Matt say within the confines of his mind made the thought of being one of the first people to make contact with the aliens exciting. "I'm all in," he said confidently.

Paul nodded, but his reluctance was evident.

~ * ~

"We have landed," Dragger announced. "It is time for us to set foot on the soil of our new home."

Nina undid the safety harness holding her to the reclining seat at the control panel. She could hear the others getting ready to depart from the ship. The thought of danger ran through her mind, but she dismissed it. She trusted her father and as the pilot of the ship, he knew what he was doing in bringing them here.

She allowed her parents and the elders to leave the ship, before Nina and the younger members of their party followed suit.

As soon as she stepped foot on this alien planet, she caught her breath. A party of men were approaching them and she feared the worst. To her surprise, these men were no taller than the women of her race.

"We come in peace," Dragger announced.

The older man from the group took a step forward. She tried to see if he carried a weapon. To her relief he held his hands out as though welcoming them.

"You are expected. I am Irv Clark and I welcome you to the Nazca Plains. It is said this area was once the home of the ancient aliens. All of the stories told by the native people of this area say in the future the Gods will return."

"I am Dragger and we are not Gods, merely mortal men who many years ago, learned the secrets of travel through the Galaxy. We have always known the ancients had intended to return. Until now, our people have not been inclined to make the journey. You see our planet, Plantas, is dying and through the writings of the ancients, we knew it was time to return to the planets where we once visited in order to pass on the knowledge to the inhabitants. I bring with me my wife, daughter, and friends. We want only to live in peace and co-mingle with the people of your planet."

"You said planets. Are you saying there is more than one planet you have visited in the past?"

"Our ancestors visited three planets. One third of our population returned to each of these places. We came here, whilst others went to Seros and Nalo. We know those who landed on Seros were welcomed but we have not had contact from those who went to Nalo."

Nina watched as the leader of the small group took count of the number of people who just landed on his planet.

"Surely there were more people on your planet than the number in your party. Even if they represent one third of your population..."

Her father held up his hand for silence, cutting the man off in mid-sentence. "There were many ships sent to your planet. We will be landing in various locations in the same manner as we have landed here. We pray we will all be welcomed as you are welcoming us."

Among the party of strangers who were greeting them, Nina noticed two young men. One of them towered over his companion. It was possible he stood at a height that possibly rivaled that of her father. She assumed they were close to her age. The one with hair the color of straw looked as though he was frightened of the people they were meeting. The other one with hair as red as the sunset on a perfect day carried a different aura. He was the taller of the two and perhaps her assumption about his age was wrong and he was but a youth who had not yet reached his mature height. Despite his youth, he seemed to be anxious to step forward and introduce himself but deferred to the older man in his party.

Nina heard her father say her name and assumed he was introducing those who made the journey with them to the strangers. She immediately brought her mind to the present and hoped the man would introduce the other men who came with him.

One by one he introduced each of the twelve men in his party. She watched intently as each of them stepped forward to shake her father's hand. This strange custom must be one of greeting and friendship for these people. Finally, the man named Irv Clark indicated the two young men who caught her attention.

"This is Paul Mathews," he said, indicating the frightened man. "This is Randsom Jacobson."

While the man named Paul hung back, Randsom eagerly stepped

forward. "I am pleased to meet you, Sir. I was told something important would happen while I was on this dig. I never expected to be granted such a great honor. I hope we will become friends. That said, my friends call me Rand."

"You are a brave young man, Rand. I am also honored to meet you. If I were in your position, I don't know if I would be as excited about welcoming them to our coming as you are. You must be a great man among your people."

Nina watched as Rand's face started to become pink with embarrassment. "I'm just a college student working on my master's degree. My degree will be in archaeology making this time of working on this dig very important in my education."

Perhaps he is mature. Her internal thoughts brought a sense of peace as well as one of excitement. Unable to hold her tongue Nina stepped forward. "This young man is intriguing, Father. I would suggest he become our companion as well as teacher in this new land."

"My daughter makes sense. She is our Science Officer and I trust her judgement. Would you be interested in joining our party and helping us adjust to our new surroundings?"

She watched as Rand's embarrassment turned to a joyous smile. "I would have to get permission from Dr. Clark. He's my boss and I need..."

"You don't need my permission, Rand," Irv interrupted. "These people are honored guests and I see there is no reason to fear our visitors. They have chosen you and I feel their choice is well made. That said, you will have to talk to the press, because this will be big news. It's not anything we can keep on the QT. Do you think you can handle this? By no means do I intend to allow you to do this on your own. I will be more than willing to help you in any way I can."

Rand's smile became even wider than Nina thought was possible.

"In that case, my answer is yes. It will take some time to find appropriate accommodations for you. If you will be comfortable in your ship while the arrangements are made, I will return with suitable transportation for you and your fellow passengers."

"I would enjoy accompanying you, Rand," Nina said, even though she knew her father would think she was too impetuous. "Would that meet with your approval, Father?"

"This is completely unorthodox, but I trust you to do what is in our best interests. I do worry about others of your people. Do you think we will be safe remaining in this area, Rand?"

Nina watched as the young man looked to his superior for guidance.

"We'll be happy to stay here with our guests while you and Nina go back to the dig to make the necessary arrangements. I suggest you talk to Stacey in the main office. I think she'll be able to steer you in the right direction. While you're there, contact the authorities and make arrangements for food to be sent up here pronto. In your absence, I'll converse with Dragger and the others about the meanings of the lines. I'm anxious to become enlightened by our visitors."

Rand stepped forward and reached for Nina's hand. As soon as he made contact with her, she felt a tingle go through her body. The only other time she'd felt something like it was when she was with Ragnar. *Am I being unfaithful to Ragnar? I don't want to be, but this man is special. I pray Ragnar will find someone on Seros. I know he will never be coming back to me.*

~ * ~

Rand stood in awe of the people who descended from the craft before him. At six feet seven inches he'd always been considered a freak. At every school he attended they insisted he should be playing basketball. He'd played in middle school and learned he was neither good at the sport nor that he liked it. Thus, ended his sporting career, giving him more time to concentrate on his studies.

Today for one of the first times in his life, he stood next to someone taller than himself. The older man, Dragger, had a good six inches on him, if not more. All of the stories pertaining to the Sky Gods said they were giants. Seeing this man, as well as his other people, he now knew the stories were true. To the smaller humans who populated the primitive areas they were, indeed, giants.

As soon as he shook Dragger's hand, he could sense these people were sincere in their offer of coming in peace. From the corner of his eye, he saw the most beautiful woman he'd ever seen. Her dark hair was long and her eyes were a piercing violet. She put the girls he'd known all his life to shame.

Behind him he could feel Paul's nervousness, even though he felt no need to be either nervous nor afraid of these visitors who came from the sky. They were definitely human and in no way Gods, but he could understand how things could have been misunderstood by the very first people they contacted.

~ * ~

Rand could hardly believe what happened in the last few hours. He never expected to be one of the first people to make contact with the alien visitors. He certainly never thought the beautiful young woman, who had been identified as the daughter of the captain of the ship, Nina, would ask for him to take care of them personally. *I hope I'm able make the right decisions.*

You will know what to do. Bridget and I will guide you. I told you great things were in your future and what could possibly be greater than this?

Matt's unbidden voice calmed Rand as he took the keys to one of the Jeeps they'd used to come up the mountain to see the Nazca Plains.

"I'm sorry this isn't an elegant form of transportation, Miss Nina."

"Please do not apologize. I can see this is a very isolated area. I would not expect anything less practical. Can you tell me about yourself, Rand?"

"I'd rather hear about you. I'm nothing special."

"I think you are. I can tell by looking at you, you are descended from the ancients."

Her statement bewildered him. "How can you tell something like that?"

"The first thing I noticed was your height. If I am not mistaken, you are left-handed, are you not?"

Rand took his time in answering as he started the truck. "Yes, I'm left-handed. What does that have to do with anything?"

"Among my people, being left-handed is a common trait. I have researched your people on our trip here and have come to the conclusion being left-handed is a sign you are descended from those of our people who first came here. What do you know of your ancestry?"

Rand shook his head, hoping the gesture meant the same thing to Nina as it did to him. "My parents weren't good to me. I was taken away from them when I was very young. I was sent to several foster homes from the age of three to thirteen. That's when I went to the home of the people I think of as my parents. They cared for me and raised me as their own. They're gone now, but I feel their presence with me every day."

"I can understand you feeling the presence of the ones you loved. What I do not understand is why parents would not be good to their children."

"From what I was told my father was never around and my mother enjoyed drugs, alcohol and men more than she did being a mother. Everyone says it is best. If she would have kept me, either she or one of the men she brought home to warm her bed, would have done me harm."

He could hear her try to choke back tears. "That is the saddest thing I have ever heard. On my planet, children are revered. They are loved and cherished. As for alcohol and drugs, I am assuming you speak of spirits. We have them also, but they are never abused. The drugs you speak of are only used by our people for their healing properties. They are not anything anyone would think of using without being under the care of a healer. What I do not understand is the part about her bringing home men. I have read about women who were prostitutes, but they no longer live among us."

"About the drugs and alcohol, it used to be the same here, but things changed. That is the dark side of life here, but hopefully your coming will help to elevate our people. As for prostitutes, on this planet what they do is referred to as the oldest profession. I am sure that is how my mother supported us, but I can't say for sure. I only know what I was told in the various foster homes where I grew up. Changing the subject, you spoke of having physicians. Do you have any medical personnel with you?"

"You have changed the subject, but yes, we do have a healer with us. My uncle studied medicine and was assigned to our ship. Each of our ships carry a healer. Just as each has a Science Officer, a captain, and many others, each with specific skills."

"I didn't see any children. Are they with you or with one of the other ships?"

"We do have children with us, but they were told to remain hidden until we were certain of the reception we would receive."

Before Rand could probe with further questions, he pulled into the area occupied by the dig. As he parked the Jeep, he thought about the possibilities of what could happen once news of the arrival of Nina and the rest of her people hit the media. In his mind's eye, he could see a frenzy of activity including the news media and possibly military intervention. He was grateful it was the weekend, meaning the dig was relatively quiet. Most of the volunteers were enjoying a weekend of no work and perhaps went into the nearest town to let off steam.

A glance over toward Nina told him her appearance here would be likely to raise more than one eyebrow. As well as being very beautiful, her manner of dress was more formal than the khaki shorts and camp shirts worn by both the men and women who worked the dig. Her body was incased in a long flowing white robe. It looked as though it was made in a seamless manner of a material unknown on earth. He also knew the violet eyes that entranced him would be an oddity among the people at the dig. It was bad enough that she stood within just a few inches of his height. Most of the women at the dig were much shorter.

"I'll ask you to wait in the Jeep for a bit while I go in and talk to the secretary."

"I am under the assumption you do not want me to cause a stir. I have no problem in waiting for you. Your Earth is very interesting. I was especially thrilled to see the glyphs at the landing field. My father tells me the ancients orchestrated them. I feel as though I have come home."

"Good. I shouldn't be long."

Rand left the keys in the Jeep and went into the office. As soon as he stepped into the air conditioned office, he could tell something had everyone in an uproar. Stacey was glued to both the phone and the Internet.

"Oh Rand, I'm so glad to see you. Is Dr. Clark with you?"

"No, why?"

"The whole world is in turmoil. There have been many landings of space craft all over the globe. There are sightings in Turkey, Egypt, England, Thailand and China. In England and Egypt, there are armed militia but the scientists from Turkey, Thailand and China are calling for people to be calm and welcome these visitors. What if...?"

"They are already here, Stacey. I have their Science Officer with me and Dr. Clark is out at the landing site meeting with the elders. Dr. Clark said you would be able to help me with housing for these people. He also said you'd be able to work with the media for the press release. We want to be careful not to bring about an uproar."

Before Stacey could answer, Nina came into the office. "I do not mean to interrupt, but my father says finding accommodations for us would be too much to ask. Until we come to some concrete decisions, we will be more than comfortable in the buildings our people will be constructing."

"H—How have been in communication with your father? He's back at the Nazca Plains and that's an hour's drive from here."

Nina smiled. "Do not your people speak through their minds?"

"Are you talking about telepathic communication?" Stacey said, getting up from her desk.

Nina turned her attention to the other woman in the room. Her face brightened and her smile was genuine. "Ah, I can see why the ancestors found the Earthly women so beautiful. I've often wondered why they would mate with those who are not of our race. Gazing on your beauty, I can better understand the thinking of the ancestors. They came to this place without their women and I can only imagine the physical need they had."

"Are—are you saying the myths are true?" Rand stammered.

"I cannot believe you are surprised. Everyone knows people from other planets have been visiting your planet for centuries. I am told our explorers come here often not only seeking gold but also because of the beautiful females. That is why I asked you about your heritage. It is quite possible one of our explorers is the man who impregnated your mother with you. You told me you do not know anything of your father. What I don't understand is your lack of communication with your mother. She must have been very beautiful to have caught the eye of one of our people."

Rand was unable to form an answer to the statements she was making. He'd been told his mother wasn't certain which of her encounters left her pregnant. Because of her drug and alcohol abuse, she'd been an unfit mother, sending him into 'the system' at an early age. If at the time she became pregnant, he could envision her having casual sex with many partners without knowing which one might have been the father of her child.

"Is there any way I could learn if this is true?" he finally asked.

"I already know it is true. As I said earlier, you are left-handed as well as having great height and those with this trait are connected to the ancients rather from the beginning of time or from a more recent contact. My mother could explain it better to you. She, like me, is a Science officer, but she has much more education than I do."

"You—you really are a—a..." Stacey began.

Nina held up her hand for silence. "I am a modern-day space traveler, as are all of our people. A third of our population has been sent to your planet so our people will not die with our world. My name is Nina. By what are you called?"

Rand could see the hint of a blush creeping into Stacey's cheeks. Was it possible she was embarrassed to be one of the first people to make Nina's acquaintance?

"I'm Stacey Petersen and I'm very pleased to be one of the first people to meet you."

She held out her hand, but instead of shaking hands, Nina stepped forward to embrace Stacey and kiss her on both cheeks.

"The honor is mine. I do have a question for you, Stacey. Why is it all of the people we have met here have two names?"

Rand thought it was strange for Nina to be asking questions of Stacey and not him, but he held his tongue and waited for Stacey's answer.

"The second name is our surname. It tells who our parents are. My mother was Norma Daykin but when she married my father, Vernon Petersen, she took his last name. All of my siblings have the same last name."

"I do not understand why the woman takes the name of the man when women are so much more intelligent. On my planet, the women are, or should I say were equal in every way to the men. We too have surnames, but they are rarely used as they fell out of fashion many eons ago. They are also very difficult to pronounce as they are in the ancient language of our people. If we did use them, it would be that of our mothers as it is from their bodies every person alive comes from. In the scientific community, this is common practice, but among the people who practice medicine, they follow the same practice as you, but not among friends."

Rand could hardly believe his ears although he had heard of other matriarchal societies. Didn't she just say that men were the space travelers? Why not send the women?

"I've always thought women were far superior to men," Stacey teased. "This proves it."

"Okay, you two, I've had enough male bashing for one day. What we need to do is to make arrangements for our guests. We need transportation from the plains, accommodations, to say nothing about press releases and food to be taken up to them."

"I told you the accommodations were not necessary. Were you not listening to me? I guess men are the same no matter where in the universe they come from."

"We weren't bashing you, Rand," Stacey said.

Rand could tell she was trying hard not to laugh at him.

"We were just stating a fact. I will contact the backers of the dig as well as the government officials. Why don't you two go down to the mess hall and get something to eat? I should have answers for you by the time you return."

"Stacey makes sense. I am hungry. Although we have enough food stores on our ship, I was much too excited to be able to eat this morning when I first saw Earth on my navigational screen."

"What do your people eat?"

"Before we embarked on this journey, we ate fresh fruits and vegetables as well as fresh meat from the local marketplaces. We could not bring these things with us so our scientists have been working for many years to perfect the nutriment pills we brought with us."

Rand wrinkled his nose. "I don't think I would be satisfied with having to eat nothing but pills. We can either have sandwiches, salads or both at the mess hall."

"You two go on. I'll be busy here. Is it possible you could bring me back a sandwich and maybe some chips? I've got water in the office refrigerator."

Rand nodded, figuring it was the least he could do.

"Before we go to this mess hall as you call it, do you think it would be possible for me to dress in the same manner as you do, Stacey? I fear I would be looked upon as being different if I were to enter this place dressed in the manner of my people."

"I should have thought of this before. Why don't you take over and read what the Internet is saying about the arrival of Nina's people, while we go to the back office and get her something more appropriate to wear, Rand?"

Rand nodded his head and watched as the two women left him alone in the reception area. Rather than stand around looking like an idiot, he sat down at Stacey's desk. He was immediately drawn to the computer and the live news feed from all over the world. In the more remote areas the news showed people approaching the visitors, much in the same manner as he and his companions approached them hours earlier. In England, near Stonehenge, reporters along with military surrounded the ship. As he watched, King William was brought to the site via a limousine.

Interested in this new twist to the story, Rand turned up the sound on the computer. He was amazed to hear the exchange between the king and the newcomers. It seemed strange to hear the aliens speaking in a precise British accent which mimicked King William's manner of speech perfectly.

"Anything new on the computer?" Stacey asked as they two women entered the room.

Rand looked up to see a completely different-looking Nina than the elegant princess he met hours earlier. "King William has come to greet the newcomers. It looks like the military is standing down. There is something strange though, Nina. How is it you sound as though you've been speaking English your entire life and the people from the craft that landed in England speak with a perfect British accent?"

Nina's eyes sparkled with mischief as though she knew a secret, which she was about to impart. "Our language is much different from yours but we are all equipped with translators. It is a chip that is imbedded behind our right ear. With this we are able to not only understand everything you are saying but we can speak a language foreign to our own. We all have them implanted at birth. That way, no matter to whom we are speaking we can not only communicate but understand everything being said no matter what language our companions are speaking."

"Why would you have something like this put in at birth?" Stacey asked. "Do you travel through space often?"

"Those among us who are trained explorers are the only ones who travel through space. We knew of the translators from the time we could understand but were given no reason why. Only now we know why this was being done. Our planet, Plantas, is dying and the people from it have need to disperse and go to three separate planets in the universe. Without the translators, we would not be able to communicate with the people we would be encountering."

Rand was speechless. This invasion of the planet Earth by these aliens, although predicted, was certainly going to throw a monkey wrench into the workings of every country and populace.

Chapter Four

Ragnar marveled at the world he was seeing as Geni sped through the countryside. The sky wasn't a brilliant lavender like it was back home. Instead it was pink, perhaps because of the red sun shining brightly in the sky.

"Your sky is very different from ours."

"I have been told the sky is different from planet to planet. Wait until you see the night sky. Not only do we have millions of stars, we have two beautiful moons. One of them is green and the other purple. One rises in the east and sets in the west, the other rises in the north and sets in the south. Our sun rises in the west and sets in the east. We love our beautiful sun and moons."

He also marveled at the color of the foliage. Rather than the brilliant shades of blue on his home planet, the colors ranged from russet to orange. Flowers of various colors bloomed everywhere.

"I was told Seros is a beautiful planet. I never expected to see something like this."

"What is your home world like?" Geni asked.

Ragnar took a deep breath in order to remember what home looked like. "The sky is lavender during the day and a dark violet at night. The foliage is in shades of blue and the flowers are mostly either white or purple. We have two suns and three moons. It's very different from here."

"Why have you come to Seros?" Geni asked.

"You must know what I've been telling everyone. It is the truth. Our planet, Plantas, is dying and so one third of our population have come here. One third has gone to a planet called Earth and the other third has been sent to Nalo. Our contingent came here because our ancient ancestors were here many thousands of years ago and helped to colonize this planet. We have been monitoring your planet and watched as you have progressed through the ages. To be truthful, my brother was here within the last turnings of the months. He has assured us we would be able to thrive here. That is why I was so shocked when open hostilities broke out against us."

Ragnar could see tears forming in Geni's golden eyes. "I am so sorry to tell you this, but my father is the head of the Military. I followed a different path and have studied astrology as well as medical science. Our scientists have been predicting your arrival for many generations. I have always told my father about this but he has been adamant the coming of anyone from other planets would signal the end of our people. I am ashamed to say it was he who ordered the attack on your people. I can only thank God for the advancements we have made in medicine to save the lives of those who were attacked."

"You mentioned God. Do your people believe in God?"

"There are many different religions but it is my belief they are all structured around the same God."

Ragnar smiled at her comment. "Our people have been called Gods on every planet we have colonized. We know, from the ancient writings, the One God ordered these journeys many thousands of years ago. We pray to the One God and know of his significance in our lives. He is the same God here, on Nalo and on Earth."

"I am so pleased to know the things I have believed all my life are real and the truth. For now, we have reached our destination and my superiors are waiting to meet with you."

Nina looked at herself in the reflection glass, or as Stacey called it a mirror. Even though the clothing provided to her were far different from the robes she, as well as all the women of her people wore, they were comfortable.

"What are these clothing pieces called?" she asked.

"This is a camp shirt," Stacey said, indicating the piece of clothing covering the upper part of Nina's body. "The shorts are called khakis. They're more practical for working on the dig. We all wear work boots, rather than the sandals you were wearing, more for protection than for anything else."

"I like the shirt and the shorts, but the boots are very constricting on my feet. I can see the practicality of them though. This is a very harsh planet. I was expecting more vegetation. This seems like a desert."

"It's called a high desert because we are high up in the mountains. It is a harsh land, but don't judge the entire planet on this location. Below us are jungles, rivers and lakes. It is a very diverse landscape."

Nina nodded her head, taking in the information Stacey was so generous in imparting to her. Already she saw so many differences between her home and this planet. The sky on her home planet was lavender during the day and deep violet at night. Here the sky was a beautiful pale blue with white puffy clouds and only one sun. When they prepared for their arrival the night before she noticed the night sky was black and glistened with a multitude of stars, the biggest difference being this planet had only one moon. It would all take getting used to.

When they stepped back into the office where Rand waited for them, she noticed the look of approval on his face.

"Wow," he declared. "As much as I liked seeing you in the robes you were wearing when you arrived, this outfit is a knockout."

"Knockout?" Nina questioned. "Don't know what this expression means. The translator tells me knockout means to render someone unconscious."

Rand laughed at her. "I'm sorry, 'knockout' is slang meaning you look great. I tend to forget the difference between proper English and the slang we use in our everyday lives. I'll try not to confuse you in the future."

"If you were to come to Plantas, you would be just as surprised when we use slang in our daily speech."

In the background she could hear something ringing and she turned at the sound. It surprised her to see Stacey pick up a strange looking instrument and put it to her ear. Nina tried not to listen in on the conversation Stacey was having until she held out the instrument to Rand.

"It's Dr. Clark. He wants to talk to you."

Her extraordinary hearing could pick up what Dr. Clark was saying now that Rand held the instrument to his ear.

"Are there any reporters there yet, Rand? From what we've picked up on the Internet the whole world has gone bonkers over these landings ."

"Nothing here, yet," Rand replied. "I just saw that the military stood down in England, though. I praise King William for defusing the situation."

"If we're lucky you'll miss the press. Tell Stacey not to say anything to anyone about what's going on here. Once you bring Nina back, we'll come up with a plan."

"Yes, Sir, we're almost ready to leave. Nina and I just have to get something to eat. While we go to the mess hall, I'll have Stacey make arrangements to have food sent up to your location."

"Don't bother with that. Dragger assures me they have enough provisions to survive. They also have started building accommodations. It's the most fascinating thing I've ever seen. They have already put up a multi-story structure. It's like magic. Dragger tells me it was how the ancients built the stone structures we have wondered about for centuries."

Nina quit listening. She knew what her people were capable of doing. Just from the short time she'd been with Rand and Stacey, she'd come to realize the inhabitants of Earth weren't as advanced as her people. Perhaps that was why her father and the others insisted on coming here at this time.

As soon as the thought crossed her mind, she chastised herself. It was possible these people weren't ready for them to return to the planet they'd helped to colonize but her people had no other option. Plantas was dying and they needed to survive at all costs.

Ragnar marveled at the sheer size of the building Geni called her estate. It reminded him of the high-rise apartment buildings of his home, only it was laid down on the ground.

"This is your home?" he asked in astonishment.

"Yes, it is. Is your home not like this?"

"Hardly. The size is about the same, only instead of being on two levels it rises high into the sky. I live, with my parents, on the twentieth floor."

Geni nodded her head. "We have buildings like this in the cities, but in the country, there is more room to build. If what you told me about your people is true, the stone structures we have found scattered across the planet now make sense. Were your people always so interested in building temples that reached for the sky?"

"Our planet is much smaller than yours. We have always lived in the cities. I know there are people who live in the countryside and grow the food we consume. I have visited the farms and they fascinate me. At first it was hard to come to grips with the amount of land the farms cover. Space in the city is at a premium."

"The way I see it, you have missed something special. I will make sure your visit to the countryside is a special one. Although I am a scientist, I do hire men and women to live on and work the land. There are many small homes for them to use while they tend to the fields as well as the animals."

Ragnar was intrigued and looked beyond the sprawling home to the fields of vegetation being cultivated for food for the people. He hadn't seen any animals but he was certain they too would be amazing to see.

As soon as the hovercar stopped and was parked, Geni pushed the button to open the doors. Once they swung up, he stepped out of the vehicle. To his surprise a man in military dress, like those who attacked his people shortly after they landed, stood just outside the house glaring at him.

"Why have you brought this Alien here? For that matter, why are there several others of his kind in your home? Don't you see the danger you've put yourself in?"

"There is no danger, Father. These people do not come to harm us, they come to..."

"I know what they come to do, Geni. They've come to conquer us and perhaps feast on our bodies."

Ragnar stepped forward and raised his hand in the traditional greeting of his people. "I assure you we do not come to do harm. We are merely returning to this planet because in the long-forgotten past, the one god told us to come here to give your people the knowledge of mathematics, written language and medicine. Now our planet is doomed and as has long been prophesied we are returning. We only want to live peacefully among your people and share any other knowledge we have

36

which might be helpful to your people."

"I don't know how you survived our attack, but it is my duty to make certain you do not contaminate our people."

Before Ragnar could take a defensive position, the man he now knew was Geni's father, raised a strange weapon like the ones he'd seen during the attack and pointed it at him. It was Geni who rushed to her father's side and pointed the weapon down toward the ground.

"I have told you. Ragnar and his people do not mean us harm. They are refugees, like the many people we have taken into our society because of war and famine. We have not turned them away and it will not be done now. My personal physicians have been caring for those you tried to kill at the landing sight. Only Ragnar was captured. From what I saw at the hospital in town, he was treated worse than a lab animal. When I found him, he was strapped naked to a gurney and had not even been fed. Now allow us to pass so I may get him a meal as well as something to drink."

"You will regret this, Daughter. When you are murdered in your bed, do not be surprised."

The man holstered his weapon and stormed away to a strangely-colored hovercar much larger than the one Geni brought him here in.

"I'm sorry about the way my father treated you. As I told you he is the head of the military. They see your arrival not as a wonderful occurrence but as a threat to our lifestyle. It will take time, but he will soon see the benefits of your arrival."

"I know you said the people who were with me have survived, but I know what I saw when your military advanced on us. I need to see for myself what you are saying is true. I also want to know what has happened to the other landing parties who arrived on your planet."

"Of course, you do. You also need to have a nourishing meal. I called ahead and had my cook prepare you a meal of roast lamkin as well as spring vegetables. As soon as your body has been fed, I promise I will ease your mind about the people who were with you."

He followed her up to the house and through the spacious entryway before going into the area where a table had been set with linens and china. Also, on the table were steaming bowls of food that made his mouth water in anticipation.

Without asking permission, he seated himself at the table. As much as he wanted to pile his plate high with food, he took a moment to give thanks to the one god for bringing this woman to him to save his life and give him this bounty of food to eat.

As he raised his head, he saw Geni watching him closely.

"I didn't know you gave thanks before eating."

"Is this not something you do?"

"It is, but I never thought those not of our planet would give thanks in the same way as we do. Now that you have given thanks, please help yourself to this meal. I know you must be hungry and cook does make a good meal."

He eyed the extra place setting at the table. "Are you not also hungry? Will you be joining me or must I eat my meal in solitude?"

For the first time since the confrontation with her father, she broke into a genuine smile. "I would be honored to share this meal with you. I am certain you are not familiar with our food. In this way, I can explain them to you."

She took the seat next to him and passed each dish to him after explaining it to him. "The meat is lamkin. It is a staple in our diets along with the edible fowl and the fish we catch in the lakes and rivers. The white starch is tonakin and the vegetable is maze."

Ragnar tasted each dish. They were all familiar to him, only with different names. He thought of the nutrition pills they'd been living on during the voyage to reach this planet. Although the pills kept him nourished, he still enjoyed the sensation of chewing his food and savoring each flavor.

A goblet of water sat by his plate as well as a glass of what Geni called wine. After one taste he realized it was the same as the spirits served in the home of his family on special occasions. "Are you celebrating a holiday?"

"Why would you ask something like this?"

"Because spirits are only served on special occasions."

"Wine is a common drink served to the adults at meals. It's not enough to become intoxicated but enough to enhance the flavor of our food."

Ragnar nodded his approval. He always enjoyed drinking spirits with his parents.

The joy of eating quickly overrode his concern about the family members he'd seen murdered at the site when they landed their craft.

Chapter Five

Before leaving the compound, Rand carefully stowed Nina's garment in the back of the Jeep. He also made a stop at the mess hall to pick up sandwiches and lemonade for them to indulge in on the trip back to where her family had landed their craft. He remembered to bring a sandwich and a bag of chips back for Stacey.

"I picked up something to eat."

He handed Nina the waxed paper-wrapped sandwich as well as the Styrofoam cup with a cover and an opening for her to drink from. Straws had been outlawed many years earlier. He remembered using them as a child, but for environmental reasons, they were no longer in fashion.

"I am not familiar with this food. How do you eat it?"

"I'm sorry. It's wrapped in waxed paper. Let me unwrap it for you. This is a ham sandwich with mayonnaise and mustard along with a dill pickle. The cup you have in your hand is lemonade. You sip it through the hole in the lid."

After unwrapping the sandwich, he tapped the cover of the drink so she would know what he meant.

"This is, indeed, interesting-looking food. I'm familiar with the bread but I'm not certain what this meat you call ham is." She took a bite of the sandwich and smiled as she chewed the unfamiliar meat. "This is very good. It reminds me of the cured meat we had at home. I'm not familiar with the pickle, but it is intriguing."

As soon as she tasted the pickle, the dill made her pucker her lips. Rather than make a comment, Rand put the jeep in gear and backed out of the parking place closest to the office.

"How did you like your pickle?" he asked as soon as he pulled out onto the highway.

"It like nothing I've ever eaten before. I think it must be an acquired taste. It's neither distasteful nor unpalatable. I think it is something I would enjoy eating again. The lemonade reminds me of a drink my mother used to make at home. She used the juice of fresh fruit. I always enjoyed it."

"It seems as though our food isn't much different from yours. I'm glad you're enjoying our lunch."

Throughout the hour-long drive, Rand ate his sandwich and finished his lemonade. He wished he'd brought along a thermos with more lemonade, but he hadn't thought of it.

"I must say it is more satisfying than the nutrition pills we have been having since we left our home. Of course, now we are becoming settled on your planet, we will be able to rehydrate the other food we have brought with us. It will be good to be able to once again eat food that is familiar to me."

"Do you think your people will be able to adapt to our foods?"

"We will have to if we are to survive in your world. In the ancient past, those of our kind who came here and helped your ancestors did not have the technology we have today. If they wanted to survive, they had to learn to eat as those they were helping ate. It will be the same with our people."

Rand drove in silence for many minutes thinking of the hundreds of questions he wanted to ask the beautiful woman sitting next to him. Even though he didn't think they'd been on the road long enough to reach their destination, he saw a multi-story building rising amid the famous lines on the Nazca Plains.

"Ho—how is this possible?" he stammered.

"Our people are known for their ability to build structures quickly and accurately. Have you not seen the many structures our people have constructed in the past?"

Rand's mind raced. He thought of places like Puma Punka as well as the great pyramids of Egypt, Stonehenge in England, and other places around the globe with beautiful structures that in no way could have been built by the primitive people who inhabited the earth.

"I've seen pictures. This is the first big dig, out of the country, I've ever been on."

"You called the place where we went before a dig. I do not know what this means."

"It means digging into ancient places to try to see how the people lived. There are many digs in the United States where I used to go, but they were never as exciting as this one. I've wanted to come to Peru ever since my foster parents took me on my first dig. I never thought I would receive an invitation like this without yet having my doctorate."

Nina nodded. "Academics is something I understand. I have been studying all my life."

Rand looked at her and for the first time wondered about her age. "All your life is a long time. How old are you?"

"I am, in your society, twenty-two. I have gone through the elementary schools as well as those of higher learning. I earned my doctorate, as you call it, just before we left our home."

Rand mentally calculated her age as much older. In the schools on earth she would have had to go through eight years of elementary school, four years of high school, four years of college and even more years of post-graduate work.

"I'm not saying I don't believe you but you're much too young to have had so much schooling."

Nina smiled at him before answering. "I have studied your education system as we came here. On my home planet we start school at the age of three. We do not have what you call high school. By the time we finish our elementary education, we are ready to go to university. It's a much more accelerated education than what you receive. Since you have asked my age, may I inquire as to your age?"

"I am also twenty-two. I've completed elementary school, high school, and university. I won't be starting my post-graduate studies until I return to the States."

"I do not understand when you talk about this being Peru and you have come from the States."

"I think the geography lesson will have to wait until another time. I see your father and Doctor Clark coming toward us."

~ * ~

Ragnar enjoyed the food Geni's cook made for him. He hadn't thought of his hunger while being probed at the hospital, but once he started eating, he realized his body was starving for nourishment.

"Was the meal satisfactory?" Geni asked.

"More than you will ever imagine. Although the food was different from what I am used to eating, it was very delicious. Your cook did a good job. Now can I see my family?"

"There is no reason why you shouldn't. I just have to check with the doctors who are caring for them to see if this is the proper time for a visit. I will be right back."

Ragnar's apprehension was growing by the minute. Geni rescued him from the hospital, defended him against her father, and served him an excellent meal, so why was she hedging about taking him to see his family?

Before he could formulate an answer, Geni returned, her smile radiant. "I just talked to the doctors and your family is as anxious to see you as you are to see them. If you are finished eating, we can go to the infirmary."

He pushed his chair away from the table and got to his feet. Even though he'd walked from the hospital room to the vehicle and from the vehicle to Geni's home, he could feel the pull of the gravity on this planet. It was certainly different from his home.

"Are you dizzy?" Geni inquired.

"I think I'm just exhausted. The gravity on this planet is stronger than I am used to."

Geni nodded. "It is best if I take you to the infirmary so you can reunite with your people and be checked over by our doctors. Even though you were not wounded, I tend to agree you are exhausted. You are too important to the future not only of those of us in the scientific community but to our entire planet. We are ready to move to the next level and I am positive you will help us to get there. I have long been a believer in the Ancient Astronaut Theory. There are too many unanswered questions about our past to not believe we have been visited before and we will be visited again."

With Geni's assistance, Ragnar walked the short distance to the area of the house she called the infirmary. He hadn't known what to expect or if he should believe his family was still alive. As soon as he entered the room, he saw his father, mother, brothers and the other members of his landing party.

"Son, we are so pleased to see you," his father said. "When they brought us here and cared for our wounds, we were told they hadn't found you. Where have you been?"

"Ragnar will be able to talk to you soon, but for now, the doctors who have been taking care of you want to check him over. He is also exhausted and needs to rest."

He didn't argue with Geni. Between the gravity pull and his lack of sleep he was anxious to be taken to a bed.

"I am Dr. Yano," the man in a white coat said, as he helped Ragnar to lie down on the waiting bed. "I hear you haven't been treated very well since your arrival. I am sorry for that. I just need to make certain no one has harmed you."

Ragnar waited while the doctor took his vitals, in much the same way as the healers he'd known all his life did.

"I have been treating your family and friends. I was appalled to think our military would take such action against you. I, like Geni, am a firm believer in the theory that says our planet has been visited in the past by people from other worlds. I never thought the return of the space travelers would be in my lifetime. You will never know how honored I was to be given the opportunity to heal their wounds."

"Are they truly going to be all right?" Ragnar asked as soon as the doctor took the thermometer from his mouth. "Neither my family nor myself are used to such violence we saw as soon as we landed on your planet. From everything my brother told me about the times he has visited in the past this is a veritable paradise. I fear for the safety of the other landing parties from our planet."

"You have every right to worry. I can assure you I have been watching the news reports and this is the only area where the military intervened before the scientists could greet our visitors."

"I was told you had the ability to watch things as they happen on the other side of the planet. We have had this technology for many thousands of years. I am pleased you have also had the ability to bring this technology to your people."

"We will have much time to talk of this in the days to come. For now, you must rest. Your family, as well as your people will need you strong to lead them, for you are the strongest of them."

"How can that be? My father is a strong man, so are many of the other men in our party. I am but a child in many respects. I am still going to university and completing my education. I am completely unworthy of such an honor as you are giving me."

"It is nothing you do not deserve. For now, I must insist you rest. I will give you a sedative because I can see your mind is reeling with everything that has happened since your arrival on Seros."

The doctor slipped a needle into Ragnar's arm. He could immediately feel the sedating liquid enter his bloodstream and make his eyes heavy with the need for sleep.

Chapter Six

"I am pleased to see you have returned my daughter to me safely," Dragger greeted them. "What I do not understand is why she is wearing these strange garments."

"These are the clothes worn by the women who work at the dig, Father. Rand's friend, Stacey, gave them to me so I wouldn't appear to be different from the others we will be encountering during our time here."

Anger flashed in Dragger's eyes. "What have they done with your robes? Were they destroyed?"

Rand could see Dragger's accusations hurt Nina. He'd seen how excited she was to wear the shorts and camp shirt. Now he could tell she felt shame for wearing them. "Do not blame Nina. We didn't want to have her feel differently from the other people in our world. As for the garment she was wearing, I made certain it was handled with extreme care. I would never destroy anything that represents Nina and her past. You are honored guests among us. My only thought was to make certain she was not considered to be different from everyone else she might meet while we were at the dig."

"Dr. Clark has explained about the dig where you are working. I remember reading of the area you are uncovering in the archives of our ancestors. They revered the people who inhabited this area. They taught them many things about the sciences including astrology, architecture, medicine and mathematics. When we first arrived, they were a primitive people. When we left, they were a great society. We promised we would return. The time has now come and I am pleased with the reception I have received from Dr. Clark and your young friend, Paul. Have you heard if it is so with the other landing parties from our planet who arrived on your planet?"

Rand took a deep breath. "Those who arrived in populated areas like England and Egypt were met with military presence. I did watch a report of King William arriving at the landing site near Stonehenge and asking the military to stand down. He greeted your people like the honored guests they are. In the less populated areas, the people who greeted those who came in your crafts were accepting and welcoming. I saw nothing about open hostilities, but Egypt is such an unstable area, anything is possible."

"Did you alert your authorities of our presence?"

"I talked to Stacey about what we should do. She said she would contact the backers of the dig and ask for their guidance in this matter. You must know, your arrival is big news. As Stacey said when we first arrived the whole world is in chaos. Many people on our planet have been waiting for countless generations for your arrival. We are far more advanced than our ancestors. We do not see you as Gods, but as members of an advanced civilization. As such we know you have much knowledge to impart to us and many questions that have been left unanswered in the past will now be resolved."

Dragger nodded his head, a sad look in his eyes. "It was not our intent to come to your planet and cause problems. We thought since our ancestors were beneficial in helping the primitive people of Earth, we would be accepted as refugees from a dying planet. I pray none of our people have lost their lives in the process."

Dr. Clark put his hand on Dragger's shoulder as a gesture of friendship and compassion. "I have a feeling there will be reporters as well as scientists coming to greet you in the next few days. Thankfully, this is a rather remote location. I think I should go back to the dig and try to deal with them before they come to your location."

Dragger nodded his agreement. "I can understand your position. If it were you who would have landed on our planet, I pray our people would become friends with you as you have with us. I would appreciate it if you would leave Randsom here. We have several questions about Earth. I'm certain he will be able to answer many of them. Never fear, he will be treated with the upmost respect, given lodging and food."

Rand could hardly contain his excitement about possibly being able to stay with Nina and her people. He felt completely unworthy of such an honor but prayed Dr. Clark would be agreeable. The only problem he could foresee was what kind of food he would be served. In no way could he see himself satisfied with nutrition pills.

"I know this is an amazing opportunity for Rand. Even though we don't know you very well, I can see no reason to distrust you."

He turned his attention to Rand. "Do you have anything you'd like us to bring with us when we return?"

Rand thought quickly. "I'll need more clothes and my shaving kit. Otherwise, I'm sure Nina and her people will take good care of me."

"Are you sure, Rand?" Paul asked.

"I know you're concerned for my safety, but Dragger allowed me to take Nina to the dig. I'm certain he worried but he gave his permission nonetheless. I'll be fine. I'll see you in the morning. I'm sure Dr. Clark will need your help dealing with the local authorities as well as the press. Let's face it, you're more of a public relations man than I am. You'll do just fine and so will I. The one suggestion I'd make is that you call your folks and let them know we're both okay."

Paul pulled him into an embrace as though he thought he would never see his friend again. "Until morning," he said, almost choking on the words.

Rand watched as Dr. Clark, Paul and the others got into their vehicles to turn down the road leading from the Nazca Plaines. For a moment he was filled with apprehension. The people who were familiar were leaving him and he was staying with the unknown. What if they required a human sacrifice as he'd read about other ancient societies? Would his friends return to find him with his heart cut out? He couldn't think of that now. He had to trust Nina and her people.

"I fear you are having mixed emotions about staying with us," Dragger said, putting his hand on Rand's shoulder.

"Like anyone I'm worried about the unknown. I'm excited about learning more about your people, but at the same time, I know I will be leaving the familiar behind."

"Well said. It was the same when I allowed Nina to accompany you back to your dig. As you can see, our builders have been busy. Our accommodations are almost ready for us to move into them."

"That is amazing. How can you build something like this in such a short time? Did you bring your building materials with you?"

"As you can see, our ships are very large. Our materials have been stored ever since before we began our voyage. What we could not bring with us we were able to glean from the area around us."

Rand looked around and noted two more vessels that weren't visible before. He wondered if they'd been cloaked in invisibility until Dr. Clark and the others left. "Why didn't I see the other ships before?"

"It is always best to err on the side of caution. Since you are a trusted friend, we are allowing you to see the extent of our people. We are not much different from you, but we do fear what others of your people will think of our arrival on your planet. Until such time as we feel comfortable, we will use the invisibility shields when dealing with others who could pose a threat to us."

More questions crowded Rand's mind. "I see plenty of rocks. How were you able to transport them?"

"It was done in the same ways as any of the stone structures around your globe were made. We were able to transport them with sonar waves. This is something our people have been doing for eons. I am a pilot but not a technician. I do not know how this is done, only that we can do it."

Rand was amazed. He followed Dragger to the high-rise building that had grown almost magically on the edge of the Nazca Plaines.

~ * ~

Ragnar awoke. He'd slept peacefully for the first time since landing on this planet. Dr. Yano stood on the far side of the room talking quietly with Geni. For some reason, he didn't feel as secure on Seros as he had hours earlier. He couldn't help but wonder what her agenda could actually be.

"You're awake. I'm certain you're hungry and you'd like to spend some time with your family. They are all feeling much better and are anxious to see you again."

"Before I do any of that I want some answers to my questions. First, why were we fired on when we first landed?"

49

Geni sighed heavily before answering. "I have been a follower and believer in the ancient astronaut theory. Everything I've studied pointed to your return and I've been anticipating it. My father, on the other hand, believes, when and if you came to Seros, it would be to take over our planet with force. There is a faction among our people who fear the unknown as well as the people who might invade from the heavens."

Ragnar nodded. He knew the rumors of invaders from the skies ran rampant on his planet for years before the news of the destruction of his home became common knowledge.

"Why did you choose to save the lives of my family and come to the hospital to take me out of the bad situation I found myself in?"

"I first heard about your landing on the scanner. Your craft was spotted days before it actually landed. I knew what my father was planning and more than anything I wanted to stop it. Unfortunately, I arrived at the landing site too late. The military thought everyone but you were dead. They were wrong. My people rescued the other members of your crew, but I didn't find out where you'd been taken. After I located you, I had to cut through a ton of red tape in order to bring you to my estate so you could be reunited with your family and friends."

Ragnar gave much thought to the answer she gave him. "We are safe here, but what will happen when the day comes when we are all well enough to leave your protective custody? Will the military attack us once again if we try to establish our own community within yours?"

"As we speak, the leaders of our country are making arrangements to come here to visit with you and your party. They will be bringing the media with them so you can make a statement about your peaceful mission. After that I am certain the leaders will ask the military to stand down. Once people know you have come to join our people and not conquer them you will be readily accepted."

"Ours was not the only landing party to arrive on Seros. Do you know the fate of the others who landed at the same time as our craft did?"

"I am afraid I do know their fates. The ones who landed in the most remote area were greeted as returning Gods by the natives. The ones who, like you, landed in more populated areas met with resistance much the same as you did here. There were causalities among those our people were not in time to save. All in all, the causalities were minimal. Of course, even one causality is one too many."

The thought of any of the people from his planet losing their lives in the relocation from their home to this surrogate home brought sadness to Ragnar's heart.

"I know your friends and family are ready to go into the dining room to break their fast. I will give you a moment of privacy so you can take care of your morning needs and get dressed. Once you are done, I will be waiting for you outside your door."

Ragnar waited until Geni left before moving to the far side of the room. He'd seen a glassed-in area. Walking to it, he was surprised when the wall seemed to anticipate his arrival and slid open to show an area for relieving his bodily needs as well as a bathing area and a receptacle filled with steaming water along with a razor so he could shave off the stubble of his beard. It was as though the area knew exactly what he would need to not only cleanse his body but also so he could shave off the unwanted beard from his face.

Above the steaming water was a dark screen reminding him of the computer screen he'd been studying with at home, as well as on the flight. As soon as he stepped closer the darkness of the screen disappeared and it became a mirror. The reflection of his image came as a surprise. He immediately reconsidered shaving off his facial hair. He'd never allowed it to grow before and he liked the look of it. With a little trimming, it would make him appear to be more mature than his twenty-two years.

Once he'd washed the stink of the lab where he'd been held from his body, trimmed his newly-acquired beard and brushed his teeth, he dressed in clothes resembling the ones Geni brought for him to wear the day before. He had to admit he enjoyed the feel of the fitted trousers and the garment she called a shirt. Throughout his entire life he'd worn the loose-fitting robes everyone on Plantas wore. He'd seen the doctors both at the lab and here at the estate wearing the trousers as well as white shirts Geni called lab coats. Geni, on the other hand, wore a garment that reminded him of his robe, only it fit tighter to her body and covered only from her waist to her knee. The upper part of her body was covered with a more feminine version of the shirt. At the neckline he could see not only her skin but also the hint of cleavage. Although he knew what the female body looked like, the women he knew wore the unisex robes like everyone else.

Once he finished with his morning rituals, he finally left his room. Like the door to what Geni called the bathroom, the door leading into the hallway magically opened before he reached it. True to her word, Geni waited for him.

"You do look handsome in our clothes. I've seen the robes your people wear but I think they must each have new clothing made for them. After talking with your family and friends, I have heard their opposition, but I would prefer to have all of you looking more like our people. In that way you will be able to assimilate into our society much easier."

Her approving glance moved from his clothing to his newly-trimmed beard. "Now your beard is perfect. You will fit in with the young college students in the city. They usually go through a period when they experiment with their facial hair. I must say your beard is one of the better ones I've seen in a while."

Ragnar appreciated her complimentary comments. If he had concerns of how he would fit into her world, they were now dissolved. He could easily see himself dressed in these clothes and looking more like the people around him. They were all as tall as his people, so they wouldn't be an oddity among them.

Rather than going through the infirmary as he had the night before, they walked across a sitting room before coming to the dining room. It pleased Ragnar to see several small tables filling the space. At them were his family as well as several other members of their party. Some of them were dressed in their traditional robes while others wore clothing like that he and Geni were wearing.

"It is good to see you, Son," his father greeted him as he awkwardly got to his feet.

"Please, Father, remain seated. I can see your injuries are not completely healed."

He noticed his father hadn't adapted the new clothing into his lifestyle as had his brothers and sister as well as his mother and many of their other friends. "Have you not tried on the new clothes, Father?"

"My injuries are such that they would not be practical at this point. I am excited to be able to wear them in the same way as you and the other members of our family. Dr. Geni has told us you would be joining us and we have saved you a place at our table. She assures us the meal to break our fast will be up to the same standards as the meals we were served while we were confined to the infirmary."

Ragnar took a seat at the round table with his parents as well as his two older brothers and his sister.

"I like your new look," Patra said, as she put her hand to his face to touch his facial hair.

"I thought it might make my new life more interesting. I see you are wearing clothing like those which Geni wears."

His sister laughed at his comment. Finally regaining her composure, she looked down at her new clothing. "Dr. Geni told me this is a skirt and a blouse. She has a seamstress coming to the estate tomorrow to help me build a new wardrobe. I am excited to wear something other than the dreary old robes we have worn all our lives."

"Now, Patra," their mother admonished, "I find these new clothes different but not quite as comfortable as our robes. There is something to be said for change in our lives. We are hoping to fit in with these new people. Although I will miss my former attire, I am certain I will become comfortable in these new clothes."

Their table conversation was interrupted when servants presented them with what Geni called breakfast casseroles. There was one open space at their table which Geni filled. Ragnar as well as his brothers were quick to get to their feet to hold her chair for her.

Ragnar bowed his head and waited for his father to say grace before eating any of the food placed before them. It pleased him to see Geni follow his lead and echo their A-Men with one of her own.

"This is delicious," Ragnar's mother, Signe, exclaimed. "What are the ingredients?"

"They are peahen eggs, cured meat and mutton cheese. It is a favorite in my family and I am pleased to think you are enjoying it. I have spoken to several members of your party and although our food may have different names, they are things that I am sure you will recognize from their flavors."

Ragnar enjoyed the food as well as the table conversation. "I know we talked about this before, but I think it would put my parents' minds at ease to hear about your religion."

"I am afraid I am not very good at practicing my religion. I have allowed science to take over my life, but as a child I attended services with my parents on a regular basis. I believe in God, I just don't make it to the services in the manner I should. Ragnar has told me you believe in the one god as do we. Before your arrival, I didn't think our beliefs were shared by others in the Galaxy. To be truthful it was sometimes hard to believe people like us existed beyond our planet."

Ragnar's father, Blankes, smiled at Geni's description of religion on her planet. "In my world, I am active within my temple. At one time, I aspired to be a priest, but my life took a different direction. I would be honored to attend one of your services. I know I am of the older generation, but perhaps I can follow my dream and become active again."

The thought of his father returning to the religion he loved so dearly, brought a smile to Ragnar's lips. He'd always known of his father's desire to be active in the temple, but the pressures of life as well as raising a family conspired to get in his way. He could have never supported his family on the salary priests were given. Ragnar often wondered if the reason the life of their planet had come to an end was because more and more of the young people were no longer practicing their religion. In his family, it had been mandatory to attend services and they had all embraced it willingly. He knew it wasn't so with many of his friends.

Chapter Seven

Rand awoke still amazed at how quickly accommodations had been erected. Even though sleeping arrangements were little more than blow-up mattresses, he'd spent a comfortable night. He had to admit, he missed the bountiful buffet served at the dig, but the nutrition pills were filling and satisfying. He knew he would be grateful when Dr. Clark brought up fresh provisions this morning.

After getting dressed and cleaned up for the day, he went down to the commons area where he was told breakfast would be served. As soon as he arrived, he found pandemonium. Outside of the complex, television and radio vans were assembled along with armed guards from the military.

"I am sorry about all of this," he apologized to Dragger. "I was hopeful Dr. Clark could keep this quiet for a while."

"Do not apologize, my son. This is expected. Our return to your planet has been predicted ever since our people left many millennia ago. As for the media coverage, we have monitored it ever since you became advanced enough to have such things. I have always known this would be a newsworthy event. I would appreciate it if you would be our spokesman. You know these people and can speak for us."

Rand was overwhelmed. He knew many of the reporters would be Spanish-speaking and he prayed his knowledge of the language would be of help to him.

Rather than eating breakfast, he went out to meet with the reporters. "Good morning," he said as soon as the first reporter approached him.

The man pushed a microphone in his face. "Are you one of the aliens?"

"No, I'm an archaeology student working at the dig. I have been asked by the leaders of this group to stay with them and become a spokesperson for them."

"Why have they come here?"

"Their people came here because this is where they first landed thousands of years ago. Their planet, Plantas, is dying and they have returned hoping to be assimilated into our society. They are far more advanced than we are. They have much to teach us and we have things to teach them as well."

"Who built this structure? I've been to this area many times and I've never seen it before."

"It was constructed by their architects. To witness this process was awesome to say the very least."

"Are you staying here as their prisoner?"

"I am nobody's prisoner. I am here as a representative for our people and have been treated as an honored guest."

"Will the aliens be coming out to speak to us? Are they the Grays? Are they Lizard People?"

"Allow me to answer your questions."

Rand turned relieved to see Dragger standing behind him.

"The Grays, as you call them are androids we have used for exploration of your planet as well as two other planets in the Galaxy. As for the Lizard People, they are no longer a threat to any of us. Many thousands of years ago, we fought them in a great battle. We were victorious. Their armies were defeated and their civilization no longer exists. They were evil and rather than allowing them to thrive our ancestors thought it best to eliminate them."

The information Dragger imparted to the reporters caught Rand completely off guard. All his life he'd heard of the Grays as well as the Lizard People, but to hear about them from this man from the stars came as a complete shock.

"There have been other landings around the globe," another reporter shouted. "What can you tell us about them?"

"Plantas, the planet we call home, is dying. One-third of our population have landed on Earth while the other two-thirds of our people have been sent to two other inhabited planets in the Galaxy. Those of us who came to Earth were sent to the areas where our ancestors visited thousands of years ago. For this reason, we came to Nazca. Others of our people went to Egypt as well as England, Turkey, Thailand and China; each landing party is returning to their roots on this planet."

"How is it you are so knowledgeable of the areas of our planet?"

"We have been sending the Grays to this planet for several hundred years. They have kept us updated as to the evolution of your people. Before you ask your next question, allow me to tell you everyone on our planet has a translator implanted behind their ears at birth. With this we are able to understand any language that is being spoken to us."

Rand realized the questions were becoming tedious. It soon became evident Dragger was ready for this question and answer session to be over.

"Please allow me to intervene here. Dragger and his people have been traveling for many months to arrive here. You must understand they are trying to adapt to a new planet and that means they will have to learn to eat new foods, regulate their bodies to a change in gravity and learn to breathe in our atmosphere. I am certain you can understand their need for rest and recuperation."

He took Dragger's arm and escorted him back inside the building. To say he was more comfortable within the air-conditioned confines of the high-rise Dragger and his people now called home would be an understatement.

"You did well, young Rand," Dragger complimented him. "Have you handled things like this before?"

Rand suddenly felt self-conscious. "Not really, but I've watched enough television and seen enough interviews on the Internet to know how these people can be. I call them predators. They are out to get the first bite of any story that comes their way. Today you and your people are worldwide news. Don't get me wrong, you will be newsmakers for a long time to come, but tomorrow there will be another story that will grab the headlines."

"People who report the news are no different from planet to planet. I understand the need for such things, but as you say they can become predators. I do thank you for putting an end to their questions."

Nina hurried to meet them as they entered the building. "Why did you go out there, Father? From what I could tell, Rand was handling things very well."

"It was necessary, Nina. Rand would not have been able to answer the questions those people posed. I have monitored the people of this planet longer than you. I know they have known of our existence and at the same time been concerned for the safety of their lives when we return. I wanted to put those rumors to rest."

Rand marveled at the older man who allowed him to stay with them and learn firsthand of their culture. Never in his wildest dreams had he thought he would be one of the first humans to make contact with visitors from the far reaches of the Galaxy.

~ * ~

With the new day, Ragnar became uneasy. If he were on his home planet, he would have been outside working in fields where he researched the edible vegetation looking for new cures for old diseases. Although he said nothing of his background to Geni, if he were at home, he would be starting his post-graduate studies in order to become a healer as had many of the men and women in his family. Those of his line served in the medical community. At the time, it seemed best to keep his knowledge of life outside the city a secret. Just as it was best he kept his knowledge of living in the country as well as working in the fields secret until he felt the time was right to disclose these things to the people of Seros.

He'd been particularly interested in the life-saving techniques of the doctors who attended to the wounds received by his family and friends. From what he could tell, only his father still suffered from his injuries.

His thoughts turned to Nina. He wondered if her landing party had been met with open hostilities as had his. He knew he would never see her again. Still, he longed to talk to her and compare experiences. He also wondered what happened to the other landing parties on Seros. Was it possible those of his party who had been saved were the only living remnants of his fellow space travelers on this planet? Even though Geni assured him there had been only a minimal number of casualties, he didn't know if he could believe her. Only time would tell.

"You're awake."

Ragnar turned his attention to the doorway of his room as soon as he heard Geni's voice.

"I have been awake for a few minutes."

"Good. Your brothers have requested a tour of our city and countryside. I told them I would come and awaken you so you can join them. They are enjoying the morning meal and are anxious for you to join them."

He thanked her and said he'd meet her in the eating area as soon as he finished his morning rituals. Even though he knew he was in her debt, he was still apprehensive of the woman. He'd seen those of her people shoot down members of his party. Although he had not been injured, he had been taken prisoner. How could he be certain his family as well as the others here in this compound were really those he knew? Was it possible they were merely clones and he was the only survivor?

Refreshed by his morning shower, he made his way to the room where his family waited for him.

"We thought you were going to sleep the entire day away," his brother, Karten, greeted him.

"It sounded like a good idea to me. Unfortunately, I'm a creature of habit. I was awake before Geni came to my room to tell me you were eating and soon would be ready for a tour of the area of where we landed."

"I've been so excited about this tour, I could hardly sleep last tonight," his other brother, Milono, added.

"I can understand why. The idea excites me as well. Are you joining us, Patra?"

His sister gave him a brilliant smile. "Mother and I are planning to spend the day with Geni's cook. She has promised to acquaint us with the food this planet has to offer our people. We have been very impressed by everything we have been served since our arrival and want to learn as much as we can about its preparation. As for Father, he is meeting with Geni's father. As the head of the Military, Father has many questions for him and hopes to form a friendship. We have been told the man thinks we have come here to harm rather than to join with them. I pray his meeting is a successful one."

Ragnar nodded his agreement as he loaded his plate with the food from the buffet. He wondered if he was imagining things or did his sister's voice sound different to him. He knew he was being paranoid, but his overactive imagination had always been a problem for him.

How can I be sure these people are my family?

To his shock, his inner thoughts brought a reply.

My son, you are right to question, but we are all here. Despite the way you were treated when they captured you, we have been treated with the best of care. These are people you can trust.

His father's reply to his silent questions brought a smile to his lips. They would be accepted here and find a place in this new world where they found themselves.

With the morning meal finished, Ragnar joined his brothers as they all went outside. For him it was a repeat of when he was brought to the estate, but earlier Milono said no one else left the estate since their landing.

"Why haven't you been outside in all this time?"

It was Karten who answered his question. "Our injuries were severe. To be truthful, I didn't know if any of us would survive. The doctors here have been very good to us. They have skills I know will be beneficial to our people. Of course, we have not told them of our medical knowledge. We have as much to learn from them as they do from us. I doubt even our senior healers could have saved our lives. From what I've gleaned from listening to them, I find they still struggle with cures for diseases we eradiated from our planet centuries ago. I think our coming here will be a boon to both of our societies."

"Geni told me there were casualties among the other landing parties. Do you know which of our friends have died?"

Milono was the one who answered him. "I have been in mind conversations with the pilots of the other ships. Although the casualties were few, I am afraid we have lost the great mathematician, Cletos, one of the educators, Nala, and her daughter, Shana. Others were injured but like those of our party, they were rescued and saved. As far as we know, you were the only one who was taken prisoner and studied as though you were a lab animal. Mostly, our arrival has been considered a success by the elders, like our father."

They continued their discussion until they saw Geni coming toward them. Even if Milono felt comfortable openly discussing their private matters, Ragnar was far more careful in what he said within the hearing of the people who were now their hosts. It was best to keep some th ings private until he was certain he could trust Geni and the others.

When Geni joined them, she didn't bring the hovercraft she brought to the lab on the day she freed him from his captors. Instead she brought a vehicle that looked like the ones that gre eted them at their landing. It was large enough to comfortably seat everyone. The windows on either side of the vehicle allowed each of them an unobstructed view of the countryside through which they traveled.

"The area we are traveling through is basically used for farming. Our farmers grow the food that graces our table in an organic way. They also breed and grow many meat animals, which also provide us with milk, cheese, and hides for leather goods. They take great pride in their farms. "

"Would it be possible for us to speak with some of these farmers?" Ragnar asked.

"It would be not only possible but also I'm certain they would enjoy speaking with you as well. You see, we have done extensive research on the information found on the computers of your craft. If I am not mistaken, you are all scientists as well as medical personnel. I'm certain you will find the process by which we grow not only our food but also our medical herbs very interesting. This is but the first part of everything we plan to show you. In due time, you will be allowed into our scientific labs as well as our teaching hospitals. If I am not mistaken there is much you can teach us."

"How did you gain access to our computer files?"

Karten's question held a note of anger. Ragnar wondered i f Geni was able to detect it.

"You must know that any alien craft to land on our planet will be confiscated by the government. When you first arrived, we had no idea if you were friend or foe. That is the reason the Military met you with such aggression. Our scientists were quickly on the scene but not before you suffered many significant injuries. We thank God we had the ability to treat your wounds and restore you to good health. I am only sorry the scientific community did not get to your landing site be fore the Military arrived. My father has always been paranoid about an alien attack that would be disastrous to our people. While I, on the other hand, am convinced about a peaceful party coming to learn about our people."

Ragnar agreed with everything Geni said. He knew if a craft such as theirs landed on his home planet, the reaction would be much the same. People were always fearful of the unknown.

They drove for over half an hour before pulling into the dooryard of one of the well-kept farms they'd seen as they'd driven through the countryside.

"This farm belongs to my Uncle Canaan. He's one of the most prosperous farmers in the area. My great-grandparents started farming here over a hundred years ago. My grandparents inherited the farm. My father was their oldest child. He didn't want to be a farmer and gave up his birthright to his younger brother Canaan. He was the one interested in the farm. My father loved the military and wanted nothing more than to be the best at what he wanted to do. The arrangement made everyone happy. Uncle Canaan loves the land and has made great strides in developing new strains of fruits and vegetables for the betterment of the people."

Ragnar looked at the man coming toward their vehicle. He'd expected to see someone about the same age as Geni's father. Instead the man was closer in age to Geni.

"You said your uncle was your father's younger brother, but this man could easily be your brother rather than your uncle."

The smile on Geni's face told him she'd heard the same statement before. "My father is the son of my grandfather and his first wife, Lorna. She died when Dad was fifteen, leaving Grandfather to raise my father and his sister, Aria. Dad was in his middle twenties when he married Mom. Six months later, Grandfather married his second wife, Toni. They had Uncle Canaan about six months before I was born. We were brought up together, since Grandfather and Toni were killed in a freak accident. At that time, my parents lived on the farm and Father was renting out the land. Uncle Canaan took over as soon as he finished his education and received his degree in agriculture."

The man approached them with his hand outstretched. "You must be our visitors. The news has been filled with stories of your arrival. It pleases me to think you are interested in our food production. I would like to invite you to spend some time on my farm."

Ragnar's interest was immediately piqued. Even though his primary goal in life was to be a healer, he'd taken a special interest in the time he'd spent on the farms on his home planet. It came as no surprise when Karten immediately accepted Canaan's invitation while Milono would not be comfortable remaining on the farm.

"How about you Ragnar?" Milono asked. "Will you be coming back to the city with me to confer with their physicians?"

"I think I'd like to stay with Karten. Even though we both want to study medicine, the process of growing food as well as perfecting new plants and cross-breeding animals intrigues me. Perhaps I'm not cut out to be a physician but instead a scientist."

It was the first time Ragnar ever put voice to his innermost thoughts. While they were in school, Nina often told him of her desire for the two of them to become scientists and do their research work together. Now they were separated by many light-years. It was entirely possible the path his life would take on Seros would be entirely different from what had been planned for him since the day of his birth.

"My wife and I would be pleased if all of you would take the midday meal with us," Canaan said, breaking into Ragnar's thoughts.

"I was hoping you would ask us, Uncle. It's a long drive back to the city and my stomach has been growling for the past several minutes. I'll go up to the house and see if I can help Aunt Mimi."

Ragnar watched Geni leave them and realized he would miss being in her presence. Even though it seemed impossible, he was beginning to have feelings for her.

"You look like a lovesick boy, little brother," Karten teased.

"That's nonsense. It's just she's the only woman I've seen since our arrival here. Unlike the two of you, I'm still young enough to appreciate a beautiful woman."

His statement brought jibes from both of his brothers. "Old, are we?" Milono questioned as he punched Ragnar in his arm.

"Well, neither of you are as young as I am. I also know before we began this journey you were promised and those women are back at the estate waiting for you."

~ * ~

Blankes watched as his sons left the estate with Geni. He would have enjoyed seeing the countryside as well as the farms that supplied the food for the inhabitants of this planet. As a youth, he'd worked on a farm as part of his studies to become a healer. His professors insisted he must learn the benefits of knowing the origin of the food the people ate. For a time, he'd considered giving up medicine and becoming a farmer. It was only the insistence of his father that sent him back to his medical studies. Now as he envied his sons their adventure into the countryside, he knew the decisions made in his life had been for the best.

As soon as they left, his wife and daughter also went to learn of the food preparation from the cook who provided them with their meals. Along with them went some of the other women from their party, while the other men were taken to explore the areas where their expertise was also practiced. With them leaving, he'd been left alone in the room where they went for their meals.

Earlier Geni told him her father, General Ledling, would be coming to interrogate him. Her choice of words could have been much better. This meeting could turn into an interrogation with him feeling like a criminal rather than a respected healer.

"Good morning, Blankes," General Ledling said, as he extended his hand.

Blankes got, shakily, to his feet. "Good morning, General."

"I think, under the circumstances, it would be best if we were on a first name basis. My friends call me Leddy."

"Do you expect me to consider you a friend when upon our arrival on your planet, you tried to massacre my people? Had it not been for your daughter and her colleagues, we would have all perished."

"I do apologize for what happened when you arrived. As a military man, I saw your coming as a threat to our planet. I have since conferred with my contemporaries who have had crafts similar to yours land in their areas. Each one tells me the same thing. They all agree your people have come in peace and are the people our ancients called Gods. I'm certain you will tell me the same thing."

Blankes reluctantly clasped Leddy's forearm, in the manner of greeting his people used. He was surprised when Leddy seemed to be comfortable with this form of greeting.

"I am pleased to think others of your people have accepted our people as the friends we have come to be. Our planet is dying. We have come here in peace, returning to where our forefathers gave your ancients the knowledge of mathematics, architecture, medicine and the written word. We were told, by our scouts, your people had advanced enough to accept our return. Perhaps they were mistaken."

Leddy motioned for Blankes to return to his chair. "It is I, as the head of our military, who was mistaken. Unfortunately, I have allowed fiction writers as well as the media to taint my impression of the things happening around me. My daughter has informed me of the reason for your mission. I can't believe the few people who have landed on our planet can be the entire populace of your planet."

"We aren't. There were three missions sent out to three planets. One to Seros, one to Nalo and the last one to Earth. I have had no word of the other missions. I only know of ours. Those of us who were to be saved were based on which families visited them in the far distant past. My family was the one who came to Seros, therefore those of us coming here are all related, although remotely, to those ancestors. We left behind the aged and infirmed. Only the best of our people were chosen for this journey."

Blankes could see anger building behind Leddy's dark eyes. "Are you telling me you left them to perish?"

"They would have perished because of the rigors of this journey. We have had years to contemplate how the evacuation would be conducted. Everyone on the planet was included in the talks. It was a unanimous vote that those unable to withstand the journey would be left behind. Had they accompanied us, they would have never made it this far. Space travel is not as easy as some people led us to believe. It has taken its toll on even the strongest of our people. It was more humane for us to leave them behind than to watch them die far from their homeland. Their deaths were quick and relatively painless. I left behind my parents because they insisted there was nothing I could do to stop the natural ageing process and their deaths."

The thought of having to have left his parents behind drained his strength. He'd been one of the people who had argued long and hard about how unfair it was to leave the old and infirmed behind. It broke his heart to see his parents as well as those of his wife left behind. They'd been away from the planet for several days, when the final throws of life for their dying home made themselves evident in the black sky of space. He knew he would never forget seeing the blast that obliterated not only his home but also many of the people he loved.

"I fear all of this talk has tired you, Blankes. Perhaps we should postpone these talks until another time. I feel you have exhausted yourself. I merely came to ask for your forgiveness for my rash behavior upon your arrival. I suggest you take your rest. We will have many other opportunities to talk to each other in the future. I have spoken to our physicians and they are making arrangements for those in your party who are in the medical field, to be honored guests in our hospitals. I am certain they have things to teach to you as well as what you can teach to them."

Blankes agreed. He was, indeed, tired. The morning drained his strength and made him wonder why he'd been chosen to make this journey. It was possible it would have been better for him to stay behind and die with the others. As soon as the thought crossed his mind, he knew he'd made the right decision. He could never have been able to watch his sons, daughter and wife leave the planet without him, knowing his inevitable fate of dying with the old and infirmed. Had they left him behind there would have been no one to comfort him in his final hours. Even knowing the one god promised eternal life, he was not ready to begin that journey just yet.

"Before you leave, Leddy, I would like to ask something of you."

"I don't know what I could give you, but I will try. What is it that you would like?"

"All my life I have been a very religious man. At one point I pondered the idea of becoming a priest, but to appease my father I went into medicine. When I am stronger, I would appreciate it if you could take me to one of your temples."

A slight smile crossed Leddy's lips. "That would be an easy thing for me to do. Although I privately worship God, I do not always have availability to a temple. Now that I am stationed close to my daughter's estate, I have been going to the temple to reestablish my relationship with

Him. Before I came to see you this morning, I went to the temple to ask forgiveness for my rash actions when you first arrived. My answer came quickly, not only did God forgive me, He insisted before I could ease the ache in not only my mind but also my soul, I must come to you. In doing so, I was to beg for your forgiveness as well."

Blankes was touched by Leddy's confession. "As a follower of the one god, I have learned it takes a strong man to confess his wrong to his one time enemy and beg for forgiveness. I hold no ill will for you and forgive you for that which occurred. I would be honored to call you my friend."

Rather than clasp Blankes' forearm as they did in greeting at the beginning of their meeting, Leddy, pulled Blankes into a tight embrace, the universal symbol of true friendship. Blankes was pleased to know this tradition had continued many millennia after the first time his ancestors came to this planet to bring knowledge and civilization to these people.

Chapter Eight

Nina changed into the robes of her people. She had to admit she much preferred the shorts and shirt the woman, Stacey, gave her to wear when she went to the dig. She found it much more practical than the robes that constricted her movements.

"Why has Father forbid me to wear the clothes of these people we hope to join? They are more adaptable to this world than our robes. This area is hot and dusty, unlike our home where keeping our clothing clean is not as hard as it is here."

Moorea sat in silence for a moment leaving Nina to believe what she said angered her mother.

"What you say has merit, Daughter. I will confer with your father and tell him of your arguments. I doubt it will take long for our people to duplicate the manner of dress of these people. To be truthful, if we want to become one with them, it would be better if we dressed in like manner to them. I'm certain with such an argument, your father will agree with me."

Nina breathed a sigh of relief. Even though she wanted to dress in the same manner as Rand and the others at the dig she knew to do so would go against her father's wishes.

After speaking with her mother, she made her way to the kitchen where the nutrition pills were being rehydrated. Even seeing the food she'd eaten all her life, she couldn't help but think about the sandwich and lemonade Rand brought her from the cafeteria. She enjoyed the taste of the meat he called ham. The lemonade, although unlike the fruit drink her mother used to make, was unique and refreshing.

A flurry of activity outside the kitchen diverted her attention. She hurried to investigate. She smiled to see Rand along with his friend, Paul, unloading boxes of food. She recognized several of the vegetables as well as the meat. Along with the fresh food were live fowl as well as live animals.

"Good morning, Nina," Rand greeted her. "I hope these vegetables along with the meat animals will be palatable to you. Paul and Dr. Clark brought along one of the chefs from the dig to show your people how to prepare the food."

"I'm certain our cooks will be grateful. There are so many new things on your planet, we are grateful for any assistance your people can provide us. Our cooks have been rehydrating our nutrition pills. Would you care to join me for a meal from our planet?"

Paul looked a bit apprehensive, but Rand enthusiastically accepted her invitation.

"I would like to see what the pills I was given for dinner last night and breakfast this morning really are. They were satisfying but I do like to know what I'm eating."

"I can assure you that you are in for a treat. So far, our cooks have rehydrated bovine steaks, baked tubers, and a vegetable I'm particularly partial to, the ones called legumes."

She watched as both Paul and Rand broke into wide grins.

"I don't think you'll have problems acclimating to your foods," Rand commented. "What you call bovine is beef to us, tubers are potatoes, and legumes are green beans. In their rehydrated state, they look very tasty. I would imagine the meals I've eaten while with your people are also things I would recognize."

The two young men went out to help with the unloading of the other vehicles of supplies. She stood looking in their direction for a moment longer, before her mother called for her to come back to the kitchen the cooks set up earlier in the day.

"You should be careful. You don't know these men."

She turned at the sound of the voice of her friend, Lora. "Why would you say such a thing? Rand is our friend."

"Perhaps that is true, but haven't you seen the communication we received from Seros this morning?"

"What communication? I saw the one about them being treated like gods."

"This morning the communications officer from Ragnar's ship sent a message saying after they were met with adulation, the military opened fire on them. It was only when a young scientist and her people came to their rescue, that they were saved. They have been taken to a hospital and given medical attention. Were it not for her, they would have all perished."

"What of Ragnar?"

Lora's eyes filled with tears. "I do not know. The communications officer said he'd been captured. They presume he's been either imprisoned or is dead."

Nina felt her heart sink to the pit of her stomach. Even though she knew she and Ragnar would never be together as they once planned, she didn't want to think of him being lost to everyone.

"Did you hear what I said?" Lora asked.

"Yes, I did. Are you sure?"

"No one is sure of anything other than the lives of most of the crew has been saved, but to suffer what fate? It's entirely possible the same thing could happen here. I fear for our safety."

With no reply, other than a slight nod of head, she left the kitchen area and made her way to the command center to read the communication from Seros for herself.

Her mind raced with thoughts about what would happen if the military came to their encampment as they did to the landing site of Ragnar's party? What if Lora's prediction was right? Rand and the people she met at the dig were friendly enough, but was it only a ploy to gain their trust? Would their lives, their very existence be in danger?

No sooner had the thoughts crossed her mind than she heard a loud whirring noise. It was so loud in fact it forced Nina to put her hands over her ears in an attempt to block it. In fear she looked out the window and saw several big machines both on the ground and more descending from the heavens.

"What is that?" Lora shrieked. "Are these people coming to kill us like the people on Seros did to our friends? Have we come this far to be killed? I'd rather have died with our planet than to have things happen in this manner."

Nina had no answer for her friend. She too worried about their fate but clung to the friendship she'd established with Rand and the other people from the dig who were the first to make contact with her people.

~ * ~

"What the hell is going on?" Rand asked as he joined Paul and the others who were unloading the provisions for Nina and her people.

Paul was standing next to one of the supply trucks watching as several helicopters landed on the flat plain surrounding the alien encampment.

"Dr. Clark told me several dignitaries from every country in the Americas were coming to welcome our guests," Paul shouted to be heard over the sound of the rotating blades. "I can't believe we're actually going to get to meet the President of the United States."

Rand shook his head. "They aren't coming to meet us. They're here to talk to Dragger and the others. We're little more than peons where these men are concerned. I'm going back inside to put Dragger and the other's minds at ease. This must be very frightening to them."

Rand turned and walked toward the structure to find Dragger.

"Do you know what the meaning of this is?" Dragger asked as soon as Rand stepped into the main room of the building. "Has your military come to murder us as they did to our friends when they arrived on Seros?"

Dragger's questions sounded more like accusations. "It's not what you think Dragger. The helicopters are bringing the heads of state from every country in the Americas."

"I do not understand. Is there not one world government? On our planet we became one many centuries ago. It brought the end of war as well as famine when everyone was a citizen of the same nation. We even standardized the languages although several people retained the original language of their regions."

"I wish that could be the way it is here. The Americas are comprised of two continents North and South America as well as an area referred to as Central America. North America has three countries. The language of my country, the United States, is English, Canada speaks English and French, and Mexico speaks Spanish. The Central American countries as well as those in South America speak Spanish with the exception of Brazil where they speak Portuguese."

"What of the other continents of this planet? I am told there are seven continents in all."

"There are. Antarctica is too cold to sustain life other than the explorers and scientists who go there to study the area. Asia has many countries and several different languages depending on the area. China, for example, is so big there are many dialects spoken. It's the same with Africa and Europe. We're a diverse planet, to say nothing of having been at war in one region or another since the beginning of time."

Tears formed in Dragger's eyes. "I am so sorry to hear this. War is so unproductive. I prayed your world would have progressed further before we arrived."

Rand pondered Dragger's statement. "Perhaps your arrival will bring about the world peace we all pray for."

Dragger nodded sagely. "I am certain I will be expected to meet with these people. On our planet, I argued against the language chips because we all spoke in the same manner. Now I see the advantage of it. I must ask if you will agree to be at my side when I meet these people. I am afraid I will be overwhelmed. You have a way of dealing with the press that will serve me well today. On my planet, you would be considered a great diplomat."

Dragger's words were flattering. Rand was pleased to be so highly regarded. As much as he wanted to protest, he held his tongue. It was best to accept praise rather than deny the words of one he considered a very important man.

"I'm afraid I'm too young to be a diplomat, but I am honored to think you regard me in this way. Have no fear, I will be with you. I do speak fluent Spanish even though Portuguese is a language I'm not familiar with. I am certain they will be bringing people to interpret for them. If nothing else, I can offer moral support."

Their conversation was interrupted when Nina came into the room. "Father, I am so frightened. There are strange crafts landing around us. I just heard how the military attacked Ragnar's party. Are we going to be killed?"

Rand stepped to her side. "It's nothing like that. I have been informed the heads of states of all the countries in the Americas are arriving to meet with your father. Because of the remoteness of this location, coming by helicopters is the most practical mode of transportation. Believe me, these men are seeking peace, not coming to do harm. Your father and I are preparing to meet with them. I think having you present as well would ease the minds of these dignitaries. Anyone coming to take over the world would not bring their women. They would come armed for attack."

He could tell by the expression on Nina's face she was skeptical. The only way he could prove anything to her was to have her accompany them.

"I agree with Rand," Dragger assured Nina. "We want these people to trust us. What better way to gain that trust then to show them we have come to settle and have brought our families with us. Neither Rand nor I will allow any harm to come to you."

~ * ~

Rand could feel his nerves kick in as he, along with Dragger and Nina, stepped out of the building. Before them were representatives from many news stations along with several well-dressed men. Among them he recognized the presidents of the United States, Canada, Mexico and Peru, having seen them on television. He assumed the others represented the various countries of the Americas.

Dr. Clark was standing on a makeshift platform and motioned for Rand and the others to join him. "How is everything going?" he asked Rand.

"It was going better before all these helicopters arrived. They have these people really spooked. Why weren't we warned they were coming today?"

"I got here as fast as I could, but the helicopters were already landing when I arrived. I was just informed of it myself. Are you here to help Dragger?"

"You know I am. We all decided it would be best if Nina joined us as well. I told them I'm fluent in Spanish and can help with those dignitaries, but I'm at a loss with Portuguese."

For the first time Dr. Clark smiled. "That's not a problem, I worked on a dig in Brazil for a couple of years. I can help out with that. Of course, with Dragger's ability to understand any language, we might not be needed."

"That is where you are wrong, Dr. Clark," Dragger said. "On my planet, I was a member of the governing board, but only because of my knowledge of science as well as history. I was never called upon to be a diplomat and I am the first to admit the sheer number of people who have come to this place is intimidating to me. I trust you and Rand to ease the tension I feel about meeting so many people at one time."

The delegation of the leaders of the Americas was led by the President of the United States.

"Dragger trusts you," Dr. Clark whispered. "Why don't you handle this one?"

Rand swallowed the lump forming in his throat. He was barely out of his teens and wondered how he would handle such a great honor.

"Mr. President, I am Randsom Jacobson. I'm doing some post-graduate work on the dig near here. I was with Dr. Clark when he made first contact with these people. This is their leader, Dragger. Although he understands everything we are saying and will be able to speak with you, he wanted me to make first contact."

The President looked past Rand to where Dragger and the others were standing. "You speak very well, young man. I am pleased to make your acquaintance. I am also pleased to be able to meet and confer with Dragger. I recognize Dr. Clark, but who is the beautiful young woman standing beside you, Dragger?"

"I am pleased to meet you as well, Mr. President. This is my daughter, Nina. She is the chief Science Officer on our mission, just as I am Historian and Leader of our people. As you see, we have brought our families with us and want only to settle in peace."

"Is it true you are descendants of those who are rumored to have come here in ancient times? The ones the primitive people call Gods?"

"It is true. Many millennia ago my ancestors came to this planet and helped the people they found here to learn language, astrology, medicine and many other things. We helped them to build the many stone structures you marvel at today, here as in many other places around your planet."

"Why have you come back?"

Rand watched as tears formed in Dragger's eyes.

"Ever since we first left this place, we have sent androids to check on the process of your people. Even if the time is not right for us to return, the time for us has come, as our planet is dying. We came here as well as to two other planets in the galaxy to preserve our race. Ours is not a mission of war, but one of peace, harmony and friendship."

Dragger held out his hand and the President took it.

"It is a pleasure and an honor to meet you Dragger. Believe me I speak for all of the people here when I say we welcome this opportunity to meet with you. Is there some place where we can speak in private?"

Dragger's moment of sorrow about the reason for their return to Earth quickly turned to one of pleasure at the question posed by the President.

"We have a room within our structure where those of us in command will be able to meet without the prying eyes of those recording our every move. I would appreciate it if not only Dr. Clark but also our friend, Rand, will be able to attend."

Rand felt a blush creeping into his cheeks. He was far from prepared to be in on a diplomatic meeting. His position with Dragger as well as Nina now seemed to dictate his attendance.

Chapter Nine

Ragnar reluctantly went back to the compound with Geni. He wanted to stay on the farm with Canaan and learn more about their farming practices. Even so, he knew he wouldn't be allowed to do so. Gina and her team of scientists wanted to do more physical and physiological investigations not only on him but on the other members of his family who were now at the compound.

"You're very quiet," Geni observed. "Is it possible you would have wanted to remain with my uncle and learn more of his farming practices?"

"You know too much about us. On our planet, before one can become a healer, he or she must study the way the foods as well as the medical herbs are grown. Before we left, I worked on the farms for two years. I was about to enter the university for the remainder of my medical studies. Our professors felt by our studies on the farms we were much better equipped to understand how foods and medicines worked in our bodies. I, personally, believe this is a great boon to anyone who wants to pursue a career in the medical field."

Geni nodded her head. "I tend to agree with you. Would you and the others be willing to confer with the professors at our university? I think it would be valuable for our medical programs to implement such programs."

Ragnar was surprised by her comment. "Of course I would. My brothers feel there is much we can learn from your physicians as well. They said the way their wounds were treated and the speed of their recoveries was remarkable. It is possible both of our people can learn and grow from our interaction."

They continued talking, oblivious to the others in the hovercraft. By the time they reached the compound Ragnar decided he now had a better comprehension of the people of this planet.

"We're glad you're back," Blankes greeted them.

Ragnar was surprised to see his father deep in conversation with General Ledling. A chill of fear ran through him. What was this military man planning to do? Wasn't it enough that he'd already opened fire on the people as they exited their craft?

"I hope you had an educational trip with my daughter," the general added.

"What do you want with us, General? I thought we were safe here and now I see you with my father. Wasn't it enough that you tried to murder us when we first arrived?"

"Simmer down, son. Leddy and I have been conferring off and on all day. We are much the same, as I realize our military would have been frightened of anyone who arrived in the manner we did. Leddy and I have resolved our differences. We both realize our people have much to teach each other. The real reason I am so glad to see you is we have had communication from Dragger and his party."

The mention of Dragger brought to mind a vision of Nina. Had she been greeted with the same hostilities as they had? Was it possible the woman he thought was going to be his life partner was dead?

"Is she...?" He couldn't bring himself to say the word dead. He didn't want to imagine her being dead. It was bad enough she was light-years away from him and they would never see each other again.

"Don't jump to conclusions. Our communications officer has received a transmission from them. Their party was met by people from an archaeological dig not far from their landing place. It seems there was a young student with them who has become very important to the mission of our people. His name is Randsom Jacobson but he insists they call him Rand. Dragger is quite taken with this young man. I think they are in a position much as we are enjoying. They are accepted and being treated as though they are honored guests."

Ragnar breathed a sigh of relief. Even if he never saw Nina again, he knew there was a chance she could find love with this young man her father held in such high esteem.

~ * ~

Rand could see the day of meetings with the dignitaries from the various countries of the Americas was very tiring for Dragger. Even so, the older man insisted the two of them needed to meet in private before they retired for the night.

"You wanted to see me, Dragger?" Rand asked when he entered Dragger's apartment.

"Yes, I did. I have been studying the history of our people for many years, most of my life to be exact. In them I found our people were known by many names. Star People and Sky Gods, to name just a few. I also learned of this landing place and the markings that would lead us to the heart of the civilization established by our forefathers. Our scouts have told us many of the places we helped to build have gone to ruin. Being an archaeologist and having studied the antiquities of your planet, I am hoping you can tell me what you know of these places."

Rand smiled. "There are many places of which you speak, but over the centuries the jungle has reclaimed them. They are just now being rediscovered. Machu Picchu is about five hours away from here by car. Another place that might be of interest to you would be Puma Punka. Unfortunately, that is in Bolivia and not Peru. The trip by car would take us over fourteen hours. I'm afraid it would be a tiring journey."

"Earlier the leaders of the countries came to us in flying machines you called helicopters. Would not these machines take us to these places in much less time?"

Dragger's perception amazed Rand. "Yes, they would. If these are places you want to visit, we can speak with the representatives from these countries and see if they would be interested in taking you to these national treasures."

"I don't understand what you mean by national treasures."

"Unlike in past generations, we now see these places built by your people eons ago as monuments to be revered rather than ravaged. What the grave robbers and treasure hunters did in Egypt was deplorable. They weren't interested in what they could learn from those who had come before them in the past. They were only interested in the monetary gains they could make for themselves. So much of the knowledge of the past was lost because of their greed."

Rand could see sadness in Dragger's eyes. "I fear it is the same in most civilizations. From reading the ancient texts I learned how those of my race also destroyed the knowledge of the past before they realized exactly what it was they had. You spoke of other sites. Are they close by?"

"Not really. In Mexico, there are many beautiful pyramids as there are in other countries of Central and South America."

Dagger nodded. "This morning I spoke with a man who speaks the same language as you. As I recall he was the President of the country from which you come. Do you have such cities?"

"I'm afraid not. In the Southwestern United States, we have several societies who worshiped the Sky Gods, but their cities do not rival the ones in this area. There are many petroglyphs all over our country and people are still debating as to who drew them or what their meanings are."

"I must see all of these places and want you to come with me along with my daughter, Nina. We have much time to go to these places. Will you be content to stay with us for as long as these explorations take?"

Rand thought for a moment. He had nothing to return to the states to do other than to pursue his Ph.D. and be able to become a highly-respected archaeologist like Dr. Clark. If Dragger and his people wanted him to stay with them for an extended period of exploration who was he to say no?

"I would be honored to accompany you to these sites. As a child, my foster parents took me to many sites in the United States and I've always wanted to explore all of the sites in the Central and South America. By accepting your offer, I will be fulfilling a dream of a lifetime."

Dragger shook his head as though Rand said something that was beyond his comprehension. "I do not understand what you mean by foster parents."

The words Dragger just spoke were surprising. With the communication chip was it possible he could not understand the word foster? "When I was taken away from my mother, because she was an unfit mother, I became a ward of the state. Since they didn't have the ability to care for children like me, they find people who would take us into their homes. It was meant to be a good experience for us, but many of the people wanted nothing more than the money the state paid them. I was abused in several homes until I went to stay with Matt and Bridget Scott. They treated me like their natural son. I think they would have adopted me, but the state told them they were too old and so was I as I was a teenager at the time. Nevertheless, they paid for my college education and left enough over in my inheritance to pay for my post-graduate schooling."

Again, Dragger looked perplexed. "I must come to the conclusion these foster parents are no longer living. The thought of that saddens me. I am also saddened to think someone might have to pay for education. On Plantas, all education is without charge for anyone who seeks it."

"That's the way it is in some of the European countries. The U.S. hasn't decided to do anything like that yet. College is expensive and so is grad school. Many students graduate with enormous student loans hanging over their heads. I am one of the fortunate ones who had the funds to pay for my education in full and not have to work part-time for spending money."

"Does Paul carry such debt?"

"His parents planned for his education and he received several scholarships and grants. Still he does have about ten thousand dollars in student loans and I'm sure he will have to take out more loans for grad school, but I don't think it bothers him as much as it would have me. He is studying carbon dating and once he graduates, he will be in high demand. As for me, I will never garner a high salary so the inheritance from my parents will help me to be able to live comfortably, just relying on the interest from the investments both they and I have made."

Dragger nodded his head as if in dismay. "I grieve for the young people who have to go into debt in order to obtain an education. Perhaps this is the perfect time for us to arrive and help the governments that allow this atrocity to happen."

"I do hope you can do something about this, but it's been going on for years. Every president has promised to do something about it and it hasn't happened. It's a growing epidemic and I see no end in sight."

"This is a debate that will take much more time than we have now.

For tonight you must get some rest. I will speak with Dr. Clark tomorrow to make arrangements for the journeys the three of us will be making. I must ask, can you fly one of these helicopters?"

"I'm afraid not. I'm little more than a college student. I had enough on my plate with my studies. I was lucky to have my education paid for by my parents, but the cost of learning to fly something like a helicopter was far beyond my means."

"That surprises me. Our children are schooled in the operation of every kind of craft used on our planet. If it were necessary, Nina could pilot the ship that brought us here. Are you telling me your young people do not receive such training?"

Rand smiled at the thought of Nina being able to fly a massive starship. "I'm afraid not. I know how to drive a car, but to fly a plane or a helicopter is something that is extremely expensive to learn. Perhaps if I'd gone into the military rather than opting for an education I might have had the opportunity to learn those skills."

Dragger shook his head. "I see we have much to learn about your planet. I must admit I was shocked to see the vehicles you arrived in. Long ago we banned the use of the combustion engine. We travel in hovercrafts. Do you not have such vehicles?"

Every science fiction book Rand ever read as well as the movies he'd watched brought to mind the kind of conveyance Dragger referred to. "I'm afraid these things are only in the planning stages. Several years ago, a company brought out a hover board, but it was so dangerous they were taken off the market."

"I don't understand what you are talking about."

Rand wished he had his computer so he could do a Google search for information about the now-outlawed hover board. "Here we have a sport called skateboarding. It's very popular, but many years ago there was a movie about someone who went into the future and instead of the board with wheels everyone is familiar with the kids were all riding boards that floated on air. Unfortunately, in reality, when they were put into production, they burst into flames even when they weren't in use. They were immediately banned as there was too much of a threat concerning them."

"That sounds logical. I have studied the history of the hovercraft. It has always fascinated me. As I recall the first prototypes were prone to burst into flames. Fear not, technology will eventually perfect the product. Among our people there are engineers who understand the needed technology. I am sure they will be helpful to those who work in the production of such vehicles. We are here to bring your people our knowledge as well as to learn from you. Tomorrow will be a busy day for us, so I suggest you return to your quarters and get the necessary sleep."

Rand thanked Dragger and headed for his own room. It had been an exciting day and he was suddenly exhausted. Never in his wildest dreams did he ever think he would be involved in a project of this magnitude.

As he made his way to the floor where he'd been given a room he was surprised to run into Nina. She stood just ahead of him looking out the window at the stars in the night sky. Before he could approach her, he could hear her sobbing softly.

"Nina? Are you all right?"

She turned and he could see her tearstained cheeks as well as her red eyes. "I will be."

"Do you want to talk about it?"

"I shouldn't bother you, but..."

"It's not a bother. What's wrong?"

She wiped at her eyes with her hand as though the gesture would stem the flow of her tears. "We told you there were three delegations sent to three different planets. The man I always thought I would marry was on one of the ships going to Seros. We have received a transmission from their communications officer saying the landing party was met with open hostilities. Although many in the party were gravely wounded, a group of scientists rescued them and tended to their wounds. Unfortunately, Ragnar was captured and is presumed dead. Even though I knew once we left our home Ragnar and I would be separated by many light-years, I still mourn his loss."

Rand engulfed Nina in his arms. He knew of loss, but not on the same level. Even though he had only vague memories of his birth mother he ached every day over the loss of his foster parents. He knew it was a different kind of loss than the one she was feeling. This was the man she'd planned to spend her life with, perhaps even have his children. He thought back over the girls he'd dated both in high school as well as in college. There were none of them he ever considered marrying.

"I'm sorry for your loss. I can never say I know how you're feeling, but I will be here if you ever need to talk."

He could feel her tears soaking into his shirt. All he could do was hold Nina tightly and comfort her to the best of his ability.

As he held her, he realized this woman could easily become very important to him. The minute the thought crossed his mind, he dismissed it. Nina wasn't the woman for him. Nina's intelligence far exceeded his own and if he wasn't mistaken, she was of the upper class of her society. In no way could he ever begin to be good enough to have her in his life.

Chapter Ten

Ragnar couldn't stop thinking about the farm he'd visited earlier in the week. Even though he knew the examinations by the doctors at Geni's compound were a necessary evil he still longed to return to the farm run by her uncle, Canaan.

"Good morning," Geni greeted him as soon as he entered the dining area to break his overnight fast.

"The same to you. What examinations do you have scheduled for me today?"

Geni smiled at his question. "None really. The professors from the medical school have asked to meet with you and learn of your education. They are especially excited about how your students go to the farms to study the production of food and are hoping you would be willing to help them to institute it in their curriculum."

Ragnar beamed at the compliment Geni just paid him. "Is it possible for you to speak with your uncle and see if he would be willing to allow students to study on his farm?"

"Before I contacted the professors at the university I spoke with my uncle. When I told him how medical students studied on the farms, he thought it was a marvelous idea. He told me he's talked to several of his other neighbors and they've all agreed to join in the initial experiment through the university. They have already started building a dormitory along with an extension to the university on a field in a central location."

Ragnar felt his pulse quicken. He had no idea Geni would have taken his casual comment to heart and instituted such a program. "I don't know what to say. I never thought I could bring something useful to this planet."

"I hoped you'd be as excited about this as I am. I know several others in your party have found their place in our society. There were several military men and women in your landing party. They have been conferring with both your father and mine about joint efforts to make our military better."

Ragnar nodded his head in a mixture of amazement and disbelief. "I realize your father and mine have become friends. With all of the examinations I have been undergoing, I didn't realize our military people have joined with yours."

Geni beamed at his statement. "Your arrival and the assimilation of your people with ours has been a dream come true. I've been an avid supporter of the ancient astronaut theory for many years. My mother has always been a supporter of the theory as well. I think that is why my father and mother's marriage didn't last. The more active she became in the movement, the further apart they grew. My father always wanted me to follow in his footsteps like my brother did, but I was happier exploring my mother's beliefs."

Ragnar thought of his parents. They were totally committed to one another. He'd heard of people not being able to remain married to one another but had never met anyone in that situation. "You spoke of your mother as well as your brother but I have never seen either of them."

"My mother works in the headquarters for our movement. Her people met another of your ships when they landed. Thankfully, there was no military interference. My brother is stationed on one of our moons. There is a military base there and they were the first ones to warn us of your arrival. Unfortunately, I haven't been able to see him in the last two years. His unit is due to return home sometime in the next year. As children, we were very close but when our parents separated, he went with Father while I remained with Mother."

Ragnar pondered the life Geni led. In no way could he imagine being separated from his siblings as they were growing up. Rather than make any comment he followed her into the room where he knew breakfast would be served.

As soon as they entered the room, he saw what could only be called a delegation of several men and women already seated at the table. The man sitting at the head of the table was immediately on his feet with his hand extended.

"You must be Ragnar, young man. I'm Dr. Claymore, the head of the university's medical program."

"It's a pleasure to meet you," Ragnar said, as he grasped the older man's forearm in greeting.

"Geni has been telling us of the differences between our medical studies and those of your people. We would be pleased if you would join the faculty at the university."

The offer took him by surprise. "I—I don't know what to say. I haven't finished my formal studies. I don't know if I am qualified."

An attractive older woman got to her feet. "I am Dr. Reanie Patros. It has been my assignment to investigate you. In that quest I have spoken to many people from your party and been given access to your computer files. From what I have learned you are more than qualified to teach the courses we are planning to implement into our medical training. At the same time, we will be giving you the opportunity to finish your degree and receive your doctorate. From the information I have gathered, you are very close to having both your degree and doctorate. What you are missing is your hands-on training."

"I realize I am close to the end of my formal training, but from what I have observed, your medical practices are far advanced to ours."

"That is where the hands-on training comes into play, my boy," Dr. Claymore replied. "It will take us several months to implement the new program. During that time, you will be working in one of our best hospitals and learning from the top physicians. With your training completed, you will have earned the title of physician and be able to go into private practice if you so desire. Of course, we are praying you will join the academic field. Your knowledge will be invaluable to our students as well as the university."

Ragnar took a deep breath. "I am honored and accept your offer. I must admit, I feel the agricultural education is very important in the training of medical students. When I toured the farm of Geni's Uncle Canaan I was reluctant to return to the compound. It was as though I felt more at home there than I did in any of the classrooms I have ever sat in. I will accept your offer and look forward to this new chapter in my life."

~ * ~

Ragnar was still reeling from the breakfast meeting with the professors when he went to seek out his father.

"Did you know what was going to happen today?" he asked once he told his father of the events of the morning.

"I did. I have been having meetings with not only Leddy but also with the professors. I assured them you would be a good candidate for the position they are creating. I know how much you enjoyed your studies on the farms. I've been in contact with one of your professors who was on another of our crafts that has landed on the opposite side of this planet. He also spoke with Dr. Claymore and recommended you highly. I am so very proud of you."

"I hope I am up to the challenge. Do you not think one of my brothers would be better suited for this position?"

"I have talked to them and they are both promised to women who came with us. They want to be joined as soon as possible and would rather be practicing medicine than to be teaching. Had this been offered to them another time without the prospect of joining their lives to the women they love they might have accepted the offer."

"I agree with you and can see why my brothers would not be in a position to take advantage of the opportunity I've been offered. I do wish I had the materials I used to study when I was at university."

"That is not a problem. Your professors were able to upload their files to our computer system before we needed to evacuate. They have transferred those files to our system so they will be available to you."

Ragnar thanked his father and went out to the garden to put his thoughts into perspective. He wished he could talk to Nina about the new change of events in his life. Would she be happy for him or would she be concerned that his new position would jeopardize their relationship?

As soon as the thought crossed his mind, he was reminded she was light-years away and a new man had entered her life. Any thoughts of him were no more than a memory for her. Fate tore them apart and they would never again be together as they once planned.

~ * ~

It took several days and, in some cases, weeks to arrange permission of all the countries where the ancient ruins were located. Even so, they had not been idle waiting for the verifications of their travel plans.

Many scientists from both North and South America met with Nina and her team. Other authorities met with Dragger to discuss the history of both planets, while still others met with the astrologers, and medical personnel.

~ * ~

Nina prepared for the journey she was about to embark on with her father and Rand. Although she found the helicopters to be an archaic form of transportation, she anticipated the exploration they were about to do.

Rand told her their first stop would be Machu Picchu, even though she knew her father was more interested in Puma Punka. The reason for the initial flight to be to Machu Picchu was because the Peruvian government had given permission and they were still waiting to hear from the government officials from Bolivia.

Rather than the robes she would have normally worn at home, she opted for the khaki shorts and camp shirt worn by the people at Rand's dig. Her father didn't approve of them at first, but when Rand told him they would be more suitable he relented and accepted a pair of khaki pants and a shirt to wear as well.

"Nina, I am so glad I was able to catch you before you left the compound."

She looked up at the sound of the communications officer's voice. "Has something happened? Have you had word from the delegation sent to Nalo?"

"I'm afraid not. It is apparent their mission has failed. We received one transmission from them and it was a distress call. They were encountering a field of meteors and had already lost two of their ships. We were in contact with them for several minutes before their transmission was suddenly terminated. I am afraid we have lost that portion of our population.

"What I have to tell you is we have been in contact with the delegation to Seros and Ragnar has been reunited with the remainder of their party. He has been under the care of the best of their medical professionals and has gained great favor with one of the top scientists, Geni Ledling."

Ragnar was safe and that was all that mattered. Even though they were separated by many light-years, he was still her first love and she knew she would never forget him.

"Are you ready to leave?" Rand asked, breaking into her thoughts.

"Yes. I am anxious to see the ruins you have been speaking of. Are they as fascinating as you say they are?"

"I think they are. They are part of the Inca Empire from the fifteenth century. They aren't as old as many of the ruins but I think they are very special. I realize your people were long gone before this empire existed but I can't help but wonder if they didn't have help from the 'Star People.'"

Rand's reference to the 'Star People' brought a smile to Nina's lips. She considered herself no different from the people she'd met here. If they'd been from different countries, she felt they would have more in common than she did with Rand as an intruder upon his world.

~ * ~

Even though Rand only wondered about the interventions of people like her, she knew the truth. The Incas, like the other people of past, had been visited and assisted in the building of the places Rand referred to as National Treasures.

"I am excited to see this area of your world. I am certain my father will be able to shed some light on the origins of these ruins."

Together they made their way to the waiting aircraft. The first thing she noticed was the horrific noise the machine made as it lifted into the sky. As much as she wanted to cover her ears to block out the racket Nina sat quietly waiting for the flight to be over and for them to back on solid ground.

The flight took several hours but at last they landed. If Nina thought she'd been overwhelmed by the beauty of Nazca, with its lines drawn into the hard earth, she could hardly begin to compare with the beautiful stone structure in various stages of excavation.

"This is amazing," Dragger exclaimed. "It is more breathtaking than any of the accounts I have read in our history books."

"Your people have been here before?" Rand asked, astonishment sounding in his voice.

"Of course they have. Every aspect of wonder on this planet have been touched by our ancestors. I have studied the ancient drawings brought back to our people so we could understand what has been accomplished here."

The admiration showing on Rand's face warmed Nina's heart. Once and for all the mysteries of the past were going to be revealed and her people would receive the adulation they deserved.

Walking around the ruins, Nina listened to her father explain how each of the structures were constructed with the help of their people.

"Why? Why help these people construct these magnificent structures? Why have they been allowed to be return to the jungle?"

"You have many questions," Dragger answered. "Not all of them are easily answered. Our prophets told of the marauders from the East who would come and scatter the people. They said these people would come in the search of the gold our people needed and showed the natives how to use it to form their artwork. It happened because the people began to worship the gold rather than the gods who came from the sky. As soon as our scouts told of the discovery of what you call national treasures, we knew it was time for our return to your people and to encourage your belief in the One God."

"Why aren't these stories incorporated into the histories I've been studying ever since we left Plantas?" Nina questioned.

"There is so much history there is no way you could have studied it all in the short time needed for our journey. I have committed much of the oral history to memory but it has taken a lifetime. Now that we are here, you will be learning more every day. Just open your mind to what will be disclosed in the coming weeks and months."

Dragger turned his attention to Rand and began to explain the building of the structures stretching out across the clearing in the jungle. As Nina listened, she could see the ancients using the powers of levitation to help the natives with the building of the structures that now stood in ruins.

I am your ancestor, one of the people in her vision said within the confines of her mind. *We came to this site to educate those called the Inca. We helped the people with our advanced methods to build the buildings you see here. Once we were secure in the knowledge we had helped them all we could, we returned to our home.*

The man, who closely resembled her father, smiled at her and returned to the work of building the magnificent structures left behind when her ancestors returned home.

"Can you believe everything your father told us?" Rand asked, breaking her concentration and dissolving the vision of those from the past.

She prayed what her father just told them mirrored her vision. "It is a miraculous story, to say the very least."

Her father took a step toward her before putting his hand on her shoulder. "I know you heard not a word of what I said, for I also saw your vision while I was speaking. The man who spoke to you was one of our ancestors, known as Malock. He was a great explorer as well as a builder of magnificent structures."

"How—How did you know?"

"As I related the story, I saw the faraway look in your eyes. As I followed your glance, I saw the story as I told it come to life for me as well."

"I'm amazed," Rand commented. "I wish I had the same powers as you."

"They are not powers, Rand. They are memories that are imbedded in our genes at the time of our birth. I was able to experience the same vision as Nina because I have seen it all before as I read the histories left by our ancestors."

~ * ~

Rand was still pondering all the information Dragger shared when the pilot of the helicopter approached him.

"I have a radio message for you, Rand."

"For me? Are you sure?"

"Positive. The man on the other end of the transmission said to tell you it was Paul Mathews calling."

"Paul? What could he possibly want?"

Without waiting for an answer to his question, Rand made his way back to the helicopter.

"Just pick up the microphone and press the button when you're ready to speak."

Rand nodded as he took the mic and depressed the proper button. "Paul, what's going on? Is something wrong?"

"Nothing's wrong, Buddy. I just wanted to warn you a visitor has come here to see you."

"A visitor? Who?"

"Cyn and she's hopping mad."

"What does she have to be mad about?"

"What do you think? She's been watching the news reports back in the states showing you and Nina together. In other words, she's practically green with jealousy about Nina."

Rand took a moment to think about what Paul just told him. He thought he'd seen the last of Cynthia Adams when he came to Peru. He couldn't call her a gold digger because her daddy had more money than Rand could ever imagine making working as an archaeologist.

"Can't you get rid of her? You know, send her packing back to the States?"

"I tried, Buddy. She's not budging until she sees you. Just thought you should be warned before you got back. Speaking of getting back, when will you be here?"

"It's getting late. We're going to be staying at the dig that's close by. Probably won't be back until late tomorrow afternoon."

"See you then. In the meantime, I'll try to keep the lovely Cyn at bay."

"If you think she's so lovely, why don't you wine and dine her? It would get her off my case."

"You've got to be kidding. Cyn isn't my type. I could never go for someone who is so self-centered."

"Give it a try and I'll be forever in your debt."

Rand broke the connection and sat down on the ground to contemplate what his return to the dig would be like.

"Is something wrong? Has someone sinned? If so, why are you so concerned?"

Rand looked up to see Nina standing in front of him. "Nothing's wrong, not really. It's just someone showed up at the dig looking for me."

"Did that person sin?"

"No, that person is Cyn, it's short for Cynthia. She's a girl I dated before I came down here."

"Is she your girlfriend?" Nina had a sly look in her eyes.

"Hardly. We broke it off when I took on this assignment. It was a case of I dumped her before she dumped me. She was looking for someone with a lot of money who could support her in the manner to which she was accustomed and I just didn't fit the bill. Her dad is a very wealthy man and she's been spoiled rotten. In other words, whatever she wants, she gets. I could never offer her anything like that. Besides, she is very self-centered. She cares for no one and nothing other than herself."

"I don't understand. What does that mean?"

"She wanted to be with someone who wasn't heading off to Peru to work on an archaeological dig for three months and who had a lot of money to spend on her. She had her heart set on the guy who just passed the bar to become a lawyer. She thought they were going to live happily ever after. When she left my place, she went to his townhouse and found him in bed with another girl. That's when she hotfooted it back to me in the hopes I'd change my mind about coming down here." In desperation Rand ran his fingers through his hair.

"So why is she here now?"

"Paul says it's because this has all made the news and she thinks I'm going to be someone important and maybe I'll make a lot of money she can spend. I told Paul to try and get rid of her, but he says she's not budging, so I guess I'll have to deal with her when I get back to the dig. I just wish you wouldn't have to be around someone like her. I even suggested that

Paul should become her next boyfriend. He wasn't interested. Of course, you could avoid her altogether if you stay at your complex..."

"You could stay at the complex," Nina interrupted. "Why do you have to go back to the dig?"

"You make a tempting offer, but I can't stay there forever."

"In that case, I'll go with you to the dig. I want to see what this woman is like. How will I be able to fit into your world, if I don't meet all different kinds of people? She sounds interesting and just a little...what's the word I want? Oh, yes, jealous. I know I'm jealous of the women Ragnar will meet on Seros."

Rand shook his head. Cyn had no right to be jealous; it wasn't like they were a committed couple like Nina and Ragnar had been.

Chapter Eleven

Ragnar settled into the routine of studies at the university's medical school. He was readily accepted by the other students who populated the dorm. It surprised him when he was assigned a roommate, a young man by the name of Eros.

"Are you as tired as I am?" Eros asked as he entered their small living quarters.

"I feel like I could sleep for a week," Ragnar replied. "I've heard horror stories about the hands-on portion of the training, but I always thought I could handle it."

"Is it the same on your planet as it is here?"

Ragnar nodded. "Our people are very much like yours and so are our modes of study. I must admit I've learned much more here but I also see a lot of thing we do differently. As much as I have to learn from you, I feel you can learn as much from me."

"I've heard rumors you're going to be a professor when you finish your residency. Is that true?"

Ragnar hesitated for a moment. He'd purposely kept his plans for the future a secret, but somehow the information had leaked.

"I've been approached to teach medical students about the benefits of studying agriculture. It's something we do at home and Dr. Patros and Dr. Claymore seem to think it would be beneficial to add to their program."

"Wow, Patros and Claymore. You don't mess around. They're the most important people at the university. I just don't understand what agriculture has to do with being a doctor. I don't plan on treating animals or shoveling their waste."

"Maybe not, but how much do you know about the food you eat? Do you know how it's grown or what it does for your body?"

The blank look on Eros' face spoke volumes. "What's there to know? Our cook makes our meals and I eat them, just like I do in the cafeteria here at school."

"Your family must be very well off to afford a cook. In my family, my mother does our cooking. Since everyone in my family is in the medical field, we are all very aware of what we eat. Since pesticides were banned on our planet, everything is organic. We know what foods are best to eat to prevent many medical problems. When we first arrived here, I was taken to one of the organic farms outside of the city and their operation fascinated me. It was enough to make me question my chosen profession. By teaching about agriculture, I will have the best of both worlds."

"It sounds interesting. As for my family being well off, we aren't. Having a cook is a necessity since my mother was murdered during a period of unrest on our planet. Many extremists wanted to take over the planet. My mother was a high-ranking member of the government and they decided it would be best if they took her hostage. Before they were exterminated, they murdered her. My father never recovered. It was the government who brought in a cook, housekeeper and a governess to help him through those bad days."

"I'm sorry, I didn't know. It must have been a terrible time for you."

"I only know what happened by what has been told to me. I was a small child when the uprising happened on Seros. My older siblings were more affected than me."

Resident Ragnar, report to the commons area. The announcement came over the intercom installed in each of the dorm rooms.

"I guess there's no rest for the wicked," Ragnar said, getting up from his bed. He was aware he hadn't showered or changed his clothes since his shift in the hospital. He decided it was best if he answered the call dressed in his scrubs.

"I'll try to be quiet when I return so I don't wake you."

"Don't worry about that. I'm so tired, I think I could sleep through just about anything."

Rand put his shoes back on before going out into the hall to get to the bank of elevators at the far end.

Why would I be summoned to the commons area after working a thirty-six-hour shift?

The question no more than formed in his mind when the elevator door opened and he saw Geni waiting for him.

"Is something wrong at the compound?"

"Not wrong, really. It's my Uncle Canaan. He asked me to come here and speak with you."

"I don't understand. Has he decided not to participate in the program?"

"It's more like he wants the program to begin immediately. The dorms have been built and the planting season is ready to begin."

Ragnar wondered about his ability to take on the added responsibility and still finish his residency.

"I can see you are torn. If you are concerned about your residency, don't be. I've spoken with both Dr. Patros and Dr. Claymore and they say your expertise far exceeds that of your classmates. Your graduation is set for tomorrow. After the ceremony you will be moving out to the farm. Your classroom has been set up. There are two agriculture professors in residency and ready to begin conferring with you. I've been sent here to get you packed and ready to return to my estate as soon as you graduate and earn your doctorate. I know you just came off a long shift and must be exhausted. I will be back in the morning to help you pack up and be ready to begin your new career."

He was torn. He'd made friends in the residency program and was reluctant to leave them. "You are right, I am torn, but I'm excited to begin this new venture. When I haven't been on call, I've been meeting with Dr. Claymore and we've been discussing the criteria for the class. Between the hands-on training and the planning for the class, my head is spinning with the possibilities."

In an unexpected move, Geni, put her arms around his neck and kissed him squarely on the mouth. "I am so pleased to think you will be closer to me than at the university. I have missed you, Ragnar."

A warmth he didn't think possible crept into his body. The only thing he could equate it with was the love he felt for Nina before fate separated them forever. Without hesitation, he pulled Geni into a tight embrace and deepened the kiss they'd shared just moments earlier. Until now he hadn't had time to think about missing her. He was anxious to put that part of his life into the past and perhaps open a new chapter that included Geni.

~ * ~

Rand spent a restless night at the dig close to Machu Picchu. Thoughts of confronting Cyn with Nina in attendance kept sleep at bay. How could Cyn have come here? Was she looking for notoriety by being close to him and his position with the people who came from the stars? He had no doubt her father financed this trip. It was even possible he brought her here in his private jet. From what he heard, commercial travel to the area was curtailed until the newcomers could be assimilated into society.

"You look tired," Dragger said, as they ate breakfast.

"I didn't sleep well. I'm concerned about seeing Cyn when we arrive back at the dig."

"Do you love this girl?"

Rand wanted to laugh at Dragger's question. Instead he tried hard to suppress the urge. To do so would be disrespectable. "She was someone I dated. We never slept together. I knew I was just the boyfriend of the month and was ready for both of us to move on when we finally separated."

"I do not understand what you mean by sleeping together."

Rand thought about the promise he'd made both to himself and his parents. With the possibility of sexually transmitted diseases and unwanted pregnancies, he'd promised not to have sex until marriage. Now having to explain this to Dragger felt uncomfortable. He found it easier to say sleeping together than to explain sex.

"Is this something that's troubling to you?" Dragger asked, when it took Rand a few moments to answer.

"It's just this is a sensitive subject. It involves sex. Since I promised my parents as well as myself, I wouldn't engage in casual sex before marriage, it made dating difficult. In this day and age, it seems like no one wants to be together without sex. That was part of the problem between Cyn and me. She's a party girl and I was more the let's take in a movie and get a bite to eat guy."

Dragger broke into a wide grin. "It's been a long time since I've heard anyone speak of casual sex. When I was a child, it was widespread, and so were sexually transmitted diseases and unwanted pregnancies. It was then the world government banned all sexual relations without the benefits of marriage. I am pleased to think you adhere to the same principles as our people. I do take it you are in the minority on your planet."

Rand relaxed. It was good to know the problems of his home planet with sex was universal. It wasn't surprising to realize Dragger's people eliminated the problem years earlier.

"You do understand. One of the reasons I don't want Cyn here is because of her ways. You have many young men in your delegation. I'm afraid of the effect she might have on them."

"Don't underestimate our people, Rand. I think they can handle someone like your Cyn. For now, it's time for us to return to our landing area."

~ * ~

After the flight from Machu Picchu to the landing site of Dragger's people, Rand was more than happy to be on firm ground again. As they had every time Dragger made an appearance, the press was there to ask their never-ending questions.

Once they finished with the press, they made their way toward the multi-story building used as housing for Dragger's people. He wasn't paying attention to much of anything than getting inside and taking a nap before meeting with the people from the Bolivian embassy when he heard Cyn's shrill voice.

"Randsom, Randsom Jacobson, over here."

He turned to see her standing on the edge of the crowd of reporters. Just the sight of her made him groan inwardly. She wore a top that barely covered her breasts and left her midriff bare to her hips. Her shorts were so short he was embarrassed to even look at them. They only covered her from the top of her hips to just below her crotch.

Rand reluctantly went over to where Cyn was standing. "What do you think you're doing here?"

"I missed you and when I told Daddy you were a very important man here, he insisted I come down so you wouldn't be alone. I'm sure I'd be better company than that little alien bitch I've been seeing with you."

"Her name is Nina and she's an honored guest. As for being a bitch, she's far from that. She's the chief science officer for her delegation and has ten times the education of either you or me. If you're looking for a bitch, I'd suggest you look in the mirror. She's celibate which is more than I can say for you. I would also warn you that if you're thinking you can find one of her comrades to grace your bed, you're sadly mistaken. They are far more advanced than we are. They don't go around screwing everything in sight, which is more than I can say for you."

"I don't like the tone of your voice. Daddy said you're some sort of a diplomat and you'll need a beautiful wife to be with you. He also said we would make beautiful children together. You have to be nice to me. Daddy has lots of money and if he wants to, he can..."

"Enough, Cyn," Rand said. "You can't intimidate me with threats of what your father can do with all his money. We dated, nothing more. We certainly weren't committed to each other."

"Are you saying you'd turn down an offer of a position with Daddy's company if we were to get married?"

Rand laughed at her question. "You've always known I had no desire to go into business in the corporate world. My chosen profession in this life has always been archaeology."

"That may be so, but like it or not, you've moved in a different direction in the past few days. Mark my words, you'll be sorry you ever crossed either me or my father."

Rand took only a moment to think about her threat. Cyn's father held no threat to him. It was far more concerning to think about the life of a diplomat. As such he would, most certainly, have to leave his dream of becoming an acclaimed archaeologist behind. It wouldn't be long before he would have some serious decisions to make.

Before she could turn away from him, Dragger joined them. "You must be Miss Cynthia. My young friend's description of you doesn't do you justice. I'd like to have you join us for the midday meal. I'm certain my daughter, Nina, would appreciate talking to a young woman her own age. I'm afraid most of the people she's met since our arrival have been men. She will welcome the chance to become acquainted with you."

Dragger's invitation seemed to take Cyn by surprise. Once she got over the initial shock, she turned to Rand and stuck out her tongue like the spoiled brat she was.

Rand wondered if Daddy was really behind this or if Cyn just wanted to be in the limelight.

~ * ~

Nina watched as her father approached the woman who so upset Rand. She was clearly beautiful. Her hair was so yellow it was almost white, in a mass of curls like she'd never seen before.

It had been her idea that her father invite Cyn to join them. There were things about Earth, as well as about the females who were natives here Nina wanted to know, and what better way to find them out than to meet with this woman?

Inside the structure they'd built, Nina went to her mother and requested a feast be planned for Rand's friend.

"Why would you want to bring this woman into our company?" Lora asked.

"We have had little contact with the women of this planet. It is possible she can answer many of our questions about life here."

"I saw her and I don't trust her. Didn't you see her arguing with Rand? I don't think she's a friend."

"Neither do I, but Father feels she has knowledge we can use to become one with these people. From what Rand has said, she is self-centered. Perhaps it is wise for her to learn from us as well."

A commotion from the entrance of the building announced Cyn's arrival. "Nina, we have a guest. Have you made arrangements for refreshments to be brought?"

"Yes, Father. A luncheon will be served in our dining area."

She hurried into the reception area and got her first close look at Cyn. If her father thought the khaki shorts and camp shirts were revealing, what must he think of the way this woman was dressed?

"Welcome. I am called Nina and I've been told you are Cyn."

"Cynthia," her father corrected. "We are not familiar enough with this young lady to use anything other than her proper name."

"Forgive my forwardness, Cynthia. It is a pleasure to make your acquaintance. My friends and I have many questions about the lives we can expect to live on your planet."

The look on Cyn's face was one of shock. Perhaps she hadn't expected them to be able to communicate, but it was more than likely due to her shock at being accepted by these people who entered her world.

"Ah, thank you for inviting me to meet with you."

Nina could see fear in the woman's eyes. Was it possible she was worried they would take her life or the fact that everyone in the room towered over her? She was very petite, probably no more than five feet tall.

"Since we are new to your planet, there is much we would like to know. How do you choose a mate? Are the clothes you're wearing what all of the women wear? What makes the color on your lips and eyelids?"

Cyn seemed to relax. "Here we date. Don't you date where you come from?"

"I don't know what you mean by date. We get together in groups and then pair off with the person we decide to spend our lives with."

The look on Cyn's face was one of relief. "Is your intended with you?"

Nina fought the tears that threatened to spill from her eyes. "Ragnar is many light-years away from here. His family was sent to Seros. For a while I thought he was lost to me, but I have since learned he is safe. Even if I never see him again, I am pleased his life has been spared. I will never forget him and what we once thought would be our future together."

The relief once again faded but Cyn continued to answer the questions Nina posed earlier. "My clothes are especially made for me. I wore this outfit to impress Rand. I hoped it would get his juices flowing. Guess I was wrong. He really did mean it when he said we were finished. I'm not used to guys dumping me. It's usually the other way around."

She flicked her hair over her shoulder as a gesture that told Nina she was used to getting her own way.

"Oh, yes, and the color on my lips and eyelids is makeup. Do you like it?"

"I do. I would like to try using this makeup and see how it looks on me."

Cyn smiled. "I have my makeup with me. I could show you how to use it. I'm sure if you want some of your own, the people at the dig would be happy to get it for you."

"I would like to try, but I'm afraid my father wouldn't approve."

"What wouldn't I approve of, Daughter?"

Nina looked up to see her father and Rand enter the room. "Cynthia and I were talking about the face makeup she wears. She said she would show me how to wear it."

"I have to admit, I am not a fan of the way she paints her face," Dragger said. "That said, I can see no harm in allowing you to try something different. I cannot see how painting your face will enhance your natural beauty, but if you think this will make you fit in better with the women of this planet, why not?"

Nina was anxious to try the makeup mainly because it was something entirely new to her. She wasn't certain if it was anything she would want to adapt in her life on this new planet.

~ * ~

"I don't think I approve of Nina becoming friendly with Cyn," Rand observed once the girls left the room. "Cyn is the most self-centered, opinionated woman I've ever met. I don't think she will be a good influence on Nina."

"You underestimate Nina. She's baiting Cynthia. Maybe with all her questions she will be able to learn more about the women on your planet."

Rand wasn't as certain about the effect Cyn would have on Nina. It was possible Nina would have a positive effect on Cyn rather than Cyn having a negative effect on Nina.

"Have you heard from the government of Bolivia?" Rand asked in an attempt to change the subject.

"We have and they have given permission for us to go to Puma Punka as well as Tiwanaku. I have heard of Puma Punka before but

Tiwanaku is not familiar to me. Perhaps it was other people who were responsible for its existence. Do you know anything of this area?"

"I have read about this area. It is located close to Lake Titicaca and was a cultural and spiritual center for the area. I have also read about the strange activity reported in and around Lake Titicaca. It's said alien craft come up out of the lake, but that has never been authenticated. I've also seen pictures of the buildings and sculptures they've discovered there ."

"I have a feeling the stories of space craft coming out of the lake are just that, stories. I have never heard of underwater bases where life can be sustained."

"I suppose anything is possible, but the stories have continued for centuries. They must have some validity to them."

Rand watched as Dragger tried to justify the information he'd just been given. Someday it was possible the age-old stories would be either proven to be either truth or fantasy. For now, he was on the most exciting adventure of his life and he wanted to enjoy every moment of it.

"I am anxious to see both of these places," Dragger said, interrupting Rand's raging thoughts. "For now, we have had a long trip. It is time for us to satisfy our hunger for food, rest and information. The r est and nourishment are what you need. As for me, I am anxious to read about these two places I have never heard of before."

Rand agreed. He was hungry and his lack of sleep over the past twenty-four hours was beginning to catch up with him.

~ * ~

Nina watched as Cyn pulled bottles, tubes, and brushes from the bag she carried with her. The number of different products each of them represented boggled Nina's mind.

At Cyn's insistence, Nina obtained a basin of hot water along with a washing cloth. "This is my cleanser," Cyn said, handing one of the bottles to Nina.

"How do I use it?"

"First you put the cloth in the water and use it to moisten your face. Once that is done, you will squeeze some of this cleanser onto the cloth and use it all over your face."

Nina did as she was told. She'd always washed her face with the cleanser her mother made but the bits of grit in the cleanser came as a surprise. Even so, she found it refreshing. Once she finished, she again put the cloth in the water in order to rinse off the residue from her face.

"It is different from the cleanser I've used all my life, but it is not an uncomfortable feeling. What is the next step?"

"This is moisturizer. It has a sunscreen in it. I put it on every day. I especially have been grateful for it since coming here. The air is so dry here, I really need it. I don't want to wreck my skin."

"I don't understand why you would want to screen the sun. Is it not the giver of life?"

"That's what I used to think. My mother was a sun worshipper. Every summer she spent hours laying out in the sun by the pool. She always had a great tan. Unfortunately, the UV rays contributed to her skin cancer. By the time it was detected it was too late. She passed away within a year."

"I am so sorry to hear this. As for damage from the sun, we have never had to deal with such things because our planet had a natural filter to keep such dangerous rays away from us. I think this moisturizer will be very beneficial to our people."

Nina put on the moisturizer but felt as though it was a bit greasy on her skin. It was the same with the foundation and blush. The face powder seemed dry as did the eye shadow. She also didn't like the feel of the eye liner and mascara. What she did enjoy was the lip gloss as it seemed to act in the same way as the moisturizer and felt good on her lips.

"What do you think?" Cyn said as she held up a pocket mirror so Nina could see her reflection.

Nina studied the reflection intently. Even though the makeup seemed to enhance Cyn's natural beauty, the face staring back at Nina looks like a strange creature from another world. "I do not think this is something I would enjoy doing regularly but I do like the moisturizer as well as the lip gloss. Hopefully, I will be able to obtain some."

"If you can't get it here, I'm certain my father will have it shipped in for you. All I have to do is ask him for it."

"I wouldn't want to be a bother. I'm sure my mother can duplicate these products."

"Why go to all the work when one call can get it here within twenty-four hours?"

Nina marveled at Cyn. She was far more materialistic than the women from her planet. Things that were necessary were not purchased, they were made and if they were unable to be made, they weren't needed.

"Let's go and show Rand and your father your transformation."

Even though Nina agreed, she would have rather washed off the makeup that seemed so important to Cyn. "Do all of the women on this planet wear makeup? When I was at the dig, Stacey didn't seem to be wearing any."

"If you want to be fashionable, you do. I saw those girls at the dig and I would never want to be as homely as they are. I will always be beautiful no matter what happens. I don't ever go out without my makeup on."

Nina merely shook her head. The thought of putting so much makeup on her face was completely offensive to her.

~ * ~

Rand awoke from his nap, refreshed. He'd enjoyed the food the women prepared for him before he went to his quarters.

He found Dragger hunched over what looked like a computer, only the screen reminded him of the flat screen TVs people were so fond of displaying in their homes.

"Did you find anything interesting?" he asked as he entered the room.

"Very interesting. From looking at the pictures on the website for Tiwanaku I can't tell who their gods were. It is very different from any of the structures our people built. I am excited about getting to see it for myself. Considering I knew nothing of it until we were told we could visit there. This planet brings more discoveries every time I turn around."

"I know what you mean. It's why I chose archaeology as my profession. By coming here, I hoped to learn more about the ancient cultures. Instead I am learning firsthand about you and your people. I'm receiving the education of a lifetime."

"You give us too much credit. Without your help, we would have been out of our element with the reporters who greet us at every turn."

Rand was unaware of the opening of the sliding door behind them until Nina made her presence known. He turned at the distraction and stared at Nina. The makeup transformed her natural beauty into almost a carbon copy of Cyn. He'd never been a fan of the makeup women insisted on using and seeing it on Nina made him almost sick to his stomach. Instead of making a negative comment, he merely acknowledged the two young women with a nod of his head.

"Is this how all of the women of this planet paint their faces?" Dragger asked.

"All of them who want to be pretty do," Cyn replied.

"Interesting. How do you feel about this face paint, Daughter?"

"I like what Cyn called the moisturizer. In this dry climate, I feel it will be very beneficial. I also enjoy the lip gloss because my lips have also been very dry since our arrival. I have spoken with Mother and she feels she can duplicate the formula. Cyn was good enough to allow us to take samples of both products. That said, I am not a fan of what she calls makeup. It feels heavy upon my face and I do not feel it enhances my beauty."

"I don't understand," Cyn protested. "The makeup has made you absolutely beautiful with a flawless complexion. How can you say you don't like it?"

"It is not what I am used to. I am a scientist and depend on my brains rather than my beauty to show my worth to the world. I don't want to hurt your feelings, but there is a vast difference between the women of your society and those of mine. We can still be friends, but I doubt many of our women will be vain enough to think enhancing that which we have will make us more acceptable."

Rand could tell Cyn was close to tears. He'd never seen her without full makeup. Maybe things would have been different if they'd taken their relationship to a higher sexual destination, but he knew that would never happen. She wasn't someone he loved. He'd been flattered when the most beautiful girl on campus accepted a date from him, but he soon saw through her thin exterior to the real person inside the made-up body. Cyn was interested in nothing more than her position in life. She wanted a husband who had a prestigious career, lots of money, and enjoyed having a beautiful woman on his arm.

"I doubt we will meet again," Cyn said, her voice laced with anger. "I can see we have nothing in common. I thought I could make Rand love me because he needed a wife who would make him look good. I can see now he's not interested in anything of the kind. I do thank you for your hospitality, but my father's plane is waiting to take me back to the States. I've learned everything I need to know."

All of a sudden, Rand had a premonition of what Cyn was planning to do. "If you have any thoughts of going to the press and dissing these people, forget it. If I hear of anything of the kind, I will make your life a living hell. I know you thought the worst thing that could happen was when you caught Jack in bed with that bimbo but honey, you ain't seen nothing yet. I know what you've done to every guy you've ever dated and dumped. If you think I'll keep quiet, you're sadly mistaken."

"Daddy will..."

"Trust me, there's nothing your father can do that will deter me from trashing your reputation. Think about everything you've seen here and put things into perspective. It's been interesting knowing you, Cyn. Have a nice life." He enjoyed echoing the words she'd spoken to him only weeks earlier.

"Well, I never," Cyn sputtered.

Without saying anything further, she turned on her heel and stormed out of the room as well as out of his life.

"Are you certain you should have been so harsh in dismissing that young lady?" Dragger asked.

"I said nothing to her she hadn't said to me before I left to come to Peru. I soon learned, that even though I was flattered by the fact she agreed to go out on a date with me, she is a very shallow person. I remember my foster mother telling me about the girls in the 1960s who went to college not to get an education but an MRS. Degree."

"What is a MRS. Degree?" Nina inquired.

"In our society, unmarried women are referred to as Miss, married women as Mrs., and liberated women by Ms. In the 1960s a woman was expected to be married and raise a family. If they needed to work, they could be a secretary, a waitress, a nurse or if they had the education, a teacher. All of that changed over the next fifty years. Today women are employed in all sectors. They are doctors, lawyers, politicians and even the head of many countries. Physical beauty is only important to people like Cyn. She'll have no trouble in finding a man who wants a beautiful woman, with very few brains, on his arm."

Nina laughed at his description of Cyn. He could tell she agreed with him, but perhaps he had been a bit harsh. His only objective was protecting Dragger and his people from Cyn's sharp tongue.

~ * ~

Later in the day, Rand finally heard the interview Cyn gave to the press upon her departure from the compound housing the newcomers.

"Miss Adams, as one of the few people admitted to the alien compound, can you tell us about your experience?"

Cyn batted her eyes as Rand saw her do many times in the past when she wanted to impress a man. "Nina, as well as all of her family, was very hospitable. I'm certain they will enhance our planet with their knowledge as well as their abilities."

"That's not what I expected," Paul said when he turned off his tablet. "I thought she'd find something to complain about."

Rand laughed at Paul's comment. "I knew she wouldn't do anything of the kind. She's abiding by the deal we made before she left the compound."

"What kind of a deal?"

"I told her if she dissed Nina or anyone else in her delegation, I would make certain everyone knew what a shallow and self-centered bitch she really is. I have a feeling Daddy Dearest would be very upset to know everything about his darling little daughter."

Chapter Twelve

Rather than endure another trip in the helicopter, the Bolivian government sent a private jet to take Dragger, Nina and Rand to Puma Punka and Tiwanaku.

Nina enjoyed the comfortable seating and relative quiet of the flight compared to her previous experience when the noise from the turning blades of the helicopter made any kind of conversation or quiet contemplation impossible.

While Rand and her father chatted about the wonders they were about to see in Bolivia, she considered the visions she'd experienced at Machu Pichu. *Why did the ancients appear to me? Can I expect the same thing to happen to me in Bolivia?*

Not expecting an answer, she leaned her head back against the padded seat and closed her eyes. Almost instantly she fell into a deep sleep.

It is no coincidence you received a vision at Machu Picchu. You along with your family are the chosen ones for this destination. In the past, your family were considered Sky Gods. Although you and your family are mere mortals you are destined for great things on this planet.

You were right when you said Rand was descended from those who came from the skies. His relationship to the ancients is not recent but still he has been destined for this meeting with you and your family since the day of his birth.

When you arrive at the next ruins, you will again see visions. These ruins were not made by your ancestors, but they are important just the same. Listen to those who visit you in your vision, for they will give you important information.

"Nina, Nina."

Rand calling her name woke her and shattered the dream.

"Is something wrong?" she asked once she brought herself to full awareness.

"Not wrong, but we're getting ready to land. I thought you might want to get a bird's eye view of Bolivia before we land."

"I couldn't have been asleep that long."

"Oh yes, you could. You had a great nap. I wish I could sleep that soundly when I'm on a plane."

Nina looked out of the window next to her seat at the beautiful mountains below her. She knew this was the sight seen by the ancestors who came here thousands of years ago to impart their knowledge to the natives. Even so, today they looked as pristine as they must have to those long-ago space travelers.

~ * ~

Ragnar had little time to enjoy his new title as physician. After the ceremony giving him his degree, he was taken directly to the newly-constructed extension to the university close to Canaan's farm.

Although he'd been expecting to be living in the dorm with the students, he was pleasantly surprised to find his family waiting for him at a private apartment within the complex.

"What are you doing here?" he asked after greeting each family member warmly.

"Geni thought you would be more comfortable moving in to your new home if you had family here to greet you," his sister Patra said. "Along with Geni, Mother and I have been working to get everything furnished and ready for you to move in."

Ragnar looked around. The apartment had two bedrooms, two modern bathing rooms like the one at Geni's complex, a functioning kitchen with a small dining area, and a comfortable seating room. The furnishings in the larger of the two bedrooms were almost identical to his bedroom on his home planet but the smaller one looked to be more suited for a woman.

"Will I have someone living here with me?" he asked after taking the entire tour.

"This apartment is for you alone. The professors decided you needed more seclusion because of your notoriety," Geni replied.

Ragnar thought about it for only a moment before answering. In his wildest dreams he never thought he'd have a private apartment.

"I have no problem with it. If I don't feel like preparing my meals, I'm sure you will be more than able to help out."

Geni laughed at his comment. "I don't cook and you won't have to either as you are welcome to take your meals at the dormitory with the students. I'm a scientist, not a chef."

"If that is so it's a good thing my mother insisted I learn how to cook and take care of my needs by myself. At least, if necessary, I won't starve. You will always be welcome to come over in the evenings."

Geni smiled. "I doubt we have to worry about things like that. Your mother has told me how your people do not approve of sex before marriage. It is the same with my people. We will be friends and nothing more, unless things develop in that direction over the next few months. For now, we will be working together as professors at the university."

Ragnar prayed something more would come out of their relationship. He was pleased to think her morals mirrored his own. A sexual relationship was something every male of his people longed for but the beliefs of his people made it something to be anticipated rather than sought after.

~ * ~

There was little time for Ragnar to settle into his new home, as his classes started the morning after his arrival. Many of his students were female and totally excited about the prospect of learning more about the farming practices of growing the food they all needed for survival.

"You're one of the aliens who landed here, aren't you?" a pretty young woman named Napha asked after the first class.

"I am. I feel as though I have returned home. Many millennia ago our people first arrived on Seros and taught the people the skills of writing, mathematics and medicine. Now, with my planet dying, we have returned."

"Do all your medical students study agriculture?"

"We do. If you do not know where your food comes from and the effects it has on your body, how can you be successful as a physician? Food is the fuel of the body and knowing the properties of each thing we put in our bodies is essential."

Ragnar marveled at how easily the words he remembered his professors speaking came from his mouth. The lessons he'd learned stuck and now he was able to pass along the same knowledge to his students. It sounded so strange to think about his students, but they all seemed to be anxious to learn everything they could.

Being spring, the students were being taught how to prepare the soil for planting. Each student marveled at the amount of work it took in order to be ready to put the seeds into the ground. Another part of the program was learning about the care needed in the raising of the animals.

The area farmers were more than willing to impart their knowledge to the students. It was interesting to see the interaction between the students who, more than likely, grew up in the city, and the farmers who would be uncomfortable in the high-rise apartments and fast paced life offered in that very city.

~ * ~

"What are you doing after class tonight?" Ragnar asked.

Geni looked up from the papers she was grading. "Dinner at the dorm and..."

"Can I change your plans?"

Geni stared at him for a moment before answering. "What do you have in mind?"

"I talked to Canaan today and asked if he could spare a couple of steaks along with some vegetables. I thought I would like to prepare dinner for you and we could spend a quiet night enjoying some music I found on my computer."

Geni could feel her heart begin to beat a little bit faster. She'd been hoping to spend a quiet evening with Ragnar, but they'd been so busy setting up their classes by the time they returned from dinner at the dorm, they were too exhausted to think about anything other than going to their separate apartments for much-needed sleep.

"I think that would be lovely. It is a good thing you know how to cook, since if it was up to me, we'd starve."

Ragnar laughed at her comment, remembering how she told him she was a scientist, not a cook. Before leaving he promised to come to her classroom after their last class of the day.

Time seemed to drag until at last the students left to return to their dorm rooms and begin their studies for their next day's classes.

"Are you ready?" Ragnar asked, as he entered her classroom.

"More than ready. Are you sure I will be safe eating your cooking?"

"Positive. Back home we had to prepare our own meals while we were in school. We didn't cater to the students like they do here. The schools provided the food, but as medical and agricultural students we were expected to prepare it ourselves. In my dorm, we did communal meals, with each of us taking turns doing the cooking. I have to admit my meals were some of the best ones any of us ate."

"I think you're bragging, but I'll withhold judgment until after we've eaten tonight."

He took her hand in his and together they walked out of the building. The feel of his skin against hers prompted feelings of emotional attachment. Geni took a moment to think about her feelings. *Is this the love I've read about in books? I couldn't know from my parents as they were never together enough to show me what love really is.*

As they made their way to Ragnar's apartment within the dorm system, Geni marveled at how different their lives had been. She'd grown up with her mother, living in the compound she now owned. Their meals were expertly prepared by the same chefs she now employed. There had been no reason for her to learn how to cook.

On her random visits to Canaan's farm, she marveled at her aunt's ability to cook meals. Every meal she prepared compared to anything she ate at the compound. Even so, she'd never had a desire to learn the art of cooking for herself. Now she wondered if she should have spent more time in the kitchen and less in the lab.

While she was content with a private apartment, she spent no time using the kitchen her home boasted. Ragnar actually lived a life that was more like that of her aunt and uncle. She was pleasantly surprised when she stepped into his accommodations. She'd seen them when Ragnar first arrived, but at the time she'd had other things on her mind other than scrutinizing his new living arrangement. The apartment had a large sitting room, an eat-in kitchen, two bathing facilities, and Ragnar told her there were two bedrooms. It was luxurious by any standards; not as large as the estate, but enough for a single man or perhaps a couple with a child. Hers was little more than a large dorm room; her kitchen was very small and the sitting room also contained her sleeping area. It was enough for her, even though at times she missed her spacious dwelling at the complex with its myriad of servants to do the work of running her home efficiently.

~ * ~

Ragnar was pleased to see Geni's acceptance of his accommodations. He'd been astonished by the sheer size of his apartment, to say nothing of the furnishings that came along with it.

He was glad he'd been able to come home during the midday break in order to begin marinating the steak and getting the vegetables ready to steam as soon as they returned from their day at work.

A week earlier, he'd taken his students to visit a winery located not far from the school. At that time, he'd purchased several bottles of their award-winning wine. When he'd been home earlier, he'd put one in the refrigeration unit to chill to go along with their steaks. He was pleased to find not only a sweet white wine but also a pleasing red. The red would be a perfect companion to his planned steak dinner.

While wine on his home planet was reserved for only special occasions, since coming here he found he enjoyed having it with his meals. He'd also developed a taste for the local beer. At first, he found it different from the beer he'd enjoyed before being banished from his home but he soon decided he enjoyed this headier brew.

"Make yourself comfortable, while I prepare the grill and get the vegetables ready to steam."

"Can I help, or at least watch? I'm no good in the kitchen but I always enjoyed watching my aunt when she made meals."

Ragnar smiled. He'd heard all about Geni's lack of ability in the area of cooking. "If you'd like."

He opened the door leading to the patio where he'd been pleased to find a grill. It was state-of-the-art and even had a feature where he could steam vegetables and bake tubers. With such equipment, preparing a meal for Geni would be relatively easy.

"When did you have time to get everything ready?"

"Maybe I shouldn't tell you."

"Don't tease me."

Ragnar gave her a smile before telling her how he'd skipped the midday meal to a get everything ready to put on the grill as soon as they returned to his apartment.

"I know my knowledge of cooking is limited, but why are you preparing the meal outside when you have a modern kitchen?"

"Ah, my dear, you have a lot to learn about men. Even though we are adept in the kitchen, when the weather cooperates with us, we all like to use the grill and cook on the patio. It's a man thing, so I don't expect you to understand. As I recall, my mother always loved it when the weather was warm enough for my father to take over cooking for the family. He loved 'cooking out,' as he called it. I'm certain he will continue doing so in their new accommodations here on Seros."

After his explanation, Ragnar turned on the fuel to the grill and ignited the flame. He also turned on the steamer on the side of the grill where he could cook with pots and pans. It took no time at all for the flame on the grill side to be ready for him to put on the steaks.

"How do you like your steak? I usually eat mine medium rare."

He watched as Geni contemplated her answer to his question, it made him wonder if anyone had ever asked her such a question. Considering she had a full kitchen staff it was possible no one needed to ask because they'd been cooking for her all her life and knew her preferences when it came to food.

"I'm not sure. What do you mean by medium rare?"

Knowing he'd read her correctly brought a slight smile to his lips. "It's well-cooked on the outside and pink to red on the inside."

"I think that's the way my aunt used to prepare it when I visited. I would like mine medium rare as well."

The minute the steaks hit the grill they began to sizzle as they cooked. The aroma mingled with that of the steaming vegetables began to make his mouth water uncontrollably. By missing the midday meal, he was now overly hungry and more than ready to eat.

While their meal cooked, he finished setting the patio table with dishes and cutlery. Lastly, he poured the wine into glasses he found in the cupboard. They weren't the fancy wine glasses his mother owned and left behind, but they would do for tonight's dinner.

Once the steaks were done to his satisfaction, he put them onto their plates, along with the tubers and a generous helping of the vegetables.

"This meal looks as though it is fit for a queen," Geni said, once she was seated at the table. "I can't ever remember eating outside before. It is very romantic eating with the moons and stars rising. Did you plan it this way?"

"I could say I did, but the moons and stars always rise at this time of day. I often take my evening meal out here to enjoy the beauties of the night."

They'd just finished their meal and were enjoying a second glass of wine when they were interrupted by a loud pounding on the front door of the apartment.

Ragnar excused himself and went to see who would be so impatient.

"Where is she?" a young man who looked remarkably like Geni demanded.

"If you're referring to Geni, she's on the patio. We were just enjoying a glass of wine. I can get another glass so you can join us."

"Why is she here, with you, an alien and perhaps a threat to our people?"

"We are friends. I invited her to come here and share dinner with me. I'm sorry to say we have nothing left over to offer you other than the wine."

"I don't care about your damn wine. My sister shouldn't be here, alone, with a man. What kind of people are you? Do you not know of our courting practices?"

"Courting? Is that what you think we are doing? We are adults and if we wish to enjoy each other's company, there is nothing wrong with it.

Can you say you haven't enjoyed the company of women during your deployment on the space station?"

Ragnar's question seemed to infuriate Geni's brother. Fortunately, he saw the man prepare to hit him and sidestepped before his fist could find its mark on his jaw.

"Jayden! What are you doing?"

Ragnar broke his concentration and turned to see Geni entering the apartment. By doing so he opened himself to the next blow from the man he now knew was called Jayden. Caught off guard, he staggered backward, tripping over a small bench in the foyer and falling to the floor.

"Geni," the man said rushing to her side, completely ignoring Ragnar as he got up from the floor. "Have you been compromised? Has this man taken what he is not entitled to? Have you been hurt?"

"Have you lost your mind? Ragnar and I have become friends. We are enjoying a meal together."

"Alone?"

"I can see you have been on the space station far too long, Brother. When Ragnar's people landed here, they came with technology that is far superior to our own. They also brought new ideas in the training of our medical personal. Tomorrow we will take you on a tour of this extension of the university and you will see how we are putting those ideas into practice. We have also shared with them things they hadn't developed. We have made great progress in assimilating their culture with our own."

"Have you forgotten the rules of propriety?"

Ragnar listened to the conversation between brother and sister. He thought of all the things his own people would say if aliens landed and tried to change age-old customs. Getting to his feet, he addressed the man who just hit him.

"I think we should continue this discussion in a more comfortable area. Would you like a glass of wine, or would you prefer a beer?"

For the first time, Jayden began to smile. "It's been a long trip from the space station and out to this campus. I would appreciate a beer."

Geni led the way out to the patio, while Ragnar got a beer from the refrigeration unit. Once he returned to the patio, brother and sister were engaged in conversation. It was interesting watching them interact with each other. Even though he could understand their words, he knew they were also communicating through their body movements, and possibly even by telepathic communication.

Ragnar waited until there was a lull in the conversation before putting the bottle of beer along with the frosted mug in front of Jayden.

"That looks good. I probably wouldn't have needed the glass."

"This is something I enjoyed on Plantas, my home planet. The mug that has been kept in the freezing area of the refrigeration unit keeps the beer cold longer. I've always appreciated it and hope you will like drinking your beer this way as well."

While Jayden watched, Ragnar opened the beer and poured it into the mug. As though he was apprehensive, Jayden let the beer chill before taking a sip of the brew.

"I have to admit this is much better than the warm beer we had on the space station. Is this one of the new things you have brought to our people?"

"One of them. I also was instrumental in getting this school established to run in conjunction with the medical college. On Plantas, when you study medicine, you should also study agriculture. It is good to know where your food comes from and how it is grown."

Jayden nodded as Ragnar continued to explain about not only the things his people brought to Seros but also of the advances his people had made since arriving here.

"I was one of the first ones to detect your ships as they approached our planet. I'm afraid I am the one who warned my father of your coming. Unfortunately, I was mistaken about your intent, causing you and your people to suffer injuries inflicted by the military. I have spoken with my father and he confirmed his new friendship with your father as well as others of your people."

Ragnar took a moment to recall the announcement of the friendship between his father and General Ledling, or Leddie, as he said he preferred to be called.

"I remember when they told me of their friendship as well. I must be honest and say I was skeptical. I couldn't help remembering how the military attacked us only moments after we were greeted with adulation. I saw my family murdered and I was taken prisoner. I spent many hours being examined like a lab animal. I felt nothing but animosity toward the people of your planet."

"Something must have made a difference in your feelings. I am told you are the head of this annex to the university."

Ragnar glanced at Geni. Did he dare tell her brother she was the reason he changed his mind? "I got to know the people and found we have much in common. Your uncle Canaan has become a good friend. He was instrumental in getting this program up and running. Once we moved past the fear of an alien invasion, it became evident our peoples have much in common."

"You forgot to mention how we also became friends," Geni commented.

"I can understand why," Jayden said, his tone one of a teasing older brother. "I came on a bit strong when I first arrived. I was ready to defend the honor of my baby sister. I can hear your feelings by the tone of your voices and I can see it in your actions. Am I wrong in thinking you care for my sister?"

For the first time since Jayden's arrival Ragnar felt the weight of uncertainty lift from his shoulders. "You're right, I do have feelings for Geni and I hope she has feelings for me as well. If I were on my home planet, we would have known each other for our entire lives. Here things are different. Neither of us knows the other well enough for anything serious to develop this quickly. We are just beginning the process of becoming better acquainted."

"For me, I think we are further along in the process," Geni said with a wink. "I can tell you, Brother, I am totally in love with Ragnar. All my adult life I have been looking for my soulmate and when I first saw Ragnar on the examination table in the lab, I knew I'd found him. If he asked me to mate with him, I would definitely say yes."

Jayden laughed at his sister's statement. "Is this the Geni I know and love? I thought you were content to become an old maid scientist. I'm not completely happy with this relationship, but I'm willing to get to know you, Ragnar. It's good to see my sister happy, but it will take more than seeing such happiness to make me certain this will last. What does bother me is the fact you are living in the same house as Ragnar."

"I am not living in Ragnar's apartment. I have my own small apartment within the dormitory. Tonight, he asked me to share the evening meal with him. I must admit it is a welcome change from the meals cooked for all the students. I wouldn't be against sharing his apartment, but only if we were properly married. To be truthful, this is the first chance we've had to be alone since the beginning of the classes. Between our class schedules and the amount of prep work we need to do at night we usually grab something to eat in the dorm cafeteria before retiring to our own accommodations. Tonight was a special occasion for us."

For the first time since his arrival at the apartment, Jayden began to smile. "I must assume you had the meal brought in, as I know your talents don't run along the lines of cooking."

"You shouldn't assume anything. Ragnar happens to be a good cook. Unlike our people, their mothers teach their sons and daughters how to be self-sufficient. The meal Ragnar made for me tonight was as good as anything that has been prepared for us at the compound. We have much to learn from these people. Accept it, Jayden, these people have much more than academics to teach."

"It is possible you are correct, Geni, but I still advise you to take this relationship slowly. Know exactly what you're getting into before you jump in feet first."

Ragnar could feel his blood begin to boil. He did have feelings for Geni, but at the same time, he didn't feel as though he should take things to the next level until he could put his feelings for Nina into perspective. It was true he would never see her again, but she'd been part of his life for many years. Had things been different, he would have taken her as his life mate and together they would have brought children into the world. Now she was over sixty-seven light-years away and getting the two of them together was indeed an impossibility.

"I'd offer you something to eat, but unfortunately I only made enough food for the two of us. I can offer you another beer before you have to leave."

Geni picked up on the comment. "Speaking of leaving, are you planning to return to the compound tonight?"

"I cannot see why you would be going back to the compound. This apartment has two sleeping areas and there is no reason why you should travel so far tonight," Ragnar suggested.

"Thank you for your concern, Ragnar. I wouldn't think of imposing on your hospitality. Before I came here, I stopped to see Uncle Canaan. He assured me he and Aunt Mimi have a spare sleeping room where I can stay until I'm again deployed. I have about a full moon cycle before I will be shipped out close to where Mother is working. It will be good to see her again but it will also be good to be close to you so we can catch up. I'll see you in the morning. If I'm not mistaken tomorrow is a holiday so there will be no classes."

Ragnar watched as brother and sister embraced before he left the house.

"Jayden always had bad timing," Geni said once she returned to the patio with a fresh glass of wine. "Maybe it's just as well he came when he did. I didn't know how to tell you of my feelings."

"Perhaps I should tell you more of my past before things go much further. Before we left Plantas, I was very much in love with a girl by the name of Nina. Our parents were neighbors and it was a given the two of us would one day be mated. Unfortunately, her family was sent to another planet, one called Earth. I'm still getting over the feelings I had for her before we were separated. In other words, I need more time before I commit to anything or anyone."

Geni smiled and put her hand to his cheek. "I understand completely. Unless your feelings for me are the same as mine are for you, we could never make things work out. I'm more than willing to wait. Someday, maybe the two of us will be sharing this apartment. At that time, perhaps you can teach me your skills in the kitchen while I learn more about your past and you learn of mine. If I'm not mistaken the two of us are meant to be together and when the time is right it will become as evident to you as it is to me. For now, let's enjoy what is left of the evening as well as the remainder of this good wine."

Chapter Thirteen

After the plane landed in Bolivia, Nina unfastened her seatbelt and prepared to deplane. Through one of the windows, she saw a group of photographers as well as reporters, all anxious to get a glimpse of the visitors from another planet. She was getting used to seeing these people waiting for them wherever they went. Likewise, she was getting used to Rand expertly handling them. She knew her father was relieved not to have to deal with the myriad of questions the reporters insisted on asking.

"When will we stop being news?" she asked of no one in particular.

"You are news and you will be for a long time. From what I'm told, news agencies all over the world are interested in not only you but also your counterparts. You have no idea how many questions your arrival has answered. For now, let me handle this."

As usual, Nina deferred to Rand. She knew he would take care of things and soon they would be on their way to Puma Punka. She was anxious to see if she would receive any visions once they were at the now-famous ruins.

In the days prior to leaving Peru, she'd done many hours of research on Puma Punka. Seeing the pictures the Internet provided piqued her interest. How could anyone cut solid rock so precisely leaving an edge so sharp it could cut your finger?

Taking a deep breath, she stepped off the plane and was immediately inundated by the reporters anxious to ask her questions.

"How do you like earth?" a female reporter asked as she shoved a microphone toward Nina. "Is it like your home planet? Do you find our people different from yours?"

"This is going to be my home," she replied. "The planet I called home for my entire life, Plantas, no longer exists. I am adapting. To answer your second question, it is not like where I grew up, but I realize no two planets within the solar system are alike. As for the people, everyone I have met has been very cordial to us. For now, we are expected for a tour of Puma Punka. If you will excuse us, it would be rude of us to be late."

Nina felt Rand move to her side. He snaked his arm around her waist and whispered in her ear. "You're getting good at handling the press. I'll have to watch out or I'll be out of a job."

"That's nonsense. My father depends on you to help him with situations like this. He is very fond of you."

"I've become fond of all of your people, some more than others."

Nina smiled at his comment. Even with her memories of Ragnar, she found herself becoming enamored with Rand. He was handsome, intelligent, and her almost constant companion, while Ragnar was sixty-seven light-years away on another planet. She prayed he would find love. Thinking of him brought to mind the communication she'd received saying he'd survived the attack on the landing party and like the rest of his family was making a complete recovery.

~ * ~

The articles Nina read on the Internet, although informative, could in no way begin to describe the beauty of the ruins stretching out before her. The precision of the cuts made into the rock so that they fit together so precisely were amazing.

As promised in the visions she'd received at Machu Picchu, she no more than touched the ancient building blocks than she again saw the people who once populated the area.

We are the ancients. Some called us the Sky People because we were travelers from other planets. We came here through a time warp from many hundreds of light-years away. We were here after your people and knew of the massive building you helped the natives to construct in other areas of this continent.

Nina's mind spun with questions but she knew she couldn't speak them aloud. What she saw and was experiencing was visible only to her. To voice her questions would confuse the others.

There is no need for you to voice your questions. This was one of our people's most beautiful feat of engineering. We brought with us the special tools to cut the stones and used our levitation devices to put them into place. Unlike you, we knew we would never be returning to the planet called Earth. We were sent by the one god but were told never to promise our return because it would not happen. We envy you the opportunity you have to return and meet the modern people who now populate not only this continent, but also the other continents on this planet.

We have kept watch over this planet and grieve over the change in climate that turned the seventh continent into an uninhabitable place. Our predecessors told us of the beautiful land that they inhabited until the change took place. They called it a paradise but were forced to leave when the temperatures dropped and the snow refused to stop falling. It grieved them to return to our planet but it was understood they could no longer stay.

It was many years before we returned to this planet. It was then that we found this area. The weather was more tolerable. Unlike when we inhabited the seventh continent, we realized we were not to colonize this area but to give guidance to the natives who lived here. Unfortunately, before we could finish what we'd started, a war broke out. We were instructed to return to our home planet and not to return. Our leaders were not happy with the warring nature of the natives who populated this area.

"Nina, are you all right?"

She turned at the sound of Rand's voice. "I was having a vision. Where is the seventh continent? I have not read anything about it. Can we go there?"

Rand looked puzzled for a moment. "Are you talking about Antarctica? That would be the seventh continent. No one goes there except the scientists who study its frozen environment. There are rumors of an ancient society that once thrived there, but nothing has been proven."

"The people who built these structures once lived there and built similar structures. When the snow began to fall without ceasing, they returned to their home planet. Later, they found this area and came here to build what you see before you. When they once again went home it was with the knowledge they would never return to Earth as we have. It is sad, but they will never be able to share their technology with you."

She watched the shocked expression on Rand's face. "Are you sure? If what you say is right, this will turn the scientific world upside down."

"I've been having visions from the people of the past," she continued. "The people who built the structures are the ones I have seen in these visions. They were on Earth long before they came to this land. They settled in what they called paradise on the seventh continent. When the seasons changed and the snow refused to stop falling, they returned to their home planet. When they once again thought the time was right, the people returned to Earth and came to this area. They built the wonders your people now revere, but when their time was over here, they returned to the stars and were told never again would they come back to Earth."

"My daughter speaks the truth, for I had the same vision. I thought I was the only one to experience it. These people were not from our planet but from one far more advanced. From my vision, I was told of the stone cutting tools as well as the levitation devices they brought with them to create this wonder we are now seeing. I wish I could have known these people and learned of their tools. They would have had much to teach us. Now we can only imagine the marvelous tools they used to create these monuments to their great achievements. Unlike my people, they will never be able to see how the people of Earth have progressed over the centuries. Soon they will engage in a war between rival planets they cannot win."

~ * ~

Rand marveled at the visions described by both Nina and Dragger. For years, he'd heard the stories of a once-flourishing civilization on Antarctica but dismissed it as mere speculation. These revelations confirmed the rumors and he knew would spur further exploration of the frozen expanse of land Nina referred to as the seventh continent.

"I honestly don't know what to say," he finally commented. "You've confirmed the rumors that have been running rampant within the scientific community for decades."

"For now, they must continue to be rumors," Dragger cautioned. "Until they can be confirmed by your scientists and explorers, we must not speak of this to anyone other than ourselves. We have come to this world to track the progress of the people here, not to change anything. We are looking for a home, not to make waves. I think that is the right phraseology."

Rand smiled at Dragger's choice of words. "You are right in your words, Dragger. You are also right in wanting to keep this information between the three of us. If the wrong people were to learn of it who knows what could happen to our world. It's best, as you put it, if we let it be discovered by the scientists and explorers. When the time is right, they will confirm their find."

Chapter Fourteen

Ragnar enjoyed spending more time with Geni. His feelings continued to grow for her with each passing day. Just last week, he'd received a communication from contingency of their people sent to Earth.

All of the groups had been accepted and were settling in to their new homes. He'd also heard from Nina. As she had in the past, she mentioned the young archaeology student by the name of Rand. He prayed she wouldn't allow the feelings she'd once had for him to interfere with her future happiness in her new home on Earth.

"You have a serious look on your face, Ragnar. Is there a problem?"

Ragnar looked up from his computer to see Geni standing behind him. "Just reading about those of our people who went to Earth. They are adjusting to their new surroundings as well as we are to life on Seros. It makes me sad to think our friends who were dispatched to Nalo have not been heard from. I don't know if they landed safely or if their ships were destroyed while on the journey."

"You've spoken of a woman from your past, Nina. Is she adjusting well, or does she long for your touch as much as I do?"

"As you know, we were meant to be mated, but this forced evacuation has separated us for all time. In the same way as I have met you and am learning about you as well as finding my feelings growing, she has also met someone. It pleases me to think she is not dedicating her life completely to the science we both loved. She wasn't meant for the medical profession. Her life was that of a science officer while mine was to be a healer. I will always miss her, but..."

"...but you still love her. I pray one day you will love me in the same way."

"I do love you and once this session of school is finished, I want to go back to your compound to ask your father if he will agree for us to be joined. My love for you is the mature love that lasts forever, while my love for Nina is that of a young man experiencing the emotion for the first time. Nina and I have talked about it through our communications and realize even if we'd remained on Plantas, our marriage might not have stood the test of time."

"Why is that?"

Ragnar could hear the confusion in Geni's voice. "Because we were young and expected to be joined but our lives were destined to take two different paths. Had we not been separated, I would have gone into private practice and she would have spent long hours in the lab. We would have grown apart. I know it happens, so do you. Is it not so with your parents?"

Geni nodded. "You know it is, and I have always hated the fact that divorce is often allowed on our planet. I know sometimes it is for the best but in most cases, it is the children of divorce who suffer because of it. Look at my brother and me. I have followed Mother into the world of science and education while he is a military man like our father. Thankfully, he was able to stay with Uncle Canaan and Aunt Mimi while he was on leave. It has given us time to get to know each other once again."

Ragnar thought about the man who was so angry to find Geni eating the evening meal with him. "I, too, am pleased to have had the time to get to know him. It is good to know he will be stationed on this planet so we can get together often."

He glanced at the clock and realized how late it had become during their conversation. Today was the day of final exams for their students, signaling the beginning of the break.

~ * ~

Throughout the summer, the students, as well as Ragnar and Geni, had been busy working on the farm. With the harvest finished and the first winter storm predicted to arrive the following week, both faculty and students were ready for a break. They all longed for time to return to their homes and families.

Ragnar was anxious to see his brothers, sister and parents. Being at the farm, some of them came out on occasion, but mostly they were busy acclimating themselves to their new lives on this planet. He even had a new niece he'd never seen.

He was looking forward to the time away from the school. Of course, he would be working at the university hospital, but would be away from the farm until it was time for the spring planting. Once it commenced, there would be a new crop of students who, he hoped, were excited about learning how their food was grown and processed.

He was glad Geni had agreed to spend the night at his apartment in the spare sleeping space. It had been late when they finished their dinner and evening conversation. Due to the hour of the night he didn't want her going to her apartment alone. Neither did he relish walking her home and returning to his dwelling. She'd spent many nights in the spare bedroom and kept clothes there for the coming morning.

"We'd better get finished up here and over to the classrooms," Geni said. "This is going to be a long day. I know the students will be anxious about their exams and final grades. They are equally excited about going home for the break. It's hard to believe they will be starting their internships."

"I've been thinking about that. I'll also be working at the hospital. It will be strange to be working side by side with the young men and women I've been teaching in my classes this past semester."

"You'll handle it just fine."

Geni loaded the last of the dishes into the dishwasher, before grabbing a coat from the closet. Just before they left the apartment the dishwasher began its almost silent whir as it sonically cleaned and sanitized their breakfast dishes.

~ * ~

Nina checked her communicator as soon as they were airborne and headed for the Southwestern states of Rand's home country. She was surprised to see a message from Ragnar.

My dear Nina,
I think of you often and am pleased to read of your friend Rand. I,

too, have met someone on Seros. Her name is Geni and she is a medical scientist. Together we founded an extension to the university on her uncle's farm. It is much like the agricultural training I received on Plantas. We have successfully completed the first semester and are looking forward to spring when we will start the process with a new group of students.

I have finished my residency at the university hospital and will be able to be an attending physician until the school's next term.

That said, I also wanted to tell you that I've fallen in love with Geni and we have made plans to marry before the next term begins. We are an unlikely match as her father is head of the military and was responsible for the attack on our people when we first arrived.

It has come as a great surprise to find that Leddy, as her father prefers to be addressed, and my father have formed a strong friendship.

As for the others of our party who settled here, all of them are adapting well. We are all saddened to realize the ships we sent to Nalo have not been heard from. I, like everyone else, fear they are lost to us forever.

I keep you in my thoughts and pray you will find the same love as I have with Geni. I know we were destined to be mated, but fate sometimes has a way of taking the future out of our hands.

With warmest regards,
Ragnar

Turning off the screen, Nina swallowed down the tears threatening to spill from her eyes. Although she'd accepted the fact she would never see Ragnar again, it still bothered her to think he had fallen in love with someone else. He was her man. He didn't belong to someone on an alien planet, named Geni.

"Bad news?"

She looked up to see Rand slide into the empty seat next to her on the private jet.

"Not really. It's an update from Ragnar. He's been working as an attending physician at the university hospital and he's getting married. He's also the head of a new program for the university to study agriculture as part of the medical training. I'm happy for him."

"Are you? Isn't he the man you thought you were going to marry?"

"Yes, but we both understood we would never see each other again. He has gone on with his life and so will I once we are no longer traveling to the many archaeological areas of your planet."

"I hope you mean that."

The look on Rand's face was one she once saw on Ragnar's. Just looking at him she began to realize how much she'd come to care for this Earthling. Was it possible, she, like Ragnar, was falling in love with someone different from herself?

"I came up here to tell you we're getting ready to land in Santa Fe. That's the capital city of New Mexico and our stepping-off point to view the wonders of the Anasazi."

Nina nodded. She'd spent most of the trip from Bolivia reading about the ancient society of Indians who populated the area Rand referred to as the four corners. They fascinated her as did the other archeological areas they'd visited while in South America.

~ * ~

As soon as the plane touched down, Rand knew there was something wrong. He could see the terminal from his window seat but for some reason the plane was taxiing toward a hanger off to the far side of the airport.

Rather than say anything to upset Nina or Dragger, he waited until the plane was securely in the hanger. Once they came to a complete stop, he could see a set of movable stairs being put into place. They would not be coming into the terminal, but into a deserted hanger.

Before the door was opened, the captain came out of the cockpit. "We've been informed there is a large group of possible protesters in the main terminal. We were told this was the best solution."

"Protesters?" Dragger questioned. "I do not understand the meaning of this word."

Scenes from the 2016 presidential election flashed through Rand's mind. Even though he'd been too young to remember them, he studied the time period in his U.S. history class. Because there was so much media coverage, he had formed a mental picture of the events in the history books. Back then there were almost daily protests and many of them turned rather nasty. He remembered taking a class about the protests and riots in the early twenty-first century. The unrest in his home country as well as around the world had been a prelude to the peace now enjoyed worldwide.

How can this happen in my country? Aren't protests a thing of the past?

Before he could answer the question, he posed within the confines of his mind, the cabin door opened and people were being escorted off the plane. With the exception of when he moved to sit next to Nina and when he made his way up to speak with the pilot, he'd remained in one position ever since taking off from Peru. Now he was looking forward to getting off the plane and stretching his legs. He was grateful for the private jet that had been provided for them by a businessman who asked to remain nameless. There was so much security around this flight, he wondered how there could be a large crowd assembled for their arrival.

Dr. Grant was the first one to come down the ramp, followed closely by Rand, Dragger and finally Nina. To his surprise, he recognized many of the dignitaries assembled in the hanger. Of course, the President of the United States of America stood shoulder to shoulder with ranking members of the Hopi, Navajo, and Apache tribes in native dress. The others he assumed to be the Governor of New Mexico and the mayor of Santa Fe.

To Rand's surprise it was the leader of the Hopi who was the first to step forward.

"We have waited many years for the return of the Sky People. I feel I am blessed to be the holy man of my people to be one of the first to greet you. With my brothers from the Apache and Navajo, we welcome you to our sacred lands."

Dragger bowed graciously and extended his hand to the Hopi holy man. "It is our pleasure to return to this planet. Although our people came to those who live far to the south of here in the country called Peru, I hope I represent those who came to your ancestors. All of us who have traveled across the heavens have done so for peaceful reasons. I know the mission of my people was to build monuments that would last throughout the generations as well as to teach the skills of mathematics, astrology and language to those who were living on this planet."

The other Native American leaders came forward, each bowing slightly to show their respect for this alien who came to visit their lands. Rand was impressed.

Lastly, the white leaders came forward and gave welcoming speeches.

"We were told there were protesters at the airport and that is why we were diverted to this hanger," Dr. Clark said. "I thought our arrival was to be kept secret."

"Unfortunately, the news was leaked and has been reported on the national networks," the President replied. "It seems there has been another landing not far from here and people are worried. Our people are looking into it and have sent pictures of the craft that landed. We are hoping you can identify it."

The President handed his cell phone to Dragger. The expression on his face went from elation, at meeting the leaders who were gathered, to concern as he viewed the picture.

"What is it, Father?" Nina asked.

Taking the cell phone from the President's hand he turned it so she could see the picture for herself.

"How can it be? That's the ship carrying Tarena and her family. We have to go to them. They might be injured. I'm certain they are afraid of what might happen. Considering what happened to Ragnar and his party, I don't blame them."

"Since these are people from your planet you should go there," the President said, as he took back his cell phone. "Any reception that was planned can wait. I will take you and your party there in my limousine. There are scientists at the scene along with medical personnel. The site is close by. Just follow me and we will get there with the greatest of speed because we will have a police escort."

Everything moved in warp time. Rand could hardly keep up as everyone rushed toward the waiting limousines. Presidential flags flew from the first vehicle to which Dragger and Nina were taken. The second vehicle waited for Rand and Dr. Clark to get in. As soon as the door closed, the cars started driving out of the airport with sirens blaring from the police escort in front and back of the line of cars. Rand decided the additional cars in their party were for reporters as well as the secret service agents assigned to guard not only the President, but also the visiting dignitaries from the far side of the Galaxy. It was entirely possible the Native American leaders as well as the other dignitaries were also being transported to the landing site.

"This certainly isn't what I expected to happen," Dr. Clark said. "For that matter, who is Tarena?"

"I guess, since you've been hanging out with Dragger more than you have Nina, you wouldn't know. You see, Nina had two very special people who went on the same trip as she did, but in different directions. The man she thought she was going to marry, Ragnar, went to Seros and her best friend, Tarena, went to Nalo. Nina has heard about Ragnar's successful voyage and that he's found someone new. As for Tarena, there has been no communication from them since we left our home planet. For all intents and purposes, she believed Tarena was dead."

Dr. Clark nodded his head in agreement. "Yes, that explains a lot. Dragger never talks about the other missions. I'm sure he had friends going to both planets, but this is the most I've heard about the other ships that left there at the same time as those who landed here on Earth. You do know, once again we will be one of the first people to make contact with these people."

For a moment, Rand contemplated what Dr. Clark just told him. "I've been thinking about it. If the mission going to Nalo did run into trouble, where are the other ships? We know there were several ships that landed around the globe, so we have to assume it was the same with the other missions. If so, where are they?"

Chapter Fifteen

Nina tried to concentrate on the conversation going on between her father and the President, but her mind kept wandering. She recognized the craft that just landed on Earth as the one she watched Tarena and her family enter and fly away from Plantas in. The markings on each ship were unique and she had no doubt about the identity of the passengers who would soon be disembarking.

As though from nowhere, towering red rocks served as a backdrop for the ship that recently landed on this alien planet.

"There they are, Father. Can you communicate with anyone on board? Can you tell them we are here and they have nothing to fear?"

"I'm trying, Daughter. Wait...I just heard from Fragon, Tarena's father. I told him to wait until we arrived to come out of the ship."

The limousine skidded to a stop and two men in military dress were quick to open both back doors. While the President exited from the right, Nina and her father exited through the door on the left.

"Where is Rand?" Dragger questioned. "He must be here."

"I'm right behind you, Dragger."

Nina turned, as relieved to see Rand as she knew her father was. He had become their link between the people who populated Earth and those from her planet who came to Earth.

As they approached the craft, Nina watched the doors open. Fragon was the first one to come down the steps to set foot on the soil of an alien planet. She was horrified to see the condition of her best friend's father. It was evident the man was suffering from the extended travel through time and space.

Behind Fragon, Tarena's mother, Dyna, and Tarena also disembarked. Behind her, several others made their way out of the craft that had been their home for much longer than anyone ever thought they would be traveling.

Nina broke away from the protection of the officers guarding the President. "Tarena," she cried, making her way to embrace her friend. "What happened? How is it you are here? Don't answer that, we need to get you some medical attention as well as something to eat."

A flurry of activity was happening all around them, as more vehicles as well as ambulances and medical personnel began arriving. Nina turned to the President, wondering what was happening.

"Your father told me the people would probably be starving and suffering from the effects of such prolonged space travel. I had my people call for medical assistance before we even arrived."

Nina was ashamed of the fact she hadn't paid closer attention to what her father and the President were discussing on the trip from the airport to where the ship carrying Tarena and her family landed.

"Oh, Nina, it was terrible," Tarena said, speaking for the first time. "Of all the ships that were dispatched with us, we were the only ones to survive. We ran into a meteor storm and watched as the other ships were destroyed. If it hadn't been for our pilot..." before she could finish, she burst into tears.

Nina enfolded her in a warm embrace until Rand came to her side.

"I'm sure your friend has been through a horrific ordeal. The medical personnel would like to take over her care. I told them you would want to accompany her to the hospital."

She looked around to see her father consoling Fragon while more and more of the inhabitants of the ship emerged to the bright New Mexico sunlight. It was Dr. Clark, along with the President and the men who guarded him, that assured the others they were considered honored guests who would soon be receiving food and medical treatment.

~ * ~

Rand marveled at the difference in appearance of the people descending from the body of the ship and those he met months earlier. Even though they wore the same style of robes as Dragger's people, it was evident these people were starving. He wondered how this could be, since surely, they carried the same amount of food pills as Dragger's party brought with them.

He focused his attention on Tarena. He knew she was the same age as Nina, but she looked more like a waif with hollow eyes and a shallow complexion. It was true the sun hadn't kissed her face for many months, but he was afraid she was going to collapse at any moment.

"Rand."

He turned when he heard Dragger calling his name. Assured Nina would care for Tarena, he went to where Dragger and Fragon were in conversation.

"Is there something I can help you with, Dragger?"

"I want you to meet my lifelong friend, Fragon. He was a Professor of Mathematics at the university in our area of the planet."

Rand instinctively held out his right hand toward the older man. "I'm honored to make your acquaintance."

At Dragger's urging Fragon grasped Rand's hand. Fragon's grip was more like that of a limp fish, but Rand made no mention of it.

"This is a form of greeting. It shows the person we are greeting we come without weapons." He thought the explanation as especially appropriate, considering this was the area where the whites first made contact with the Native American population. He also considered how these people would have greeted the 'Sky Gods,' as they called their visitors from the heavens.

"I like your form of greeting, young man, but why do you not hold out your dominant hand. You are left-handed are you not?"

"I am, but the majority of the people on this planet are right-handed. Left-handed people are a rarity and do not adapt well to a world set for someone who is opposite from you."

"Well said, young man. Dragger was right when he said you are a great help to him as he adapts to your world."

"Tell Rand what you have been through, Fragon," Dragger urged.

"There will be time for that," Dr. Clark said, joining the conversation. "We have medical personnel who are anxious to examine Fragon."

Rand could tell the older man was about to protest, but Dragger insisted Dr. Clark was right.

"You will stay with us, Rand. I want you and Dr. Clark to hear the story my friend has to tell. Like us, he is not prepared to talk to the press."

Rand agreed and went to intercept the reporter who was coming toward them.

"Get out of my way, kid. I need to talk to the aliens and find out why they are here."

The attitude of the reporter angered Rand, but he tried hard to not let it show. "I have been asked to be the spokesman for these people. They are another contingency of the people who arrived all over the world. In the far distant past they were called Sky Gods when in reality they are mere mortals with a far superior intelligence. These people have much to teach us. For now, you can certainly see they are in need of medical attention. They have had a long arduous journey. Their need is for rest, food and fluids, not questions from the press. You surely understand the situation they have found themselves in?"

The reporter looked a bit sheepish as he nodded his head and moved back so the medical personnel could do their job. Behind him, he heard Fragon protesting loudly.

"I do not see why this is necessary. There are others in my party who deserve to receive treatment more than me."

"I assure you, sir, they are being cared for by my colleagues," the paramedic replied. "Do you know your normal blood pressure and pulse rate?"

"Let me speak for my friend," Dragger said. "Our pulse and blood pressure are comparable to yours. We are mortals, created by the one god as were the people from whom you are descended."

Rand wondered how many times that particular question had been asked and answered over the last hour since the medical personnel arrived at the scene of the landing.

"Your blood pressure as well as your pulse is a little elevated, but otherwise you seem to be in fairly good health with the exception of you being dehydrated. We will be taking you to the hospital where the doctors can examine you more intensely."

"There is no need for that, young man," Fragon protested. "The healers who are with us have made extensive examinations of each of us. What we need most is nourishment."

"The man is right," Dragger agreed. "He is more in need of food and enough to drink. I am certain my friend President Hawley will be more than happy to help."

The paramedic was taken aback by Dragger calling the President of the United States his friend.

From across the open area where the craft landed hours earlier, large refrigerated trucks were already on their way with food and water.

It took only a matter of minutes for the trucks to be unloaded and many tables to be erected. It looked like an open-air banquet hall rather than a flat plateau in New Mexico.

"I spoke with Dragger on the way here and have asked for what foods you would be comfortable eating," President Hawley said. "With that information, I was able to order plenty of fresh vegetables as well as some other nourishing food. There are chefs coming who will prepare everything for you. Of course, there are also many cases of bottled water. I am anxious to share a table with you, Dragger, Dr. Clark and Rand, if that is acceptable?"

Rand could tell by the look on Fragon's face, he was also honored by this man's words.

"My friend has told me you are a great man who is the leader of this country. I too would be honored."

If Fragon was honored, Rand was doubly so. Even though he would have been more comfortable sitting with Nina and Tarena, to be singled out by the President was beyond anything he ever thought would happen to him.

With the meal ended, Fragon seemed to have recovered from the ordeal of his long journey. Color returned to his face and his eyes no longer looked as hollow as they had when he first disembarked from the craft that brought them to earth.

Rand looked around at some of the others who made the trip with Fragon and they too seemed restored. The ability of these people to heal their bodies was overwhelming.

"Would you like to tell us how you happened to come to Earth?

Especially to the same area as your contemporaries were visiting on the day they arrived?" the President asked.

"I have no secrets to withhold from you. As Dragger can tell you, ours was the last craft to leave our planet with the destination of Nalo. We were halfway through our voyage when the ships ahead of ours were hit by a meteor shower and we watched as they were completely destroyed. Those of our people who were aboard them perished. We lost many good men, women and children. Being the last ship in the fleet, our pilots made the decision to turn around. We needed to make a decision between the only two planets that would welcome us. Earth was much closer than Seros. As for how we chose this landing spot, we had no idea Dragger and Nina would be here. Our computer system was compromised when the rest of our fleet was destroyed. The first ship carried the mainframe for everyone else, leaving us with no way to contact anyone else from Plantas. We didn't choose this landing spot. We had no other options as our fuel was running low and our food pills were depleted, even with the severe rationing we'd been doing. It was either land or crash. Our pilot made the decision allowing everyone on board to live."

Rand watched as President Hawley wiped tears from his eyes. It was then he realized he was crying as well. The thought of watching your friends and perhaps even family destroyed before your eyes, was more than Rand could comprehend.

"You are welcome to remain in our country and begin your new lives among us," President Hawley declared. "The bravery of you and your people throughout this ordeal is to be commended. Do you agree with me, Dragger?"

"The people who have just arrived have been friends for years. Your offer is a generous one. I can understand how hard it is for an over-populated country to assimilate those who are not of this planet into your society." Dragger's comment seemed to be well-accepted by President Hawley.

Rand wondered about the knowledge the people who arrived with Fragon would bring to not only the planet but also to the U.S. While Dragger's expertise was scientific, Fragon was a mathematician. Would the man be able to decipher some of the mathematic equations left by the ancients?

~ * ~

Nina watched as Rand walked to the table set aside for her father, Fragon, Dr. Clark and the president. She wished he was sitting at the table with her and several of her female friends who traveled with Tarena. She was so transfixed on Rand she wasn't listening to the conversation going on around her.

"Are you listening to me?" Tarena asked.

"I'm sorry. It seems my mind was elsewhere."

"I think it was on *someone*, mainly that good-looking young man who came with your party. Who is he and is he single?"

"His name is Randsom Jameson, and yes, he's single."

She remembered her feelings when Cynthia came to the landing site in Peru and insisted Rand should be with her. He'd made it known she meant nothing to him and wanted her to leave him alone. Would Tarena's beauty turn his head away from her? She prayed it wouldn't.

"Do you have feelings for him?"

Nina merely nodded.

"What about Ragnar?"

"He's too far away for me to continue to consider him as part of my future. He has established a new life as a healer as well as a college professor on Seros. Since his arrival he has met and fallen in love with a woman by the name of Geni. The last communication I had from him said they were going to be married. He has established a new life and I should do the same thing."

"I was hoping Randsom would be available. He is very handsome but I wouldn't interfere with someone you care for."

"I don't know if Rand feels the same way as I do. I've met his former girlfriend. She was very beautiful. I even tried to wear some of the makeup she wore. I didn't like it most of it, but mother learned how to make what his former girlfriend called moisturizer and lip gloss. I do enjoy wearing it but in no way do I want to look like the girls on Earth."

"Of course you don't," Sora said.

Sora was another of their oldest friends. Nina knew Sora had always been envious of both Tarena and Nina's appearance. To say Sora was plain would be an understatement. As a child she had been involved in a terrible accident that left her face badly scarred.

"I wanted to fit in, to be beautiful, but I didn't like the feel of it on my face. As for Rand, he is a trusted advisor to my father. Once we are settled on this new planet, he will be returning to the university to do his post-graduate studies. It is possible at that time I will not see him again. As much as I care for him, I know he has his life to live and I might not be part of it. I am comfortable with it."

"I don't believe a word you are saying," Tarena said. "This is me you are talking to. We have been friends for our entire lives. It is evident you love him. If nothing else, you have to tell him of your feelings. It is possible he feels the same way. I could tell he was torn when he was asked to go to the table with the leaders."

Nina wondered if her friend was correct. Did Rand harbor the same feelings for her as she did for him?

~ * ~

Rand couldn't take his eyes off Nina and Tarena. It was apparent they both came from the same planet, but they were as different as day and night. While Nina had beautiful dark brown, almost black, hair and violet eyes, Tarena was a blonde with what he would call hazel eyes. Both girls were beauties and would attract the attention of many of the young men they would encounter now that they were on Earth. Suddenly, he didn't want any other men looking at Nina or vying for her attention. He never thought it would happen to him, but he had to admit he'd fallen in love with Nina. He also knew he had no right to proclaim his love for her. Even with his inheritance, he had no way of supporting her. There were still many years of schooling ahead of him and once he received his master's degree, he still had no guarantee of a job.

"Did you hear what the President said?" Dragger asked.

Rand pulled his mind back from the mental ramblings that distracted him. "I'm sorry, my mind was elsewhere."

The President broke into a broad smile. "I have a feeling this young man was thinking about the two lovely young ladies seated at the far table. Am I close to the truth, Rand?"

"Too close to it, I'm afraid."

"Why would you be afraid?" Dragger inquired, a sly smile on his lips as well.

"It's too complicated to go into right now."

Dragger laughed before commenting. "I have a feeling I know what is going on. You are still a student and do not have a job. That said, you are also in love with my daughter. You are afraid you are unworthy of her. Am I correct?"

Rand nodded, ashamed to think his feelings were so obvious to those around him.

"You have done a great service for Dragger and his people," the President said. "After talking to Dr. Clark, as well as Dragger, we feel perhaps you will be working with Dragger for quite some time. Since you are doing diplomatic work, we feel you should be compensated for your time. Retroactive to the time when Dragger and his people landed in Peru, you will be considered a U.S. diplomat. As you have been, you will be living among them and working as a go between to them and the people they will be meeting. In other words, you will become a member of the diplomatic core representing our country."

Rand was so stunned by what the President had just proposed he took a moment before answering. "I don't know what to say. I'm honored. I hope I can live up to your expectations of me. I know I want to continue my education, but for now, that can wait. I have enjoyed my time with Dragger as well as all of his people I have met. It will be my pleasure to continue in any capacity necessary."

Dragger put his hand on Rand's shoulder reassuringly. "Since you are willing to continue on with us, I think it is time for you to tell Nina of your feelings. Today will probably not be the best timing, but you should do it soon."

With Dragger's permission to make his feelings known to Nina, as well as the President's offer of a diplomatic position, he knew he did have something to offer Nina.

~ * ~

"Mr. President," someone called from the crowd of reporters encroaching on the scene of the latest alien landing. "Were you alerted to this landing before it happened?"

The President nodded to Rand, indicating he should answer the reporter. Getting to his feet, Rand approached the man holding out the microphone.

"I'm Rand Jacobson, spokesman representing the aliens as well as the President. The landing of this craft was a complete surprise. The President was in New Mexico to welcome Dragger and his party to the United States. I was with Dragger when our flight was diverted to an unused hanger. We were met by the President as well as representatives of the Native American tribes of this area, the Governor of the state of New Mexico, and the mayor of Santa Fe. The news of this landing was relayed to us during this meeting."

"Is our nation under attack?"

"You must not keep up on the news. Dragger and his party, as well as Fragon and his people, are refugees from a dying planet. While Dragger's people helped with the settling and education of the peoples of South America, he was anxious to see the petroglyphs of the Southwestern United States. As for Fragon, his people were headed for another planet when their contingency was caught in a meteor shower. Of all of the craft in his party, only this one survived. It is the hope of everyone from their people, as well as the President, that they will be welcomed as honored guests. They bring knowledge of mathematics, science, and medicine and will be of great importance to our country and the world."

"Who are you to speak for the President?"

Rand took a deep breath before answering. "I am the newly-appointed diplomat from our government to these people."

"Why haven't we heard about you before this?"

To Rand's surprise, the President got to his feet. "Rand has been the go-between for Dragger and his people in South America. I have seen the way he handles himself and today I appointed him to this position, retroactive to when Dragger's party first landed in Peru. Our country can be very proud of this young man for the way he has handled his position over the past months. I am very pleased to announce my choice to the world, although I would have wanted to do it in a different way."

The President sat down, indicating the interview had ended. Rand followed his lead and returned to the table.

"I meant what I said just now," the President said, in a hushed tone. "I did want to announce this in a more official way. Perhaps this was for the best, as you will be representing not only Dragger but also Fragon."

"I hope I am up to the task, Mr. President. I'm certain there will be people who will be willing to help me relocate Fragon's people. Dragger's party seem to be content in the mountains of Peru where they have constructed living quarters. Already several heads of the South American countries have contacted the scientists, medical personnel and mathematics professors to relocate and teach at their hospitals and universities. I pray the people from Fragon's ship will be as in demand in our medical facilities and universities."

The President seemed to take a moment to think about what Rand just said. "I hope we don't ever lose you to the archeology field, even though this was your chosen occupation. It will take a few calls, but I am certain by tomorrow morning you will have all the help you need."

The remainder of the afternoon was taken up with the Native American holy men conversing with both Dragger and Fragon. Both leaders from the stars were extremely interested in the petroglyphs in the area and were excited about being taken to see the writing about the star people from the ancient past.

~ * ~

It was late when Rand and Nina were reunited and allowed a private minute alone.

"I saw you talking to the newsmen. Someone from Fragon's party told me you have been hired to help your President. Does this mean you will be leaving us?"

Rand could see the moonlight reflect on tears in her violet eyes.

"Not hardly. I have been hired to be the U.S. diplomat between our nation and your people as well as Fragon's people. It's a high honor. I just hope I'm up to the task."

"Oh, Rand, I know of no one either on my planet or yours who is better suited to the task than you are. You have to know father holds you in the highest esteem. I know you are young but being of the Gods you are an old spirit. I am afraid this new venture you are embarking upon will separate the two of us."

"Would that upset you?" Rand asked, taking her hand in his.

"I pray you know it would. I have feelings for you, ones I've felt for no one other than the man I thought I would marry. I've grieved his loss. Although he is not dead, he is many light-years away from me and has found someone else with whom to share his life. Today my friend Tarena asked me if I loved you. I confided in her how I felt about you, but I don't know about your feelings for me."

Rand felt his heart skip a beat. "I know science is your life, but would you be content to be the wife of a diplomat? I think the two of us can make a world of difference for both of our people."

Nina's tears now flowed freely down her cheeks. "I would be honored to be your wife."

Without restraint, Rand took her in his arms and captured her lips in a passionate kiss that would seal their engagement until he could find the time to buy her a ring to make everything official.

Chapter Sixteen

If Rand thought their engagement would be a short one, he was sadly mistaken. Before either of them could spread their joyous news, they, along with the people of Fragon's party, were whisked away to hotels in Santa Fe.

While he was taken to the Presidential suite with the President, Dragger and Fragon, Nina, as well as the females from the latest ship to arrive, were taken to another hotel within the city. It was the same with the single men and the married couples.

The talks between Rand and the others went on far into the night.

"Your landing in this area of our country is very advantageous," the President said, while they waited for their dinner to be delivered. "Many years ago, another craft landed not far from here. At the time our nation was recovering from a world war and were fearful of the unknown. The landing, although speculated on in the worldwide news, was kept as a military secret. This time we are better prepared to accept your people into our society."

"As you know," Fragon began. "Earth was not our original destination. Our ancestors did for Nalo what Dragger's people did for your planet. I am pleased at how well our arrival has been received by your people. I am also pleased with your choice of Rand as your diplomat between our people and yours. I would like to see more of your country before we decide on where to settle. Will you be able to go with us when we meet with the Native American holy men?"

The President shook his head. "I'm afraid I am needed back in Washington. I can stay one more day and that is it. I've already heard back from many of the top diplomats and some of them are between assignments. They will be arriving within the week in order to help Rand with his official duties. His is an unusual situation. I think these men, who have years of experience, will be invaluable to not only Rand but also to you and Dragger."

"You will be missed," Dragger commented. "I do understand the need for you to get back to the obligations that come with running a great nation. I was, at one time, friends with the leader of Plantas. Unfortunately, he was in one of the ships of Fragon's detachment that was lost. I believe the two of you would have been great friends."

"I am certain you are right about your friend. If he was anything like you and Fragon, no matter where he landed, he would have been a great asset."

~ * ~

Rand listened to the talks between the President and the two major leaders of the people who only months ago were still traversing the universe in search of the landing places of their ancestors. Although their conversation was interesting, Rand fought the urge to fall asleep.

Since the arrival of Dragger and his contingent, Rand had not received the amount of sleep he normally needed. He'd been given his own apartment within the complex erected by Dragger's people, but many nights it was well past midnight before he was able to go to bed. Even then, he had trouble sleeping because his mind was spinning with the information he'd received from Dragger, Nina and other members of their party during the day.

Added to that was the amount of traveling they'd done either by jet or helicopter. The flights drained him completely. Even on very long flights he'd never been able to sleep while traveling. It started when he was a young child. Moving from foster home to foster home sometimes meant traveling between states, often by plane. He attributed his inability to rest while traveling to the uncertainty of where he would land.

In the past months, he'd been thrown into a new world and the President's appointment of him as a U.S. diplomat had him in a tailspin. *What will my life be like? Am I up to the challenge? Am I ready to completely change the path my life is taking?*

Unbidden, the voice of the man he proudly called Father entered his mind. *I told you great things were going to be happening to you. Your mother and I were so proud of you when the President of the United States appointed you to be an ambassador from the U.S. to the people from the stars. When Dragger and Fragon speak of the One God, be assured he is the same God we have always worshiped. I was with Him when the announcement of the new path your life will take was made and he was well pleased.*

Rand shook his head, trying to digest what he just heard. For years he'd heard of the aliens who came to Earth and started the civilizations there. Now he was seeing the proof of the theory and realized that they weren't gods, but they were following the instructions of the God who surpassed all others.

"Dragger tells me it might be beneficial for you to visit the other contingencies that have landed on earth and represent our country. He is willing to accompany you so he can introduce you to the top leaders of their people. I think his idea is a good one."

Rand turned toward the President, shocked at the meaning of his statement. Just as he had made his feelings known to Nina, they were going to be apart for an extended period of time. It didn't seem fair, but he couldn't say no to either Dragger or President Hawley.

"When would we need to leave?" he asked, almost afraid of the answer to his question.

"It won't be for a while," President Hawley assured him. "I want you to do some training with some of our other diplomats first, and of course, you will be needed as a go-between for Fragon and his people as you have been for Dragger."

Rand let out a silent sigh of relief. Being in New Mexico with the newcomers would give him an opportunity for more time to spend with Nina and to plan their upcoming wedding. He wished his parents could have been there with him, but he knew their spirits had never left him.

~ * ~

Nina and Tarena talked far into the night. The horrors her friend and her traveling companions endured on the long flight between their home planet and Earth were far worse than what Fragon described to President Hawley and her father.

When they finally retired to their respective beds, it took a long time before Nina could fall asleep. On the contrary, Tarena fell asleep as soon as her head hit the pillow, as Rand would say. It was only natural after the ordeal her friend had endured.

Before Nina fell asleep herself, she received a telepathic communication from her mother. She was needed back at the landing site, and could she make arrangements to return first thing in the morning? Torn between the needs of her mother, those of her father and the relationship that was growing between herself and Rand, she knew she would have to make arrangements to return to Peru.

Once sleep came, it was laced with dreams of what would happen once she left the area where her best friend would be left with Rand. Even though they each professed their love for one another, would Tarena try to win his heart away from her?

~ * ~

Morning came much sooner than Rand hoped it would. It seemed as though President Hawley needed little or no sleep because the sun was barely up when there was a commotion coming from the sitting room of the suite.

Knowing sleep would be ended for the day, Rand got up to shower and dress before he joined the others in the sitting room. He'd just finished shaving when he thought he heard Nina's voice from beyond the closed door of his bedroom.

"Good morning, everyone," he said as he entered the sitting room.

He expected Nina to greet him with one of her fabulous smiles, but instead the expression on her face was grim.

"Is something wrong?"

"My mother telepathically connected with me last night. I am needed back in Peru. I've come only to say goodbye to you and my father."

"Is something wrong?"

"Not really wrong, but there is a delegation from Argentina and

Brazil coming to confer with me about a scientific matter. They will be arriving tomorrow, so I need to be there today. I hate leaving you so soon after we have professed our love for each other, but it can't be avoided. I'm certain we will be together soon."

Rand took her in his arms and kissed her, unconcerned about the other people in the room who were watching them. "You have to do what is necessary and I have to do the same. President Hawley wants me to confer with some of the other diplomats. He also wants me to help Fragon and his people in the same way I helped you and your people. We will be reunited soon then we can make plans for the life we will be spending together."

He knew he was giving her false hope but it couldn't be helped. It was hard to tell when or if they would be reunited. Between her scientific duties and the trips that had been planned to the various areas of the world where others from Dragger's planet had landed, it could be months before they could be together again.

They enjoyed the breakfast buffet that had been set up on the other side of the sitting room, before Rand left to accompany Nina to the airport for her flight to Peru.

"I wish you weren't leaving," Rand said as they stood in the baggage check in and security area at the airport.

"I wish you were coming with me, but we both must do what is expected of us. I'm certain we will be together again soon."

I hope she's right, but there are no promises in this life. I could be half a world away for a very long time. It is possible she could meet and fall in love with another scientist by that time.

Finally, they could prolong their separation no longer. Nina's plane was scheduled to take off in less than fifteen minutes. She would be taking a commercial shuttle from Santa Fe to Phoenix where she would transfer to a flight to Lima.

Rand worried about the transfer, but being a VIP, she would be escorted from one flight to another and would be traveling first class. President Hawley assured them the flights had been arranged for and paid for by the government, considering her status.

In a state of depression, Rand left the terminal and hailed a cab to take him back to the hotel. He'd no sooner settled himself into the backseat than his phone began to ring. He checked the caller ID and smiled to see the call came from Paul.

"Hey Buddy, I was planning to call you when I got back to the hotel," he greeted his best friend.

"I didn't know if you would even remember me, now that you are officially an ambassador. The news hit the dig last night when it was broadcast over the International Network. Congratulations. I guess this means you won't be coming back to school with me."

"How could I forget you? On another note, no I won't be returning to school. This new position President Hawley has offered me is too good to pass up. I'm on my way back to the hotel now to confer with him before he has to return back to Washington."

"So, what were you going to call me about?"

"I just dropped Nina off at the airport. She has to return to Peru and meet with some dignitaries. I would appreciate it if you could meet her at the airport when her flight comes in. Sorry I can't give you a specific time, but I have a feeling she should be arriving at about the same time as we did when we flew down there."

Paul laughed. "I know you too well. Something tells me you didn't even look at the board to see what time her connecting flight would get in. I'll check at the airport here. With someone like Nina I'm sure they have all the information since they will have to get their security teams in place."

They chatted until the cab reached the hotel. Once the connection was broken, Rand exited the cab, giving the driver the voucher President Hawley gave him just before he left the hotel earlier in the morning. It still amazed him at how quickly things happened around the leader of his country.

~ * ~

"I am concerned about Nina traveling alone back to Peru," Fragon said, as he relaxed with Dragger and President Hawley.

"You have no need for concern, my old friend," Dragger assured him.

"Dragger is right. I am told she was met by a security team as soon as she passed airport security and the government has arranged for a private jet to take her to Peru. She will be well-guarded every step of the way. She is too important to our world to take any chances with her safety."

They continued their discussion until they heard a key card slide into the slot to open the door to the suite. All three men turned their attention to who was entering the room, each emitting a sigh of relief to see Rand come in to the sitting area.

"Did Nina get off all right?" President Hawley asked.

"I hope so. You know how it is with security, even at the smaller airports. I stayed with her for as long as possible, since I wasn't allowed to accompany her to the gate."

"Be assured, her security continued when she was met with her personal security team and escorted to a private plane that will take her directly to Lima where they will escort her back to her accommodations at Nazca."

"I'd better call Paul back and let him know he doesn't have to meet her plane. I wanted to make certain she was met by a friendly face."

"Don't worry. I'll alert her team and they will be looking for Paul at the airport."

He nodded at one of the Secret Security men who immediately left the room holding his cell phone in his hand.

"Please join us for coffee and these wonderful pastries," Dragger said. "I must say I have become quite fond of this drink to say nothing of these sweets. There is nothing to compare to it on Plantas."

Dragger watched as Rand helped himself to a cheese Danish along with a cup of black coffee. He was pleased to see his young friend enjoyed the earthly morning tradition as much as he did. He had introduced Fragon to the hot drink earlier in the day. Although it differed from the tea they were used to drinking at home he agreed he enjoyed the taste of it.

He waited until Rand was seated at the fourth side of the table for the discussions of the possibilities for the relocation of the people in Dragger's party. It was Rand who told them of the mathematics classes being conducted at the University of Wyoming where both he and Paul and did their undergraduate studies.

"I'm certain there are larger schools on both the east and west coasts that are doing the same programs, but I know the school where I went is both prestigious as well as having a great mathematics program that could profit from Fragon's knowledge. Besides, it is isolated enough so that they will be comfortable without being an object of continual media attention."

"You speak of mathematics, but how advanced are they?" Fragon asked.

Rand smiled before answering. "Not only is the school of mathematics acclaimed for its excellence, but students come from all over the world to participate in the Ph.D. program they offer."

Before going further, Rand reached for his computer and brought up the page pertaining to the programs he referred to.

"I see it is a fairly large school," Fragon commented. "Since I am not familiar with the areas of this planet, can you give me an idea of where it is located?"

Rand typed in a few key strokes to bring up a map of the United States. First, he pointed to the state of New Mexico then to Wyoming. "The University is located in Laramie. They do have all four seasons, spring, summer, fall and winter. I admit the winters can become quite severe with a lot of snowfall, but I always enjoyed snowshoeing as well as cross-country skiing."

"I'm not familiar with the activities you mentioned," Fragon admitted. "On Plantas, we did have snow and I am certain many of the younger people in our party would enjoy looking into them."

"Is it settled then?" President Hawley asked. "Are you and some of your party willing to relocate to the state of Wyoming? I'm certain there will be opportunities for many of them there, but there will be opportunities for other members of your parties in several of our states depending on their abilities. I wish I could stay until all of the arrangements have been made, but as I said yesterday, I am needed back in Washington. I suggest we go to the restaurant where I have made reservations before I am scheduled to fly out this evening."

Dragger looked at the clock. He was surprise to see it was nearly four in the afternoon. During their talks, the time had gone from the morning meal to the evening one without any of them even considering stopping for the noon meal.

~ * ~

Nina looked back for one last look at Rand. Less than twenty-four hours earlier, he'd asked her to be his wife. On Plantas it would be referred to as mating. She never thought of mating with anyone but Ragnar, but now she realized they would have grown apart as they became embroiled in their chosen professions. Medicine was as a demanding calling as was scientific research. As much as she'd been upset about the message from Ragnar about the woman he planned to mate with, she now understood how he could have feelings for someone as alien to him as Rand was to her.

She was surprised to hear someone call her name from behind. Turning, she saw two men and a woman in suits coming toward her. For a moment, she could feel fear building within her. This was the first time since arriving on Earth that she had been completely on her own, without the protection of her father, Dr. Clark or Rand.

"Miss Nina," the man closest to her said. "We have been sent to accompany you to Peru. We have been assigned by President Hawley as your personal security team. There is a private jet waiting for us."

"A—a private jet?" Nina stammered. "I thought I was flying commercially."

"This was the order from the President. Your security is our utmost concern. My name is Hunter Hall, and my companions are Collette Yonkers and Alex Brown. If there is anything you need, you should ask any of us and we will be able to accommodate you."

"Thank you, I think. I have never had my own personal security guards before. I am just a scientist, not an important person like my father or our friend Fragon."

Colette came up and held out her hand in greeting. "I beg to differ. You are a very important person, just as those who came with you and those on the ship that just landed here, in New Mexico. After permanent relocation, there should be no need for security, but when you are traveling, you will be our responsibility. The President thought you would be more comfortable with a woman on the team. I know these two guys can be rather intimidating, especially for a young lady such as yourself."

Nina nodded her agreement. "I am pleased to make your acquaintance and I am more comfortable with a woman on my security team."

Together, the three security guards, along with Nina, made their way through the terminal and out to one of the hangers housing a private jet through an underground tunnel. As soon as they boarded and fastened their seat belts, the engines of the jet came alive as they began their taxi out onto the runway in preparation for takeoff.

Looking out the window, Nina was struck by the lack of commercial planes using the runway as they soared into the air on their way to Peru.

They were airborne for about a half an hour when Hunter came to where she was sitting. "I have been informed that a man by the name of Paul Mathews will be meeting us in Lima. Do you know him?"

"Yes, I do. He is Rand's friend and he works at the dig close to the location of our complex."

"That's good, because you will be able to identify him when we arrive. I've been told he will be arranging transportation to your complex where you will be meeting with the scientists from Argentina and Brazil. We've also been advised there is a delegation of scientists coming from Venezuela."

Nina nodded. She prayed she would be knowledgeable enough to speak with the scientists who were coming to see her. She would have been much more comfortable with her father at her side, even though his expertise was as a historian rather than a scientist.

Chapter Seventeen

Ragnar waited nervously for the joining service to begin. As much as he wanted Geni to be his mate, he wondered if he was making the right decision. Was he ready to be committed to one person for the rest of his life? He knew he was but, even with this knowledge, he could feel his hands begin to sweat and his mouth become dry.

"Are you having second thoughts, brother?" Karten asked.

Ragnar turned to see both of his brothers standing behind him. "No second thoughts, I'm just nervous. After today I will be joined with Geni for the remainder of our lives. Will I know what to do on our wedding night? What if I don't satisfy her?"

"You amaze me," Milono said. "You are not only a doctor but also a college professor. You know how things are between a man and a woman. How could you be so uncertain about the marriage bed? We can both assure you, once the two of you are alone, let your bodies tell you what to do. It is evident you love each other very much. If you're thinking about Nina, she is your past. Geni is your future. Karten and I were both nervous before we were joined but once we were alone, we encountered no problems whatsoever. It will be the same with you."

Ragnar hoped his brothers were right. With no prior sexual experience, the wedding night could possibly not be the bliss Geni deserved.

"The joining service is about to begin," Blankes announced, as he entered the room where all three of his sons waited. "You look a little pale, son."

"He's nervous about what will happen after they are joined together," Karten replied. "We have tried to set his mind at ease about the marriage bed. Maybe he's too young to be taking this step in life."

"I am not too young," Ragnar fired back. "What I am is nervous about what will be happening once Geni and I are joined. As I recall, both of you were nervous before you were joined with your mates."

"You are so right, little brother," Milono agreed. "It's always been so much fun to tease you. Everything will be just as you have expected."

I expected to be doing this with Nina. Had things been different, we would have been joined and I would never have found true love with Geni. This is the way things should be. I pray Nina will find the same happiness on Earth.

Blankes held open the door and ushered his sons from the room where they had been waiting for the service to begin.

Ragnar watched as Geni's friends walked to the front of the room where the service would be held. When Geni started her walk down to where he waited for her, he gasped at how beautiful she looked in the flowing white gown she wore. She looked more like an angel than a woman walking toward her future.

Even seeing her father in full military dress was impressive and not as terrifying as it would have been when they first arrived on Seros. As he stood on Geni's right side, holding her arm protectively, her mother, Alina Leddington, took the same position on her left side. The resemblance between Geni and her mother was striking. While Jayden resembled his father, Geni inherited her appearance from her mother. Even knowing Alina had to be close to the same age as his parents, he was amazed by how much more youthful she looked than they did. Perhaps it was because she hadn't experienced the prolonged travel through space as his family endured.

"Who gives this woman to this man?" the officiate asked.

Ragnar was surprised by the question the man posed. Why would anyone think they would consider giving another person away as though they were property?

"We as her parents do," Leddy and Alina said in unison.

Still confused, Ragnar accepted the grasp of Leddy's hand on his arm, and the soft peck on the cheek from Alina. It was possible this was a tradition on Seros, but it was unfamiliar to him.

At last Leddy placed Geni's hand in his it was as though he was transferring ownership of his daughter to Ragnar.

You are not my property, my love. You are my equal and perhaps my superior in so many matters.

The smile on Geni's lips told him she had received his telepathic message.

The remainder of the service meant for the joining of Ragnar and Geni passed in a blur. The words he waited to hear were soon pronounced, joining their lives together for a lifetime.

~ * ~

The party that followed their mating was held at Geni's estate. Ragnar still thought of it as hers, although now it also belonged to him as well.

Many of the dignitaries from the other groups that came to Seros were in attendance as well as family and friends of Geni. Also, there were doctors from the hospital and students from his classes at the extension to the university.

Once each guest had been greeted, they were free to partake of the bountiful buffet set before them by the chefs Geni employed. Along with meats, vegetables, and tubers, there was an entire table devoted to sweets of too many varieties to begin to count.

"Eating like this, we will become too fat to enjoy the wedding night," Ragnar whispered in Geni's ear.

"I was just thinking the same thing. My chefs have outdone themselves with this feast. They certainly wanted to impress our guests. As you know we don't always eat and drink in such a gluttonous way. If we did, the floors and furniture wouldn't hold our weight," she whispered back.

Ragnar followed her lead and took only small portions of the bounty spread before them. At the table of sweets, he chose only his favorites rather than sampling one of each of the offerings spread before him.

With the meal completed, musicians started tuning up in the ballroom. Geni's friends and family as well as the doctors and students joined in the dancing while those from Plantas watched in amazement at the unique dance steps. Ragnar was glad Geni had insisted on teaching him

160

to do the dances so he would be part of the festivities.

One by one, couples from the people who accompanied Ragnar to this new world began to join, trying their best to mimic the steps of the other guests. As soon as the new dancers took to the floor, ones who had been dancing before took them as partners to show them the dances. It was very interesting to see the two groups mingling as though they'd known each other all their lives. The memories of the open hostilities that greeted them were fast fading as each member of his group found their place in this new society.

"I am pleased to see our two peoples joining together," Geni said, as they danced across the floor. "So much has happened, it is hard to remember when you weren't among us."

Rand made no reply. He too easily remembered the reception he'd received at the hands of Geni's father and the military who were now dancing at the reception for his mating with Geni. He also remembered the long journey through space to come to Seros from his dying planet. He'd left behind loved ones who would perish, and watched as lifelong friends went to other planets, never to be seen again.

The music stopped and he watched as the communications officer from their ship stepped up to the microphone.

"I have an announcement to make. The contingency that was sent to Nalo has been accounted for. Although the majority of the ships were destroyed in a meteor shower, the ship captained by Fragon has landed on Earth where Dragger and Nina were able to greet them upon their arrival."

A cheer went up from the people who had accompanied Ragnar and his family to Seros. Spurred by their enthusiasm, the people of Seros also cheered. For Ragnar, the news was bittersweet. He was pleased with the knowledge his friend Tarena and her family were not lost to the meteor storm but hearing Nina's name on his mating day brought a lump to his throat.

Geni's hand on his made him turn to face her. "Just hearing her name brings back memories, doesn't it?" she whispered in his ear.

"Yes, it does, but today is for the two of us, not for old memories to be resurrected. You are the woman I have chosen to mate with for life. Even with the party still going on, I think it is time for you and me to sneak away to the suite I have reserved at the hotel before we leave on our mating trip."

"A hotel? I thought we were going to use one of the many sleeping rooms here at the estate."

"There are too many people around here for us to have the privacy we deserve. Besides, I am anxious to drive the new hovercar your father gifted us. I checked it out earlier and I will be like a child with a new toy."

"I thought I was going to be your new toy. Will I always have to come second to your hovercar?" Geni pretended to pout.

"You know you won't. For tonight, we will both be pampered before we leave for the mating trip I have planned for us on the far side of the planet."

"Is this what people call a vacation?" she asked coyly.

"Why yes, I do believe it is. Haven't you ever been on a vacation before?"

The look of sadness in her eyes gave him his answer before she answered. "My parents were both too busy with their careers to be bothered with something as frivolous as a vacation. I'm afraid I patterned my life after theirs."

"In that case, you are in for a treat. My people believe that everyone should take at least four weeks of vacation a year. Two weeks are for travel and exploration, one week is for education and one is for complete relaxation. This is one tradition I feel should be shared with your people. Not only will they be happier at their jobs, but they will be better educated and more relaxed."

"I can hardly wait to experience what you are talking about. For now, let us go to the hotel where you have made reservations and enjoy our mating night. As a scientist, I know what transpires between a man and a woman but I have yet to experience it for myself."

Ragnar nodded his approval and discreetly they left the reception being held in their honor. He knew the night would prove to be one of exploration and experiencing new sensations for both of them.

Chapter Eighteen

Nina was relieved to see Paul waiting for her in the baggage claim area. He embraced her as a dear friend and was filled with questions about what transpired in New Mexico.

After introducing Paul to her security detail, they made their way out to the parking lot where Paul's vehicle waited to take them to Nazca and the compound that now housed her people from the crafts that had landed months earlier.

"How was Rand when you left him?" Paul asked, as he pulled out of the parking lot and onto the highway.

"He was good. I'm sure you heard about him being admitted to the diplomatic corps. It all happened so quickly, I doubt he's had time to process the implications of his new position. He's already been told he will be doing a lot of traveling. He did ask me to marry him. I'm sure that means the same as mating on Plantas."

"It certainly is. Let me be the first to congratulate you. The two of you will make a great couple."

"Time will tell. With my duties back at the compound and his as a diplomat it could be a long time before the two of us are together again. For now, my duties are here and his are going to be in Wyoming where our family's friends Fragon and Tarena will be relocating."

"How ironic. After I finish my extended rotation at the dig, I will be going back to the University of Wyoming to start my post-graduate studies. My folks have a ranch not too far from there. Hopefully, you will be able to come up and see what we call 'God's Country'."

"I am confused. What do you mean by 'God's Country'? Are not all of the known creations 'God's Country'?"

"Of course, it is, but we think Wyoming is especially so. The sky is clear and the mountains beautiful. In other words, it is a special part of the

United States to those of us who call it home."

Nina smiled. "I guess I could say the same thing about Plantas. Unfortunately, it no longer exists. With its death came the deaths of our sick and elderly. I lost both sets of my grandparents as well as a handicapped uncle and aunt. It was very sad, but I know none of them would have ever been able to survive the journey we made to Earth. I can only be consoled with the knowledge that death came swiftly and relatively painlessly for them."

"I'm sorry. I have heard the story of what happened to those you left behind but didn't stop to think about how it would have affected you. I don't know how I would handle losing loved ones in such a way."

"It's all right. I've had a long time to come to grips with their loss. I know their souls are now with the one god and when I die, I will be reunited with them."

"We believe the same thing about our God and the afterlife."

Paul's statement made Nina nod her head in agreement. "That is because no matter what name we give to our religions we all worship the same God. The one god created everything in the universe and at one time or another He sent His Son to become our savior, as well as yours, by sacrificing his life for our sins."

The look on Paul's face was one of bewilderment. She'd been on earth long enough to understand the Christian religion that mirrored the teachings of her own faith. Once again, she knew the teachings of her God were repeated many times over throughout the populated planets of the universe. It was no wonder the early space travelers were able to educate the peoples of the planets they visited and build magnificent structures that stood the test of time to endure into the modern times.

"I never thought about God being worshipped on other planets. Of course, everything I've ever believed about life on other planets in the galaxy over the past months has been shot to hell. I guess I'm open for just about anything at this point."

"I feel the same way about the people on Earth. I don't know what I expected to find, but it wasn't the character of the people I've met since we arrived. Even you, Paul. I remember well your fear and concern when we first landed. So much has changed and now I regard you as a trusted friend and ally. I know you and Rand are best friends and this change in his life has to be hard for you. I assure you, no matter where your paths in life lead you, I will make sure your friendship is never compromised."

"You don't sound so positive. Are you worried about your relationship with Rand once he begins traveling for the government?"

Nina considered her answer carefully. "Our lives often take courses other than the ones we want. Right now, I have no reason to doubt Rand's love, but I have no idea what this separation will do to either of us. We have been together every day since we first landed here. I have had no chance to explore any other relationships. It is possible I will meet someone who shares my interest in science. It is also possible that Rand will meet someone special from Plantas when he visits the other colonies that have been established on Earth. Only time will tell what the final result of each of our travels will be."

~ * ~

Night was falling when they finally arrived at the dig. Knowing how treacherous the mountain roads leading to the location of the compound where Dragger and his people established their residency were, Paul suggested they all spend the night at the dig.

"I know these aren't the luxurious accommodations you have at Nazca but I feel it would be too dangerous to drive up there in the dark."

Paul watched as Nina contemplated what he just said. Before she could speak, Colette made the decision for them.

"Paul is right," Colette said. "We are here to insure your safety and navigating mountain roads in the dark is not in anyone's best interest. Are you certain there will be accommodations for us?"

"Of course. Dr. Clark maintains a three-bedroom home here. Since he is traveling with Dragger and Rand, the house is vacant. You are more than welcome to use it for the night."

"We appreciate the offer," Alex commented. "We'll take three hour shifts throughout the night."

"Why all of this security?" Nina asked. "I have been flying all over South America visiting many archaeological digs. I haven't had a security detail until now. Why is that?"

"When your flight was diverted from the main terminal to the hanger in Santa Fe," Hunter replied. "The diversion was because of protesters. Many of them threatened to do harm to your people and anyone associated with you. We have contacted the security officer for your people at the compound and they have taken the appropriate measures."

The look on Nina's face spoke volumes to Paul. He could see fear mingled with concern mirrored in her eyes.

"We've also tightened security at the dig," Paul said, in an attempt to calm Nina's fears.

"These threats," Nina finally said, "have they been substantiated? Are these true threats or just something without substance?"

"We don't know," Alex replied. "It is the reason President Hawley insisted we come here to protect you."

Paul could see Nina begin to relax, but there had been a threat. It was wise to be safe rather than sorry where everyone involved was concerned.

~ * ~

"Why have you had security guards posted to protect Nina?" Rand asked, while he enjoyed the meal with President Hawley, Dragger and Fragon. "Is there something I should know? Is she in danger?"

"We know nothing for certain, but there have been threats made against Dragger's and Fragon's people as well as anyone involved with them. Until something can be substantiated, there is reason for concern."

"What about my people?" Fragon questioned. "Are they safe?"

"You have my guarantee of their safety. The area where you landed is being guarded by the military, not to keep your people prisoner, but to make certain they are safe. The military has been in conference with your security officers and they completely understand what is going on. I will ensure nothing happens like what did in Roswell in the mid-twentieth century. You and your people are honored guests. You will be treated as such until this threat is either proven to be a hoax or the perpetrators are arrested. Should that happen, they will be dealt with appropriately."

Rand thought back to their arrival at the Santa Fe airport and the reports of protestors. At the time he questioned it, but so much had happened so quickly he'd put the incident out of his mind.

"So, have your people found anything out yet?"

President Hawley shook his head. "I'm sorry, we haven't. The threat was in the form of a letter mailed to the head of the airport security staff. In it they said the protestors would be there when the plane arrived from Peru and they would make sure Dragger and his party would be eliminated. It insinuated that, whoever they are, they feel threatened by your presence. We had this type of behavior in the late twentieth and early twenty-first centuries. I thought we'd weeded out all of these extremists. Apparently, they are still active."

Rand shook his head in disbelief. He remembered reading of the racial unrest and the white supremacists in the history classes he'd attended both in high school as well as in college. In the reports he'd read through, he cringed at the thought of not only the riots but also the killings that took place. The threats had been against anyone of color, differing religious beliefs or merely someone else's political affiliations.

Since then those ideas seemed to have disappeared. Was it possible there were sleeper cells for these people as there had been for the terrorists after the 9/11 attack on New York City and Washington, D.C.?

"Relax Rand, everyone involved is being protected," President Hawley said, as though he could read Rand's mind. "The governments all over the world have been apprised of this threat and they are on alert to protect the people who have landed in their areas. Whoever is behind this will be apprehended and punished accordingly. The arrival of our visitors from the stars has been predicted for years and they are already a welcome addition to any society where they will be relocated."

They finished their dinner, returned to the hotel and President Hawley made the necessary preparations for his departure to Washington. It was then they were interrupted by a knock on the door. One of the Secret Service men answered and there was a brief interaction between the officer and the visitor.

"There is a woman here who is demanding to see Mr. Jacobson," the officer said when he returned to the sitting room of the suite.

Rand immediately thought of Cyn. She apparently followed the coverage of the newcomers to Earth. She'd tracked him down once. Was it possible she'd found him again? Why couldn't she leave him alone? Hadn't he made his feelings known to her both in Wyoming and again in Peru?

"Who would want to be seeing me?" Rand questioned.

"She says her name is Anne Jacobson-Durand and she is your birth mother."

The name Anne Jacobson resonated in Rand's mind. It was the name on the documents he'd been given when he turned twenty-one and asked for all the paperwork concerning his journey into foster care. He mentally calculated the woman's age as about thirty-eight, as the papers said she'd given birth to him at the age of sixteen. Other than that, he knew very little. He certainly didn't remember the woman who gave birth to him and his papers gave no indication of what she might look like at the time he was taken away from her.

"Would you be with me when I meet her, Dragger?" he asked.

"You know I will be honored to be with you. How will you be sure this woman is who she says she is?"

"I won't, but if she is my mother it would be wrong for me to turn her away."

"You've made a wise decision," President Hawley said. "We will have her searched by one of our female officers before she is allowed to see you. Since I have to leave, this suite is for you to use during your stay here. I'll be expecting to see you in Washington for your training next week, Rand. As for you, Fragon, I know the people in Wyoming are expecting you as the fall semester is about to begin. They have arranged housing for you. The others in your party have also found permanent arrangements all around the country depending on their particular skills."

"I didn't think the government moved that quickly," Rand commented.

"We do when time is of the essence. Now, I must leave." The president extended his hand to both Dragger and Fragon. "It has been an honor and a privilege to be one of the first people on this planet to welcome both of you. I am certain we will meet again in the future. My term is up in a couple of years and who knows if the voters will elect me for a second term. If I become a private citizen, I'm sure I will be content to return to my family home in Wyoming. That way I'll be close to you and many of your people, Fragon."

Other than voting for President Hawley, Rand paid little attention to what went on during the campaign. He did remember something about him coming from Wyoming, and perhaps that's why he'd voted for the man running for one of the Independent parties. He knew the people made the correct choice in electing this man. He also remembered his foster father saying no matter who was elected to the office of president, he was the right man for the job at the time he was elected. It was certainly true of George Hawley.

"We have checked on Mrs. Jacobson-Durand's background and one of our female officers searched her. We feel there is no reason why she shouldn't be allowed to meet with you."

Rand turned at the sound of Officer Blaine Vaughan's voice. "Thank you," he replied.

He watched the door as the woman proclaiming to be his mother would soon be entering. Rand didn't have to wait long. The door opened and a small woman entered the sitting room of the suite. Her hair was honey blonde and she wore it in a short sassy style. Green eyes matching his own stared back at him from behind large-lensed glasses.

"I hoped you would agree to see me," she greeted him. "I'm your mother."

For him to deny this would have been wrong. He could see many of his features mirrored in her appearance. "I remember reading your name on the papers putting me into the foster care system. What I don't understand is why you let them take me away from you?"

Tears welled up in her eyes and it took her a while to answer him. "I was a wild teenager. I'm not proud of it, but it's the truth. I enjoyed sex with a lot of partners when I was in high school. To be truthful, I had no idea who your father was. My parents disowned me and rather than attending school, I had to work in order to support us. I could only make minimum wage and I still wanted to be a party girl. You were two when Social Services came and took you away from me. It was my parents who turned me in and in the end, I knew it was the best for you. I knew I couldn't care for you in the way you deserved. I prayed someone would adopt you and love you."

"You were wrong. I bounced from foster home to foster home until I was thirteen. That was when I moved in with the Scotts."

"Why didn't they adopt you? I was shocked when you were still going by the name of Jacobson."

"I was too old. We all agreed it was for the best. They were the mother and father I never had. For all intents and purposes, I was their son. You might have given me life, but don't expect me to call you mother."

Anne shook her head, a saddened expression on her face. "I know I have no right to do anything more than find you and let you know how proud you've made me. After I lost you, I realized I had to change my life for the better. I finished high school and even went on to college. That was where I met my husband, Ralph Durand. We dated until graduation before we were married. Since then we have had two children of our own."

"I have siblings?"

"Half siblings. Your brother Dane is twelve and your sister Aurora is ten. I've made no secret of the mistakes I made in being a mother to you and they have always known they have a brother named Randsom. When your name became a household word, I submitted to a DNA test. I knew your DNA was taken when you were born, so I wanted to make certain I had the right person. I understand I have no right to lay any claim to you at this late date, but I do hope we can become friends. My children would like to meet their older half brother."

Rand was taken aback. He'd never thought about his mother turning her life around, marrying and giving him siblings. "I would like to meet them, but by no means am I ready to completely forgive you for not caring enough and allowing me to go into the foster system. Unfortunately, the timing isn't good. With my new position with the government, I'm going to be traveling a good deal of time in the near future. I won't even be able to be with the woman I plan to marry. It's not that I don't want to meet my siblings, but I don't know when it will be happening."

"I understand and so do they. It's enough you know about them. We will be watching your adventures on the news. They are so proud to think they have such a well-respected brother. For now, I've taken enough of your time. I gave my name address and phone number to the officer at the door. When or if you want to contact us, we will be excited to hear from you."

"Excuse me, Madam," Dragger said as he entered the room. "I wanted to make your acquaintance. Rand has told us of you and I am pleased to see you have taken the time to turn your life around. When things quiet down for us, I am certain he will be able to reconnect with your family. I also wish my daughter, Nina, had not been called back to Peru. I am sure she would also like to meet you. Soon, our home will be in Peru and you will always be an honored guest."

Rand tried to conceal the smile crossing his lips. He honestly liked Anne Jacobson-Durand. He wished she'd been a better mother when he was small, but as his foster father, Matt, always said, everything happens for a reason. Perhaps his mother's reason for turning her life around was losing her first son to the foster system and his going there was to find the Scotts and call them his family.

Chapter Nineteen

Paul Mathews looked at his packed bags. After an overnight trip to the Nazca Compound for a reception in his honor, he would be leaving to return to the States. He'd been in Peru for two years and during that time earned his master's degree through his work on the dig and the online classes Dr. Clark arranged for him. He was lucky that there was a resident professor assigned to the dig who did private sessions with him, in addition to the structured classes.

From what he heard, Rand would be at the compound and Paul would be able to spend the night in Rand's private suite before making the trip back down the mountain for his ride to Lima to catch his flight home.

"Are you ready to leave for the compound?"

Paul turned at the sound of Dr. Clark's voice. Even though the man repeatedly asked to be called Irv, it was hard not to think of him in more formal terms.

"I think so. I have an overnight bag packed along with everything else ready to head for the airport tomorrow. It's hard to believe I've been here for two years. So much has happened and the world has been set on its ear. I wonder if I'll ever fit into life in the states again. I'm glad I was able to do a lot of my Ph.D. work while I was here, but I'll still have to endure a lot of education before I get my Ph.D."

"You don't have to get it to continue working here, you know. Other than it would be good to have you do a couple of years in the classroom setting. After that, Dr. Grant assures me you can finish your Ph.D. here like you did your master's. From the experience you've had here, I think we can get you on the fast track to getting your degree."

Paul contemplated it for a moment. "I'd like that. I agree it would be good to get back into a classroom. Dr. Grant and I have talked about that last week. She's already contacted the University of Wyoming and we should have an answer by the time I get back home. I can honestly say I'm not looking forward to those harsh winters. I've gotten spoiled working down here."

Irv smiled. "I know what you mean. Dr. Grant and I used to live in West Virginia. Granted the winters there aren't as severe as when you come from, but I can certainly tell a difference living down here year around."

"Are you two going to stand around and talk all day or are you planning to join us on our trip up to the compound?" Dr. Grant asked as she stepped into Paul's room.

"We were just discussing the future," Irv replied as he picked up Paul's overnight bag.

"Good, because the rest of us are ready to leave. Once we're gone, Paul's belongings will be picked up and shipped back to Wyoming."

"I still don't think the dig should do that, Dr. Grant."

"Nonsense. I remember having to schlep my own luggage through airports and it's a real pain. This way it will be shipped out today and will probably get to your parents' home before you do. With the coming of the newcomers, even the shipment of goods has been streamlined. It certainly takes the strain off the baggage handlers at the airports."

They left the dorm and went out to where one of the dig's Hummers was waiting for them. To Paul's surprise, several other vehicles were lined up behind the Hummer that was waiting for him to get in so they could leave.

"I didn't expect so many people would be going to this event."

"Why not?" Irv asked. "You are well liked here and your friends want to say goodbye to you tonight. Enjoy it. Once you get back to the States, you will be just another student."

~ * ~

The private air shuttle the government provided for Rand landed on the airstrip adjoining the compound. From the window, Rand could see Dragger and Nina waiting for him. Even though Dragger often accompanied him, on this last mission, he'd been alone.

For several months, Nina and her fellow scientists had been busy working on a solution to the blight that was attacking the world's vine yards. At the same time, Moora had developed a wine that, although not alcoholic, could be used as a stopgap replacement until the grape crops could be restored to a healthy state.

Nina was in his arms as soon as he deplaned. Every time he saw her, he realized how long it had been since he first asked her to be his wife. His official duties always seemed to get in the way of planning a wedding.

With Moora and Dragger's help, tonight they would finally be joined as one in a surprise ceremony. Dragger arranged for a clergyman from among his people to perform the ceremony, while Moora secretly created the wedding gown.

As much as he wished Matt and Bridget would be there for him, he'd received word that his birth mother Anne and her family, his step-birth father, Ralph Durand, and his half siblings Dane and Aurora were being transported to the compound, their arrival scheduled for shortly after his shuttle landed.

Ever since first meeting his birth mother and comparing the DNA results, he had become close to the family he hadn't even known existed. Even Matt had come to him in a dream and given his seal of approval to their renewed relationship.

"Welcome home, Rand," Dragger said, extending his forearm in the official greeting style of the people from his planet.

Over the past year and a half, Rand had met with many members of the parties of Dragger's people. It had been easy for him to adjust to their customs. Even though it was different for him to call the mountaintop compound home, he'd quickly adjusted.

"It's good to be home, Dragger. As for you, Nina, I have a question I want to ask you."

Nina's expression went from excitement over having him home, to one of concern about what he wanted to ask her.

"What question could you possibly have?"

"Several months ago, I asked you to be my wife, or as your people say, my mate for life. At that time, you said yes. I have been working with your parents, and if you are willing, I would like to make you mine for now and forever tonight."

"T—tonight," Nina stammered. "How could this have been planned without my knowledge?"

"It hasn't been easy, Daughter. Shortly, the important people in each of your lives will be arriving."

Nina gave her father a questioning glance. "Who will these people be?"

"I have contacted Fragon, Dyna and Tarena. Their shuttle should be here soon. Your mother reminded me of what good friends you and Tarena were before we came here. It is only right she should be your female attendant."

"I understand, it is no wonder Paul's reception will be held at the same time. I must come to the conclusion he will be standing by Rand's side. What I want to know is what if I had said 'no I have changed my mind'?"

Rand pulled her into a tighter embrace. "I took a chance. I want you by my side when I go on future diplomatic journeys. Even President Hawley will be arriving soon."

"President Hawley? I thought he was in the middle of campaigning for reelection to office."

"He is, but he has made the journey to be with us tonight. It will also give a boost to his image. You know, foreign relations and all that stuff."

"My answer is a definite yes. I have waited far too long for you, but what about Paul sharing your suite tonight? Where will we be staying?"

"A new larger suite has been constructed for you and Rand, Daughter. Like the one your mother and I share, it is a freestanding structure. Your mother insisted on decorating it."

Nina looked bewildered. "How could this happen right under my nose?"

Rand laughed at her question. "You and your team have been so busy working on the eradication of the blight plaguing our world's vineyards, I doubt you have had much time to investigate all of the building projects going on around the compound."

"You're right. There is no need to stand out here and discuss these things. I have much to do to prepare for this night."

"I doubt that," Dragger commented. "Your mother is waiting for you in our suite. As soon as Tarena arrives she will be taken there as well so the two of you can be made ready for your mating ceremony."

~ * ~

Riding in the lead vehicle of the caravan, Paul could see the compound come into view. There seemed to be a lot of activity. In the distance, he could see Rand's shuttle with its diplomatic markings. He'd hoped to arrive in advance of his friend.

Just a week ago, he'd had a communication from Rand asking him to be the best man at his wedding. By combining the going-away party with the wedding, many of the people who otherwise might not have been able to attend the event would be there.

After all the vehicles made their way up the mountain, Paul got out, flanked by Irv and Dr. Grant. After making their way to the compound, they were greeted by Dragger.

"It is good to see you, my friends. Rand is waiting for you in his suite, Paul. As for you, Irv, as well as your party, please come and join me in the reception area. President Hawley arrived with his wife about an hour ago and I am certain they will be anxious to see you again."

Paul thanked Dragger and made his way to the elevator bank for the ride up to Rand's seventh floor apartment. He remembered the last time he'd visited Rand. At the time, he'd teased his friend about postponing his wedding for so long. It was hard to believe that by this time tomorrow Rand would be a settled man with a secure future.

The elevator door opened and Paul made his way to the suite at the end of the hall. His knuckles barely rapped against the door, when Rand invited him in.

"It's good to see you, buddy," Rand greeted him.

"You too. I can't believe within twenty-four hours you'll be married to the girl you love and I'll be headed back to Wyoming. Are you getting nervous?"

"Not really. Ask me in a few hours and my answer might be different. Did I tell you my family is coming too?"

"I think you mentioned something about it. I'm glad you found them and they weren't out to take you for money or some such thing."

"That's not the case whatsoever. Ralph owns his own company in Utah and makes more money than I could even dream of making. As for Anne, she knows what a crappy mother she was to me when I was little. I know she was apprehensive when she first approached me, but it was Dragger who put her mind at ease. It's also great having a younger brother and sister. I don't see them as much as I'd like, but with my schedule it's not feasible. I'm just glad they were able to make it here for the wedding."

"Speaking of the wedding, Dragger sent me up here to dress for the event. I brought along my suit but I have a feeling he's talking about something else. Am I right?"

"You are."

Rand ushered Paul into the suite and pointed to the two ceremonial robes displayed on of the bed. They were of the same style as the ones worn by Dragger and the others when they first arrived over two years earlier. Unlike the plain everyday robes he was used to seeing, these were of a fine fabric that had been embellished with beautiful embroidery. It must have taken the women of the community untold hours of work to complete.

"Wow, I didn't expect to be dressed in something this elegant. When you do things, you do them right."

"As you know, Nina is a high-ranking official within this community. As the ambassador to these people, I have decided to adopt their ways as my own. What about you? Are you excited about going back to Wyoming and starting your classes?"

"Yes and no. I'm anxious to go back home, but the classes are another thing entirely. I've been talking to Dr. Grant and she has been in contact with the university. She thinks I can opt out of a lot of my classes because of my work on the dig. It's possible I'll be able to return to Peru after a couple of years of classroom work. I should know what the university decides when I register for the fall semester."

"With your experience it should be a slam dunk. Changing the subject, I think we should be taking showers and getting ready."

"I suppose we should. By the way do you have the ring? I know you didn't give Nina an engagement ring. The wedding ring had better be spectacular."

"It is."

Rand walked over to the dresser and picked up a small blue velvet box. As he opened it, Paul was surprised to see a beautiful band with a large center diamond. The band itself was encrusted in magnificent gemstones with which Paul hadn't ever seen before.

"The diamond I understand, but what are the burgundy stones on the band?"

"Among the group from Dragger's planet who landed in England were some merchants of fine gemstones. They brought several of the stones with them, hoping they would be worth as much on Earth as they were on Plantas. They gave me the name of the stones, but I can't pronounce it. Here they call them burganeese. I think it fits them perfectly. I bought the band and the diamond when I was in London and had one of the jewelers set it for me. I hope she likes it."

"What's not to like? It's the most beautiful thing I've ever seen. My question is, how did you know her ring size?"

"That was the easy part. The jeweler who made the ring has been making jewelry for her family for years. He brought all of the information about his prior clients with him on a memory chip. You wouldn't believe the talents these people brought with them."

Chapter Twenty

Nina waited for the shuttle bringing Fragon, Dyna and Tarena to arrive. Even though they'd been in contact, they hadn't seen each other since the day their craft landed in New Mexico.

At last the shuttle touched down and she saw Tarena coming toward her. Rather than the undernourished young woman who got off the space craft, Tarena looked as though she was doing well in her new environment.

"Nina, I am so happy to be able to be with you on such a special day," Tarena said as soon as they met.

"I am too, but everything is happening so quickly. I knew nothing of our mating ceremony until Rand arrived less than an hour ago."

Tarena laughed. "I didn't think anyone would ever be able to surprise you. I'm glad it's all working out. Your father told me to bring my most elegant robe. I chose the lavender one. I hope it meets with your approval. I never could wear the same bright colors as you could. Have you seen your mating robe yet?"

"No. Mother has it in their quarters and has told me not to come to see it until you get here. By any chance did you tell her what you planned to wear?

"You know I did. Let's go together now and see it."

Nina walked toward her parents' living quarters hand in hand with Tarena as they had when they were children. Her mother stood in the doorway waiting for them.

"I feel as though we were back on Plantas. It seems so good to see the two of you coming to greet me. I almost expect to hear you ask me for a sweet treat the way you did when you were children."

"Only we are no longer children, Mother. I am so pleased Tarena and her parents are able to be with us today."

Tarena embraced Moora. "I too am happy we are able to be here.

Nina said we should come here to prepare ourselves for her mating ceremony. I hope one day to be able to have a mating ceremony of my own"

Moora smiled knowingly. "I have been anticipating your arrival and can hardly wait to see both of you girls in your mating finery."

Nina followed her mother to the second bedroom of the small freestanding cottage. On the sleeping couch in the room was a beautiful deep purple robe embroidered in the finest of silver threads. Beside it was an equally lovely lavender gown with matching embroidery in purple.

"Both dresses are beautiful, Mother, but how were you able to get Tarena's dress trimmed to match mine?"

"That's an easy question to answer," Tarena replied. "As soon as your parents contacted me, I had the dress sent to your compound. The parcel service is very reliable. I must say, Moora, you have created a beautiful masterpiece out of my old robe. I hardly recognize it."

"I am glad to hear you are pleased. Now, it is time for the two of you to prepare for the ceremony. Luckily, when we had this unit built, I insisted we should both have our own bathing rooms. Once you have showered and washed your hair, two of the women who do hair designing will come in to dress your hair to make both of you beautiful."

~ * ~

Honored guests filled the reception area, while musicians played softly in the background. Rand stood with Paul waiting for Nina to enter the room.

The first person to come down the aisle to approach the altar was Tarena. Her blonde hair was dressed beautifully with purple and lavender ribbons. They both accented her lavender robe with its purple embroidery.

As soon as she started to walk toward them, Rand heard Paul take a deep breath. He hid his smile, knowing this had been planned. The more he got to know Tarena, the more he realized she would be the perfect woman for his best friend.

Paul took a step forward and took Tarena's arm to escort her to where she would be standing throughout the ceremony.

The music changed and everyone who was assembled got to their feet. Rand could hardly breathe as he watched Nina begin to walk down the aisle, clutching her father's arm. The deep purple dress she wore was embroidered in silver thread that sparkled under the solar-powered lights, making her look like a medieval princess getting ready to marry her prince charming. All he could think of was the stories he'd read about the royals of long dead societies wearing the royal color of purple. Her dark hair was dressed with lavender and silver ribbons.

How did I get so lucky to have this woman in my life?

It was all preordained. Yours will be the first union between our people and the newcomers in South America. It certainly won't be the last.

Rand had become accustomed to hearing Matt's voice within the confines of his mind. Hearing it now, as he was ready to take the biggest step in his life, brought comfort and confirmation this was what he was supposed to do.

Bringing his attention back to the beautiful vision coming toward him, he saw the look of approval on Dragger's face. Knowing this esteemed leader was willing to give his precious daughter to this man of another race was as much of a comfort as having his father's approval.

~ * ~

Nina looked into the mirror in her mother's second bedroom. She never thought of herself as beautiful, but today she felt beautiful, even without the makeup Rand's friend Cyn insisted she needed.

Looking at her friend, Tarena, she knew their beauty was natural and didn't need any of the earthly enhancements the women here seemed to prefer.

"Are you ready to go to your chosen mate?" her father asked, as he entered the room.

"I am but I'm afraid I have no commitment ring."

"There is no need for concern. Before we left our home, your grandfather gave me the commitment ring your grandmother gave him."

Dragger held out the ring and dropped it into her hand. The band was made of terrarium, one of the precious metals from Plantas, and studded with burganeese stones.

"Oh, Father, this is too much."

"No, Daughter, your grandfather meant this for you to give to the man you love. Since the terrarium conforms to the size of the finger of the man who will be wearing it, it is a perfect gift for the man who will share your life."

Nina fingered the ring she'd seen her grandfather wear for all of her life. It had such a special meaning for her. As a child she remembered tracing the pattern of the stones set into the terrarium band that had molded itself to her grandfather's finger. How had he taken it off? She was certain he was wearing it the last time she saw him. Had he commanded the ring to slip off his finger so it wouldn't be lost when Plantas was destroyed, so he could give it to her, as his granddaughter, to give to the man she planned to be mated to for life?

"I can read your thoughts, Daughter," Dragger said. "It was your grandfather's wish for you to have his ring. He was a man of great powers. He was able to command the metals from the ground to do his will. That is what makes this ring so special. When he gave it to me, he commanded the ring to conform to the finger of the man of your heart. I know you have found that man in Rand."

Nina took her father's arm and allowed him to lead her to the reception hall and the walk toward her destiny.

Tarena waited for her as the music from the musicians floated around them.

"I am so happy for you," Tarena whispered. "I have one question, who is the man standing beside Rand?"

Nina smiled. *Is it possible my friend is taken with Paul? They would make a good couple.* "He is Rand's best friend, Paul Mathews. They both greeted us on the day we landed and he has become a good friend to everyone in our colony."

"Does he have a mate?"

"He has been here for over two years and in that time, I have never heard of him speak of a mate or a sweetheart."

"I have heard the world sweetheart from the students at the university, but I didn't understand the meaning my decoder was giving me."

"It means a person of the opposite sex for whom you have feelings. From sweetheart, they become your fiancé before the two of them are mated for life. Here they call it married and the man is the husband while the woman is the wife."

"Hmm, that is good to know. Are you ready for this? I think it is time for us to meet these two men and for you to become Rand's wife."

The word *wife* sounded strange coming from Tarena's lips but it gave truth to the fact she and Rand would soon be mated for life.

Although she hadn't seen Rand's mating robe, she knew it would be embroidered with gold and silver threads. She'd seen many mating robes when her older friends had been mated. At the time she thought Ragnar would be the man of her heart. Now, she thanked the one god for separating them. She was meant to be Rand's mate, not Ragnar's. Theirs was a love built on more than friendship.

~ * ~

The young man who took Tarena's arm was even more intriguing close up as he had been from the back of the hall. As soon as she saw him, she wondered how she would be able to see him again after the evening ended. It was a long trip from Peru to the University of Wyoming.

In the time she'd been there with her father, she'd made a place for herself. Starting off as an assistant to her father, Tarena soon became a paid tutor for many of her father's students.

When the school year ended, she'd been offered a position teaching in the local high school. It came after she was sent there to do something called 'practice teaching' and made a good impression on the head people there. She was thrilled, but now she wished she would be staying in Peru to be closer to Paul.

Tarena turned her attention to the ceremony taking place between Nina and Rand. Knowing his traditions were different from the ones she grew up with, she was surprised when he sang the wedding vows to the woman he loved above all others. His voice was a beautiful tenor and made the vows come to life. Nina's response was equally special with her ethereal soprano filling the reception hall.

With the vows sung, Rand presented Nina with a gold ring set with a diamond and studded with burganeese stones. It was the perfect match to the ring Nina planned to give to Rand.

She watched Rand's face. as the terrarium band adjusted itself to fit his finger. The look on his face told Tarena he felt the adjustment.

Once both rings had been given and received, Rand and Nina sealed their union with a kiss. When they parted, the musicians began playing again. This time it was a much livelier tune. Rand and Nina turned toward the invited guests and literally ran toward the back of the reception hall.

From the corner of her eye, Tarena saw Paul reach for her hand. Without hesitation she took it and followed Nina and Rand's example by hurrying after their friends. Again, the touch of his hand sent excited shock waves through Tarena's body.

While the attention focused on Nina and Rand, Paul pulled Tarena into a tight embrace and kissed her tenderly. "I've been to the compound many times. Why is it I have never seen you here before?"

Tarena took a moment to catch her breath. She should have been horrified by his actions but all she wanted was to once again have him take such liberties with her. "I only just arrived today. Nina is my best friend but we were separated when she came to Earth and I went with my family to Nalo."

"Ah, the fated party from your planet who landed in New Mexico last year. Are you all settled?"

"Yes, Father has been teaching at the University of Wyoming and I have signed a contract to teach high school when classes resume in the fall."

~ * ~

Paul could hardly believe his luck. Nina's maid of honor was settled in the same town where he would be beginning his studies for his Ph.D. He just prayed she wasn't committed to another man. From the moment he saw her coming toward him, he knew he'd found the girl of his dreams. He thanked God, or perhaps fate, that they would soon be living in the same town with connections to the same university.

"That's where you got off to," Rand said, before Paul could say all the things he wanted to say to Tarena. "It's time to mix and mingle. There's plenty of food waiting for us and I want you to meet my birth family."

Reluctantly, Paul left Tarena's side and followed Rand to where the food gave off a tempting aroma.

Moora orchestrated the line of people waiting to partake of the bountiful buffet set before them, while directing Nina, Rand, Tarena and Paul to a table where their food would be brought to them. For some reason it bothered Paul to think he was seated next to Rand while Tarena was sitting to Nina's right.

"Don't you have some pull with these people?" he whispered to Rand. "Couldn't you have gotten Tarena seated next to me?"

"Settle down, Romeo. Tomorrow you'll be headed back to Wyoming and you'll have all the time in the world to get to know her."

"So I found out, but..."

"No buts, old buddy. From the looks on both of your faces it won't be long until Nina and I will be coming to Wyoming for your wedding. I'm sure your parents will fall in love with her."

"Speaking of parents, how did your mother take to Nina?"

"I'll tell you later. For now, they're bringing our food. It would be rude for us to be talking while we're being served."

Chapter Twenty-One

Anne Durand could hardly believe not only that she was attending her son's wedding, but she had travelled from New Mexico to Peru. She recalled when she first realized that Randsom Jacobson, who was the spokesperson for the aliens who landed at Nazca, was the child who had been taken away from her over twenty years earlier.

Ralph insisted she get a DNA test done to compare with the one the CPS people took for Rand when they took him away from her.

Those had been dark years. She'd been only sixteen when she learned she was pregnant. Her love for the father of her son faded as soon as he left her alone to give birth to and raise the child. At least she thought he was the father of her son; there had been too many parties and too many men for her to be certain which one got her pregnant. Her parents had been supportive until she started running with the wrong crowd. Even though they paid for her apartment and she worked, her money went to booze and drugs rather than things her son needed. The best thing for him had been the day they took him out of her care.

It had been a severe wake-up call for her. Without either her son or the support of her parents, she checked herself into a rehab hospital. It took her over a year to quit the drugs and booze, but eventually she did. That was when she realized that in her drunken and high state, she'd actually signed away all rights to her son.

While living in the halfway house, she'd gone back to school to get her GED and finally went on to college. She'd gotten her teaching degree and moved to Utah to begin teaching high school history. That was when she reconnected with Ralph Durand. They'd known each other in college and shared some of the same demons during their teenage years. With him, she'd found the true meaning of love.

From the beginning, she'd been up front with him about everything, from her alcoholism to the fact she was a drug addict and had her first child taken from her because she was an unfit mother. Thank goodness, Ralph didn't care. He told her he was in love with the woman she had become, not the one she'd been.

It was Ralph who insisted on celebrating Rand's birthday every year. Dane and Aurora were thrilled with another birthday to celebrate with balloons and birthday cake. Now they had been able to meet the brother they only heard about from their mother. They bonded with him immediately and when they were invited to his wedding, they were excited to take the trip to Peru and see the aliens who held their brother in such high esteem.

As a child, Anne remembered being enamored with the Nazca Plaines where there were strange lines drawn into the hard-packed earth. She wasn't prepared for the beautiful structures Dragger's people erected in a matter of hours, or so all the press releases said. They'd been taken to a suite that rivaled any of the top hotels they'd ever stayed in.

The music changed and Anne brought herself back to the present. She turned to see an elegantly beautiful tall blonde woman in a light lavender robe embroidered in deep purple threads walking down the aisle. She was met by a handsome young man who had to be an Earthling friend of Rand's.

Again, there was a change in the music, signaling Nina, the woman who stole Rand's heart, was about to enter the room. Instead of the white wedding gown Anne expected, Nina wore a gown of deep purple, beautifully embroidered in silver and lavender threads. Her dark hair was styled with ribbons and she carried only a single flower, unlike any Anne ever saw before. She had to assume it was one native to her home planet.

The vows they spoke were somewhat reminiscent to the ones Anne spoke to Ralph on their wedding day. As though his memory mirrored hers, Ralph took her hand in his. She loved this man and it was evident Rand and Nina shared the same love.

It seemed the ceremony was over within a blink of an eye. She watched as Rand and Nina ran from the reception hall where the guests were assembled.

After Anne and her family was escorted from the area where the service was held, they were directed to another equally large hall for the reception. Long tables were set with delicacies. Some of them were familiar, while others were foreign to her, but upon tasting them she thought they were all delicious.

Throughout the reception, Anne watched the alien woman who had captured her son's heart. She was tall for a woman, but Anne knew other women who could equal her height. Her dark hair and haunting eyes were one of the first clues as to why Rand had fallen in love with her.

"Anne."

She turned at the sound of someone calling her name. She was surprised to see Dragger standing behind her.

"I am pleased to see you and your family were able to join us for the joining of our children. Although it is hard to give the protection of our children to another, I feel this is a good mating. May I join you for a while?"

It was Ralph who replied in the affirmative. "We would be pleased to have you join us. I'm sure you know that I am Anne's husband, and these are our children, Dane and Aurora."

Dragger, pulled up another chair to their table and sat down between the children. "I can see the resemblance between Dane and Rand. May I ask if you are left-handed, young man?"

Dane looked at Dragger, the look of surprise on his face. "Yes, I am. How did you know?"

Anne saw the twinkle in Dragger's eyes. It was she same look she saw when she first went to meet with Rand. The man knew things they couldn't begin to understand.

"All left-handed people are of the Gods. The star people of ancient times were called 'Gods' by the people they came to visit them. They saw the women as very beautiful and their descendants are of the Gods. The mark is that they are left-handed. You are blessed, young man."

"What about me?" Aurora asked. "I'm not left-handed. Am I not special?"

"Not at all, my dear child. Your name is that of a planet on the far side of this galaxy. It is more than a coincidence this was the name you were given at birth. Even if you do not carry the left-handed gene in your body, you are destined for great things, just as both of your brothers are."

Aurora beamed at the compliment from Dragger. "Thank you, Mr. ah..."

"No, my dear, I'm just Dragger. On Plantas, there are no such titles. I am nothing more than a historian, a keeper of the history of my planet as well as that of yours."

"I didn't realize you were a historian, Dragger," Ralph said. "It just so happens I'm a history buff myself and Anne teaches history. I wish our time here wasn't so short. If we had longer I would love to talk history with you."

"As I would you. I can see no reason why I cannot make arrangements to have you return here when you would have the time to stay for at least a week. Would that meet with your approval?"

Ralph seemed to be surprised by the offer Dragger just made. "I don't know what to say. Since it's summer in North America, Anne is on summer break and being the head of my company I can arrange for time off whenever I wish. We would just have to go home and make arrangements for the children before we could take you up on your generous invitation."

"Why must you return to your home? There are many children of the same age as yours within our complex. They would have no lack of supervision while I confer with you and Anne. Have you not looked around to see the number of children in attendance? I will make certain they are all introduced. I know Dane and Aurora will enjoy this celebration more by being in the company of others their own age."

Anne was in awe of the man who was now her son's father-in-law. Although her time for the summer was hers to do as she pleased, she knew Ralph would have to make arrangements with the key people in his company for an extended stay. Of course, with the instantaneous communications from any place on Earth, he would be available if any unexpected problems should arise.

~ * ~

When the formalities of the wedding finally finished, Paul sought out the company of Tarena. She was talking with several other women. When he approached her, she left her friends and followed him to a secluded table.

"I wanted to talk to you before the evening was over," Paul said, once they were seated at a small table for two. "I will be leaving for the States in the morning. I'm afraid I will never see you again."

"I also wanted to be alone with you. The States, as you call your country is a big place. I too fear we will not see each other in the future. Fate is a cruel mistress. It was fate that brought us to earth and fate that paired us together at this mating ceremony. Had I known you were here, I would have insisted on accompanying my friend Nina to her compound rather than going with my father."

"We are together now. Nothing else matters to me. I believe in taking whatever the moment gives me. Will you dance with me?"

Tarena broke into a brilliant smile. "I would like nothing better. Do you know the steps of our dances?"

"You'll probably find I have two left feet, but I'm willing to learn. Will you be my teacher?"

"My profession is being a teacher. I am looking forward to having my own classroom when school begins in the fall. If I can teach high school students, I am certain I can teach you."

Paul held out his hand and led her out onto the dance floor. He liked the feel of her in his arms and found the steps associated with the alien music were easy to learn. Even though he'd never been much of a dancer, he did manage to not step on her feet.

He liked the fact that she was as tall as Nina. It had always been hard for him to dance with women who were much shorter than him. Like Rand, he was well over six foot five. He'd played basketball in high school but was ready to give up sports when he got to college and immersed himself in his studies. When he got back to school, he feared he would be too busy to seek out the school where Tarena would be teaching in the fall.

Inwardly, Paul smiled. He knew he would have Tarena in his life. They would both be in the same town. Laramie was a relatively small city compared the others in the U.S. It would take only a few questions to the right people to find where she and her parents were living.

Chapter Twenty-Two

The next morning, Paul kissed Tarena good-bye before boarding the helicopter taking him to the airport for his flight back to Helena. They'd spent the night together, sitting in the garden area of the complex and talking of nothing and everything.

He told her of growing up on a sprawling ranch and riding horses, while she told him of life in the city that no longer existed.

Rather than dwelling on himself, he insisted she tell him about the space flight that was supposed to take her to Nalo.

She described watching the other ships in their squadron being destroyed by the meteor shower, anguish in her voice as she told of watching people she'd known for her entire life perish in an instant. It was only the quick thinking of the pilot of her craft that they were averted from suffering the same fate. It took several days for the decision to be made to travel to Earth, as it was the closest inhabited planet to their location.

Paul tried to hide his elation when he learned she would be teaching in Laramie. He decided not to tell her he would be attending the University of Wyoming, at least until he found her. He needed time to analyze his feelings at home with his family. If things progressed the way he wanted them to, he hoped she wouldn't be upset by his deception. It would be easy to find her again and continue their relationship. She was one girl he would be proud to take home to meet his parents.

~ * ~

The plane took off from Peru and headed back to the States. His first stop would be in Dallas, Texas, where he would clear customs and have a layover of six hours before boarding the plane to Helena. He took the opportunity of stopping in Dallas to call his parents.

Instead of talking to his folks, he reached his older sister, Kathy.

"What are you doing at home?" he asked. "Aren't you busy with your kids?"

"Of course I am, but we're on vacation. Mom and Dad are off doing some shopping, so Todd and I are holding down the fort. Right now, he's out with the kids riding the range. That's what the kids call it. I think they've been watching too many of Dad's old cowboy movies."

"I can understand. I wish I was watching some of those movies or riding the range rather than being stuck at the Dallas Airport. My plane should be landing around seven tonight. I'm glad you're home. I can hardly wait to see you and Todd as well as those little wild Indians otherwise known as my niece and nephew."

They talked for several minutes before the need to find a kiosk that served coffee and maybe something more substantial overrode his desire to speak with his family.

He finally found what he was looking for and ordered a bacon, egg and cheese bagel as well as a large coffee.

"Paul, Paul Mathews?" someone called from behind him.

He turned to see a man who looked vaguely familiar but he couldn't recall why. "Yes, I'm Paul Mathews, do I know you?"

"I doubt it," the man said, holding out his hand in greeting. "I'm Gene Emery. I was a couple of years ahead you in high school. I admired your skills on the basketball court when you were on the team. Imagine how surprised I was when I heard you were one of the first people to make contact with the aliens in Peru. I've been following you ever since."

"It's good to meet you again, Gene. Since you know all about my life, what have you been doing with yours?"

"I went to school at the University of Wisconsin and graduated in three years. After that I took accelerated classes to gain my M.D. I also worked with the aliens who landed in New Mexico. I have been studying with their doctors ever since they arrived. They have a tremendous amount of knowledge to impart to us. I can't believe the advancements we've been able to make since their arrival."

"Where are you practicing?"

"I'm working in Santa Fe, but I've been in Dallas attending a conference with some of the doctors I've been working with for the last two years. I can't believe we're meeting like this. Can I buy you a drink?"

Paul looked at Gene in disbelief. He now remembered him as a wild kid in high school, not someone who would be a doctor at such a young age. "I don't drink, to say nothing of so early in the morning. I'm good with having breakfast and coffee. Of course, if you want one, go right ahead."

"I didn't mean it the way it sounded. I meant a coffee. I haven't had anything alcoholic since I suffered from alcohol poisoning in my senior year in high school. The doctors who saved my life inspired me to go into medicine. Believe me, it wasn't easy to stay sober at a party school like UW Madison, but I did it. I took the maximum number of credits each semester along with summer school courses. After graduation I entered the medical program and aced it as well. I think I was one of the youngest doctors to graduate from there."

"So, what did you find out about the aliens?"

"Quite a bit including the fact that once they received the nourishment and water to rehydrate their bodies, they were miraculously healed. Their doctors were treating them during the entire flights. Even though they suffered from the prolonged time in space, they were given medications that counteracted everything except the dehydration and the starvation."

Paul wished he could talk to Rand about what he was now learning about Nina and Tarena's people. "What do you know about a woman who was on the ship by the name of Tarena?"

"I can't say I'm familiar with her, but I have heard her name. She was the daughter of one of the elders, a man by the name of Fragon. From what I heard he was a mathematical genius and is teaching at the University of Wyoming. How do you know her?"

"I met her at the wedding of my friend Randsom Jacobson. She's a very beautiful woman and I plan to get to know her better once we're both back in Laramie."

"Have you let her know about your intentions?"

Paul smiled. "I doubt it. I told her I was going back to the states. I didn't tell her I was planning to begin my post-graduate studies at the same school where her father teaches."

"I hope I can continue to follow this story. It sounds like your life is going to get very interesting in the next few months. From what I hear, the marriage between your friend and the daughter of Dragger, the historical officer and leader of the people who landed in Peru, is unprecedented. I suggest you take things slow and ingratiate yourself to her father before things go too far. Everything I've learned is that they believe in celibacy prior to marriage. I wish our ancestors would have followed the same ideals. The old adage 'boys will be boys' made for a lot of unwanted pregnancies, to say nothing of the spread of diseases in the late twentieth century."

"Don't worry, Gene," Paul responded. "I've been around these people for the last two years. I know all about their ideals and beliefs. I'm proud to say, I'm still a virgin and I plan to remain so until I'm married."

"That's good to hear. Oh, they're announcing my flight to Santa Fe. It was good to run into you Paul. Here's my card, keep in touch. I'll be anxious to hear how you and Tarena hit things off in Wyoming."

Paul watched as Gene walked away from him toward the gate where his flight would be leaving. He took a sip of his now-cold coffee and chucked his bagel sandwich into the garbage. Gene gave him a lot of information to digest and it didn't sit well with the solid food he had desired just a little while earlier. He'd given no thought to the idea of making nice to Tarena's father. He'd met a beautiful girl and, by Earth standards, he would be able to date her without conferring with her parents. With Tarena, things would have to be different and he would need to follow protocol.

He was still sitting at the table near the kiosk when he heard his flight called. Picking up his carry-on bag, he made his way to the gate and prepared to see his family. Although they'd communicated via Skype over the past two years, he hadn't seen them in person since he and Rand left for Peru. His life changed so much, he wondered if he would fit in with his family and life on the ranch. For that matter, would the University of Wyoming be a big enough arena for him anymore? He loved the dig in Peru and the interaction with the aliens who landed two years earlier and turned the scientific world on its head.

All during the flight to Helena, Paul thought about his meeting with Gene. Over the past two years he'd come to realize there were no accidents in life. Both he and Rand had been in the right place at the right time to watch an event that would change the course of the world as they knew it and perhaps rewrite the history books in the progress.

He knew his meeting with Tarena had been orchestrated by Rand as well as Dragger. They had become close friends and confidants over the past two years and now Rand's position with the United States Government made him one of the most influential Earthlings in the dealings with these people. Paul merely worked on an archaeological dig and had ridden on the coat tails of his best friend. In such a position, he'd been able to meet one of the most beautiful women to ever cross his path.

~ * ~

The plane finally landed and Paul made his way to the baggage claim area. Even though he had no baggage with him, he knew this was where he would find his family.

"Uncle Paul, Uncle Paul, over here," he heard his six-year-old niece Amanda calling.

He'd seen her on Skype but wasn't prepared for how tall she was. She stood next to her seven-year-old brother, Timothy, along with their parents, and grandparents.

For the first time since leaving home, he realized how much he'd missed his family while working in Peru.

His mother was the first one to make it to his side and she hugged him as though he'd returned from the dead rather than from working in Peru for two years.

"It's so good to have you home, son," his father said, clasping his hand before pulling him into a bear hug.

Kathy was crying and Todd was holding her close.

"Why the tears, Sis?" Paul asked, as soon as he stood by her side.

"These are happy tears. You'll never know how I worried about you when news of the alien ship landing close to where you were working came across the television. When I found out you were one of the first people to make contact, I worried even more. I had no idea if they meant us harm or if I'd ever see you again."

"In that case, I guess they're acceptable. I hope you won't think less of me when I tell you I've fallen in love with one of the aliens."

As they drove back to the ranch, Paul filled his family in on meeting Tarena and not telling her about where he lived. "I decided I'd better run this past the family before I make an awkward attempt at meeting her on the street in Laramie."

"You don't know this girl," Kathy argued. "What if she already has a boyfriend?"

"Rand assures me she doesn't. If he can be happy married to an alien woman, why can't I? I've waited a long time and dated several women, but none of them affected me the same way as Tarena did."

"Speaking of old girlfriends," Todd said, changing the subject. "We all saw what happened when Rand's old girlfriend, Cynthia, showed up in Peru."

"That certainly wasn't a pretty picture," Paul admitted. "I wonder what happened to her."

"Oh, I can answer that," Paul's mother said. "You probably don't know it, but Cyn's aunt, Johanna, and I were college roommates. She was so upset by the scene she created in Peru, she talked her brother into cutting off his daughter's allowance. Jo said things were pretty rocky for a while, but Cyn finally came to her senses. She met a young teacher from New Jersey and they were married at Christmas time. The last I heard she announced she was pregnant and very happy with her life. Guess leopards do change their spots after all."

"Rand will be happy to hear that. She gave him a bad time when she showed up at the dig and later at the compound."

~ * ~

Tarena didn't want to see Paul leave, but she knew it was inevitable. They were two strangers who met at the wedding of mutual friends and would never see each other again. It made her long for the man she thought she would marry, Grato. He'd been on one of the crafts destroyed by the meteor shower and she'd watched him die. Maybe she hadn't seen it personally but she knew the fate of the people on the ships that were there one minute and gone the next.

She wished she could talk to Nina about Paul, but she and Rand were secluded in the home built for them on the grounds of the complex until they would leave for England on a diplomatic mission/honeymoon in less than a week. By that time, she and her parents would be on their way back to Wyoming.

Thinking of Wyoming made her realize how much she enjoyed her newly-adopted home. It reminded her of some of the rural areas of Plantas. In her mind it was a perfect place for them to relocate.

"A penny for your thoughts," Lora said, breaking into the ramblings of Tarena's mind.

"I was thinking about our new home and how much it looked like the retreat Grato and his family took me to in the rural part of our planet."

"Do you still long for him?"

"I think of him, but I doubt our relationship would have lasted. He was interested in farming the land while my life revolved around the mathematics my father taught me. Did I tell you I will be teaching mathematics at a secondary school in the fall?"

Lora looked at her in disbelief. "I hadn't heard of any such thing. Do you think you are qualified to teach on Earth?"

Lora's question baffled Tarena. "Why would you ask such a question? I have been qualified to teach for several years. Last year I assisted at the secondary school where I will be teaching. They were more than impressed by my qualifications."

"I'm also a teacher, but I'm too busy teaching the children who made this journey with us to have time to think about teaching Earthlings who are undoubtedly inferior to us. I've only met a few of them, but I'm certainly not impressed. Rand seems all right as well as some of the other people from the dig, but others I've met seem to be simple-minded. I hope you are able to instill some of the knowledge of our people within their minds."

Tarena thought her friend's words sounded prejudicial. The students she'd interacted with at the secondary school seemed intelligent and eager to learn. It was the same with everyone she'd met at the university. No matter what, she decided not to allow Lora's words to poison her mind. Once they left Peru, she looked forward to seeing her new home as well as the friends she knew would be waiting for her. Even though they knew she was one of 'the aliens' it didn't matter. They accepted her for who she was.

~ * ~

As the private plane they had used to go to Peru landed in Laramie, Tarena's emotions were in knots. She would be glad to reconnect with her friends and find out what they'd been doing during the summer break. On the other hand, she couldn't stop thinking about Paul. It was possible she'd never see him again, but she certainly would never forget him.

The house she shared with her parents looked no different than it had when she left it just a matter of days earlier. It was she who had changed. How could a chance meeting with a handsome young man change her way of thinking so drastically?

Instead of dwelling on Paul, she began preparing for the classes she would be teaching in geometry and organography when the school year started in September. Being on the planet for almost two years, she'd become acquainted with the names of months, days of the week, and the fact the year consisted of three hundred and sixty-five days rather than the shorter cycles on Plantas.

The one constant she'd found was mathematics. It was as her father always told her. Mathematical calculations were a universal language.

She was shopping when she met one of the teachers she'd become acquainted with while assisting at the school the previous year.

"Tarena, it's good to see you," Jennifer said. "I didn't know if you'd be back from Peru yet."

"It was only a short trip so I could participate in my friend Nina's mating ceremony. I think you call it a wedding. I had no reason to stay much longer after the ceremony was over."

What she didn't mention was the poisonous words Lora spoke about the people of Earth. She didn't need to have them turn her against the people she now called friends.

"Well, I'm glad you're back. I'm having a barbeque for the teachers to get together before school starts. There are several new teachers starting this year. I couldn't believe how many of our staff retired last year. It's always sad to see old friends leave, but it's fun to meet the new teachers. We'll have a great time. I'm having it tomorrow night. Can you come?"

Tarena thought about the invitation for a moment. She hoped her parents would be in favor of her going. "I'll check to see if I can make it. I have your number in my cell phone so I'll call you either way."

"That sounds great. So, can you tell me about the wedding you attended? Was it beautiful? Did the bride wear a princess dress or something different?"

"It was a surprise for my friend, Nina. She has been promised to Rand for almost two years, but he has to travel a lot for his job. Her parents arranged the entire thing. It was a mating ceremony like the ones we attended on Plantas. She wore a traditional purple mating robe embroidered in silver. I was her attendant and I wore a lavender robe embroidered in purple. Rand and his attendant wore white robes with lavender and purple embroidery."

"How interesting. I love hearing about your customs. Do they exchange rings? Was there a wedding cake?"

Tarena was pleased to think her friend was so interested in the customs of her people. "Rand had a ring made especially for her in London, by a jeweler of our people. It is a beautiful ring. The one she gave him was equally impressive. It belonged to her grandfather and as soon as it was put on his finger it adapted to fit him perfectly. It's made of a special metal from our planet."

Jennifer seemed to be entranced by Tarena's description of the mating ceremony. "I am so glad you are my friend. I love hearing about the people from Plantas and their customs. I can hardly wait for you to find someone special to love and get married. I hope when that happens, I will be invited."

"You know you will, but the man I loved and was promised to was killed when the meteor storm claimed the lives of the majority of our people. I pray someday I will meet someone who will become special in my life."

Tarena decided it was best not to mention Paul. He was someone she knew she could come to love, but the possibility of ever seeing him again was something she realized might never happen.

Chapter Twenty-Three

Paul was anxious for the fall semester to start at school. As much as he enjoyed being home, the everyday running of the ranch soon gave way to his desire to start his studies for his doctorate.

He thought about what he would do after his schooling was complete. As much as he enjoyed the time he spent on the dig, he didn't think he would be content digging into the ancient ruins for the remainder of his life. In truth, he envied Rand his position with the government, especially now that he was married to the woman he loved.

The more he thought about it, the more he wanted to teach courses in archaeology at the college level. He decided he would speak to his class advisor at the university when he went to Laramie to sign up for his fall classes.

In mid-July, Paul made the trip to the campus to look for an apartment as well as sign up for the fall semester.

After signing the lease on a two-bedroom apartment, he made his way to the registration office. It wasn't actually necessary, as he'd been accepted for the post-grad program before he even left Peru. All he had to do was register for his classes, but with his change of plans for his future, he needed to talk to an advisor.

Leaving the office where he'd leased his apartment, he almost bumped into Tarena as she was entering the coffee shop next door.

"Tarena, what a coincidence. I knew you were living in Laramie but I thought it would be harder to find you."

"Paul? What are you doing here?"

"I'm signing up for my courses for my post-grad studies. I also just signed a lease for an apartment, so I'm pretty much set for school to begin."

"That's wonderful. I was just going in to get a cup of coffee. Would you like to join me?"

Paul couldn't believe his luck. The woman he wanted in his life had crossed his path almost as soon as he got to town.

The coffee shop was one Paul and Rand frequented often when they were roommates here two years ago. It pleased him to see the menu hadn't changed. After Tarena placed her order, he ordered an iced drink that had been one of his favorites two years earlier. She reached into her purse but he stopped her.

"This one is on me. I can't believe I found you so easily. I thought for sure it would be harder for me to find you."

Tarena looked bewildered at his presence. "I didn't think I'd ever see you again. Did you know you would be going to school here when we met in Peru? If so, why didn't you say something?"

"I did know. I also knew I would be finding you once school started. I needed some time with my family before I came in search of you. I've been away from them for two years and I've missed them terribly. With family time over, I'm ready to take the next step in my life. I've been praying you would be willing to be part of my life."

A singe tear slipped from Tarena's eye, making Paul wonder if he'd made a mistake in keeping the fact he would be a student at the university for the fall semester.

"I was afraid I'd never see you again. I was hoping to hear from Nina and ask her if she knew where you were. Our meeting was but a brief one and I wanted to get to know you better."

"I'm sorry I didn't let you know I was in Wyoming before this. I just needed to get my head together. I thought I wanted to get my degree in archaeology in order to be the head of a dig like Dr. Clark is in Peru. With my interest in carbon dating, I knew I would be able to work on any dig anywhere in the world. I've come to realize I want to teach on the college level. I was planning to talk to one of the counselors today."

"Maybe you should speak with my father. Let me contact him and see if it would be all right for you to come and take the evening meal with us."

Paul watched as Tarena closed her eyes and appeared to go into a trance. He'd heard about how these people could communicate telepathically but hadn't ever seen it done. She remained in the trance for several seconds before she opened her eyes.

"Both of my parents are excited to know you are here in Laramie. They insist I bring you home with me. My father is most interested to talk to you about this new path you think your life might be taking."

Before they left the coffee shop, Paul called his parents to let them know he would be staying in Laramie longer than he originally planned.

~ * ~

Having found Paul so suddenly, Tarena didn't want him to disappear from her life again. The fact her parents were excited about the meeting made her heart sing with joy. She wondered if he would be returning to his home after they ate the evening meal or if her parents would convince him to spend the night in the spare bedroom.

Once they arrived back at her house, she found her mother, Dyna, had prepared a feast fit for any high-ranking official from Plantas.

"I wish you hadn't gone to so much trouble. I am excited to be a guest in your home, but I needed nothing this special."

"You are an honored guest," Fragon replied. "I am pleased you will be completing your studies at the university. From what Tarena transmitted to me, you are thinking of teaching on the college level. I will be able to help you with this. From what I understand from Dr. Clark, your work on the dig in Peru will give you much credit toward your doctorate. It will require a lot of hard work on your part, but I'm certain you will find the work rewarding. With my recommendations, you will be able to get a position tutoring underclassman. That should help with your living expenses as well as your tuition for your schooling."

Paul looked at Fragon in disbelief. "How could all of this be arranged so quickly? I haven't spoken of this to anyone but Tarena."

"My father is an influential man at the university. When he speaks, people listen. It was this way before we left our home. Enjoy the things he can do for you."

~ * ~

Paul was still in awe of how quickly things happened once Frag on made the necessary arrangements.

Although Fragon and Dyna insisted he could spend the night in their spare bedroom, he didn't feel comfortable. Instead, he drove back to his family's ranch.

By the end of the week, he was ready to move into his new apartment. With the help of his dad and Todd, he packed up the U-Haul with the furniture his parents had been storing for him after redecorating their house.

"I don't like you leaving so soon after you've gotten home," his mother said, dabbing at her eyes with a tissue.

"It's not like when I went to Peru. I'm only less than an hour's drive away. The way things are going, it's best I move into my apartment as soon as possible and meet with my professors. I also need to get registered with the university as a tutor."

"Then we're all coming with you," Kathy declared. "I know how bachelors live. You need us to help you decorate your new apartment."

"I thought it was just Dad and Todd who were coming with me."

"Wrong, baby brother," Kathy said. "The kids are spending the week with their other Grandma and Grandpa so we're free to help with the move. Besides, Todd promised me a couple of days in Laramie. We have reservations for the next two nights at a really nice hotel."

"It's the same for your mother and me," his father said. "We decided we needed a mini-vacation."

"What about the ranch?"

"I think the hired hands can get along without us for a couple of days," his mother assured him. "We're not ready to have you leave us so soon after you get home. Besides, I agree with Kathy. Your new apartment could use a woman's touch. We would also like to meet the young lady who has stolen your heart, as well as her parents."

Paul realized he'd talked about Tarena and her parents far too much since he returned home. He did want his family to meet the people who had become so important in his life.

As he pulled out of the driveway, he felt like he was leading a parade. He drove the U-Haul with Kathy at his side, while his mother followed in his car, his father in his truck and Todd bringing up the rear in their vehicle.

"This is a lot different from when I first went away to college," Paul said.

"Back then you were moving into a dorm and later you and Rand had that ratty little furnished apartment. I hope this place is better than that. If it isn't, Mom and Dad's furniture will really look out of place."

"I guarantee this place is much better than the one I shared with Rand. It's a two bedroom so I will have one room that can be made into an office. I assure you, both you and Mom will approve. I've grown up a lot in the last two years."

"I know you have. It's good to see this side of you."

At last they arrived at the apartment. He'd seen the building when he leased it less than a week ago. It was one of the nicer apartment buildings on campus. He was anxious to move in and begin this next step in his life.

"Not bad," Kathy observed. "This is a great-looking building and the neighborhood looks presentable. Are you sure you want to live alone? I'm afraid you'll starve. Do you even know how to cook?"

"Yes, my dear sister, I do know how to cook. When Rand and I shared our apartment, we shared the cooking duties. I think I'll be all right, but there are a lot of restaurants around here and I bought a meal plan through the university. I can go down to the cafeteria if I'm really desperate."

The others pulled in behind them and everyone agreed Paul made a good selection in an apartment.

"Let's get you moved in so we can go out to supper. You did call Tarena and her parents and told them to meet us at the restaurant, didn't you?"

"Yes, I did, Dad. I have a feeling you will have to fight Fragon for the bill. That's just the way he is."

The conversation ended there as everyone pitched in and started moving the furniture up to Paul's second-floor apartment. While the guys brought in the furniture, Paul's mother and Kathy hung pictures and decided where everything should be placed.

"Everything looks wonderful," Paul's mother declared, once she stood back to look at their handywork.

"Yes, it does, thanks to you and Kathy. I would have been unpacking for weeks. If I'm not mistaken, my clothes are already put into the dresser and hung in the closet."

"Mom also brought you an ironing board and an iron. You aren't a sloppy college student. You have to look more like a responsible adult. I didn't see one suit in your wardrobe. I hope you're planning to get one."

"I have one that I took for Rand's wedding, but with everything that was going on I forgot to bring it along with me. If the truth be known, it was terribly out of style. I know I need to go shopping but I've decided I wanted to wait until I get on my feet before I bought anything. I promise, I won't wear anything that will embarrass you."

Paul's statement brought laughter from his dad and Todd. "Let's put this conversation to bed," Paul's father said. "I'm starving and I have confidence in your ability to look presentable once school starts."

~ * ~

Tarena was nervous about meeting Paul's parents. The meeting between Paul and her parents had taken place at Nina and Rand's mating ceremony. It hadn't been like going out to meet his family at a restaurant. If she recalled what Paul said when he called they would also be meeting his sister and brother-in-law.

"You look like you are ready to turn and run," her father said. "Why are you worried about meeting Paul's family? It is no different from when he met us."

"Yes, it is, Father. He met you at a social gathering. Tonight, we will be going to a restaurant in order to have a meal with strangers. What if they don't like me? What if they condemn him for wanting to be with someone different than them?"

"You look for problems where none exist," her mother rationalized. "I plan to meet some new people and perhaps some new friends. You should be excited to meet the people who are special to Paul."

Tarena took a deep breath and resolved to make the best of tonight's meeting with Paul's family.

~ * ~

Paul was impressed by the restaurant his father chose for this dinner party. They arrived just moments before Fragon, Dyna, and Tarena.

As soon as Tarena stepped into the restaurant, she was greeted by his mother and sister. "You have to be Tarena. I'm Janice, Paul's mom, and this is Kathy, his sister. You are just as beautiful as Paul told us. I'm so glad we are finally getting to meet you."

He could see Tarena begin to relax as she introduced her parents. For the remainder of the evening, Paul's father, Todd, and Fragen kept their conversation going, while Dyna, Paul's mother, and Kathy chatted about woman things.

"I can't believe I was worried about meeting your family," Tarena confessed. "We might as well not be here."

"That's just fine with me," Paul told her. "I'd like to take you away from here to somewhere we can be alone, but since our fathers will soon be fighting over who is going to pay the check it would be rude of us."

"Paul tells us you believe in the one god," Paul's mother said.

He cringed. She was the one who insisted they attend church as children. They'd been baptized and confirmed before they went their own way. In college, he'd used the excuse he was too tired from studying to go to the services. It was when he and Rand moved in together that things changed. Rand made it a point to attend church regularly and Paul soon found himself joining his friend. It wasn't until they went to Peru and started working on the dig that Paul became engrossed in the worship services. Even when he was at the compound on a Sunday, he attended services with Dragger's people.

"Yes, we do," Dyna replied. "Since we were the only ones of our party to come here, we sought out a church that met our needs. I must say there are many different faiths and it took several months for us to find one where we were welcomed."

"That's wonderful," Katie chimed in. "We are spending the

weekend in Laramie and were wondering where we would be going to church. Would you mind if we joined you?"

Around the table men and women alike agreed going to church with Fragen and Dyna would be a wonderful experience. During the conversations, Paul and Tarena exchanged glances.

"I don't know if this is such a good idea," Paul whispered. "My mother and Kate are the most devout members of my family. What if the church your parents attend isn't exactly like the one they're used to back home?"

"I don't think you have to worry about it," Tarena replied. "We went to many churches and this one is the closest to the beliefs of our priests."

Paul cringed at the word priest. He'd been raised as a Protestant unlike several of his friends who were Catholic. If Fragon and Dyna attended a Catholic Church, he doubted his family would feel comfortable.

All talk of church ended when the check arrived. To Paul's surprise it was a three-way tussle for the check when it arrived at the table. Todd joined his father-in-law and Fragon in haggling over who would pay their meal. Between Todd and Fragon, they insisted on leaving the tip.

"Is tipping a custom of your people?" Randy asked.

"It depends on the area of the planet where our people live," Fragon replied. "Our family lived in a large city and there it is acceptable, but in the more rural areas it is frowned upon. The young man Tarena was to have been mated with was from one of these areas. They met while studying at the university. Grato had a hard time adjusting to our ways. He could not understand why the people who served us were not paid enough money to live comfortably. We tried to explain to him that it was our custom to reward people for good service. It wasn't because they weren't well paid."

"Did he come with you?" Todd asked. "Being a farmer, I am certain there would be many farms and ranches where he could be of help and maybe have new skills to teach them."

"Alas," Fragen said, using his napkin to wipe away a tear, "he was aboard one of the ships that were lost in the meteor shower."

"I didn't realize you were engaged," Paul said, his voice sounding with surprise.

"It was a custom on our planet. Grato and I were to be mated once we arrived on Nalo. I have a feeling I wouldn't have enjoyed life as a farmer's wife. We talked about it often and he insisted I would be more than an extension of him. He wanted me to teach. Unfortunately, our plans were never to be realized."

"You will be teaching, won't you?" Kathy asked.

"Yes, I will. Like my friend, Nina, what we thought would be our destiny was not to be realized. She has found love, and I hope the same will happen to me."

Beneath the table, she squeezed Paul's hand making him aware of the fact her feelings for him were the same as his for her.

"I have a feeling you and my brother are anxious to explore a relationship. I hope things work out for you."

Kathy looked at Paul and gave him a sly wink.

With the battle for the check and the tip won, they reluctantly left the restaurant.

"Are you comfortable staying at your apartment alone tonight?" Paul's father asked.

Paul contemplated his answer. In school Rand had been his roommate and living in a dormitory setting in Peru he certainly was never alone. This was a big step in his life and he was excited to begin his new journey on his own.

"I'll be fine, Dad. Hopefully, you and Mom as well as Kathy and Todd will enjoy your night at the hotel. I'll meet you tomorrow morning for breakfast."

"Brunch," Kathy interrupted. "Don't forget we will be going to church with Fragon and Dyna tomorrow. The service is at nine thirty. We have the directions and will be picking you up at eight thirty so we get there in plenty of time."

Paul groaned. He'd planned to spend his first night alone sleeping late and going out for a leisurely breakfast. Those plans would have to wait until after his family went home.

Chapter Twenty-Four

Paul took his time settling into his new apartment. He had so much to do at the university by the time he got home he was not interested in rearranging the things his mother and Kathy put away on move in day.

Just as he had no time to become comfortable in his apartment, he had little time to spend with Tarena. Since school started, she was always preparing class plans and grading papers, just as his time was filled with tutoring sessions and post-grad classes.

It was early October when Paul received a series of text messages. The first one came from Rand telling him how he and Nina were going to become parents and they wanted him and Tarena to be godparents when the time came for a christening. It was closely followed by a message from Nina as well as one from Tarena.

When can we meet? Paul texted to Tarena.

It will have to wait until Friday. Could you pick me up after school? I'm anxious to see you.

I agree. It's been too long. Will your parents insist on a chaperone?

Don't be silly. I'll meet you at the school at four, Friday afternoon.

Paul immediately checked his calendar and was relieved not to have any tutoring sessions planned for that evening. Friday was always a good day to plan things because everyone wanted to party on the weekend. Studies were for weekdays. Most of his students needed his guidance in order to graduate on time, but they also liked to make the most of their weekends.

He'd no more than finished his text to Tarena when his phone rang. Before answering, he checked the caller ID. It came as a surprise when he saw Gene Emery's name beneath the number.

"Hi Gene, I didn't expect to hear from you so soon. Is anything wrong?"

"Not wrong, Paul. I came home for two reasons; I had some vacation coming so I decided to use it to come home for a while. My folks have been asking me to come home for a visit. I also wanted to get together with you and discuss something concerning the aliens who are now in Laramie."

"Whatever could that be?"

"I don't want to go into it on the phone. Are you free for dinner tonight?"

"I have a tutoring session at three but I'm free after that."

"Good. I'll meet you at seven at Jeffrey's Bistro. I've always liked the variety of their menu."

Paul agreed to meet the man who came up to him at the Dallas airport, but was worried about the unspoken message in the call. What would Gene have to tell him about Tarena and her family that he couldn't talk about on the phone?

His tutoring student arrived right on time. The session went well, considering Paul's state of mind. He'd finally been able to lose himself in the session without worrying about his meeting with Gene at seven.

Once the student went back to his dorm, Paul showered and changed into something a little more appropriate for dinner at the Bistro. Considering his apartment was close to the restaurant, he opted to walk rather than drive the short distance.

He found Gene waiting for him.

"I hope I'm not late," Paul greeted him.

"Hardly, I just got here and I'm a little early. I did make a reservation. I never know how many people will be eating out on a week night."

"I thought the same thing. When I went to make a reservation for the two of us, I mentioned your name and the hostess told me there was already a reservation under our name. Guess we were both thinking the same way."

They entered the restaurant that had always been one of Paul's favorites. The hostess took them to a secluded booth. She left them with the menu. It wasn't hard for Paul to decide what to order. His choice was always the same, Szechuan Chicken with Shiitake Mushrooms.

"That sounds good to me too," Gene said, "but I think I prefer the Breast of Chicken Milanese."

Once their order was taken, Gene broached the reason for their meeting. "Do you remember when there were parents who refused to have their children vaccinated?"

"Of course I do. It was big news. I know my mother was against it. She said back in the nineties this movement was big but it came back into the forefront about twenty-five years ago. She insisted Kathy and I get all of our vaccinations."

"Well, some of those kids who didn't get them are now adults and there has been a big outbreak of the measles in Santa Fe. It hit the alien community there pretty hard. Thank God we didn't have any causalities. When their doctors couldn't diagnose what was wrong, I was called in. The decision was made because of my contact with them when they first arrived. There were many symptoms I didn't recognize, but there were enough classic ones for me to diagnose it. We made certain everyone who didn't get the disease was vaccinated. I need to have you meet with Professor Fragon and his family to be sure they know the danger of this disease."

Paul nodded his head, suddenly concerned for the safety of Tarena. "I read about what happened to the Native Americans, Hawaiians, and other indigenous people when they contracted that horrible disease. We can't allow the same thing to happen to the people who have settled here. Have you contacted Rand yet?"

"I couldn't get a number for him. You know how the Federal Government is about giving out privileged information. I was hoping you could get in touch with him. He's been instrumental in helping all of the colonies get settled. I'm certain he will be able to convince them to get vaccinated against the diseases we think of as minor."

Panic began to overtake Paul as he remembered hearing about an outbreak of measles on campus when he was still an underclassman. He was glad he'd been vaccinated, but several other students were hospitalized. If such a thing were to hit campus again it would be disastrous considering Fragon, Dyna and Terina would be susceptible.

"Can we make arrangements for my friends to be vaccinated right away?" he asked once their food was served.

"Once you talk to them, I would like to set up a clinic next week. Do you think they would be agreeable? I know how the people in Santa Fe felt about it. They were worried we were trying to poison them. I can't say I could blame them, but once their doctors and I explained it to them, everything went well. Even the people who suffered from the disease insisted on being vaccinated. I tended to agree, considering none of us had any idea how their bodies would react to the virus."

Once they finished eating, Paul placed a call to Fragon.

"I have been informed that Dr. Emery is coming to Wyoming," Fragon said, once Paul told him the reason for the call. "I can understand his reason for concern. One of my close friends in Santa Fe has told me of the terrible disease that he suffered from and how this young doctor who first treated us was able to cure him. He insisted I get the vaccinations Dr. Emery has to offer. When can I meet with him?"

"We just finished having dinner together. He wants to set up a clinic for next week, unless we learn of an outbreak of measles before that."

"I've spoken with my wife and daughter. Tarena immediately called the principal at her school to get his help in insisting the students be vaccinated. Perhaps you can bring Dr. Emery over so we can meet him and learn more about this disease of which we have never experienced on our planet."

Paul asked Gene if he would mind going to visit Fragon and his family and he was excited about going to the home of the man he met briefly in Santa Fe.

Ten minutes later they pulled up in front of the house. The first thing Paul noticed was Tarena standing on the porch. From the expression on her face, he knew she was frightened by the news they'd received from New Mexico.

"Oh, Paul," she said as she allowed him to embrace her. "This all sounds so terrible. I fear for the lives of not only my family but those of the other people from Plantas around the world. I also fear for my students."

"That's why Gene, Dr. Emery, is here. He's been working with your people in New Mexico."

"I've also been assigned to visit other cities around the country to make certain those people who arrived with you are vaccinated," Gene said, speaking for the first time. "Paul has assured me he will be able to contact Rand so he can make these vaccines available to the people who were the first to arrive. I'm told he is the U.S. Ambassador to all the people who arrived from your planet."

The fear seemed to fade from Tarena's eyes. Rather than standing out at the curb in front of the house, she ushered them into the parlor where her parents waited patiently.

"I'm Dr. Emery," Gene said, extending his hand. "I would be pleased if you called by my given name, Gene."

Fragon's mask of worry seemed to instantly disappear. "I remember you from when we first arrived, young man. You were very good to our people and it seems you are still taking good care of us. My friend, Parin, speaks highly of you. He told me he was one of the first people to come down with the virus our doctors could not identify. It was only because you were called in that he was healed. Our people are calling you a hero."

"I'm far from heroic, Sir. I'm just pleased to have been able to help your people. Now I hope I can be of help to you and your family as well as any students who would need a vaccination. The last thing I want is to see a breakout of measles become an epidemic."

~ * ~

It was almost midnight when Gene dropped Paul off at his apartment, yet sleep was the last thing on Paul's mind. Once Gene left, Paul picked up his cell phone and placed a call to Rand.

"Hey Buddy, do you have any idea what time it is?"

"Sure I do, it's a little after midnight here."

"Look, I'm in Washington this week. It's three AM here. This better be good to wake me out of a sound sleep."

Even though Paul felt bad, he continued telling Rand about the measles outbreak and the need for all of the aliens to be vaccinated.

"We got word about it in the briefing today. How did you hear about it?"

"I think I told you about meeting Gene Emery when I was changing planes in Dallas. Well, he was the doctor they called to take care of the people in Santa Fe. He told me he met them when they first arrived and they trusted him enough to allow him to treat them."

"I remember him. He was great with everyone he treated that day as well as the days that followed. I guess I didn't know his name or I might have put two and two together when we were talking in the meeting today."

"So, what does the government plan to do?"

"They are communicating with the heads of health and human services for the countries where the people have settled. Nina talked to her folks this evening and they are arranging for everyone to receive the vaccine. I guess bad news travels fast and this time it has brought about good results. The world owes your friend a huge debt."

They talked for several more minutes, before Paul started to feel the exhaustion of the day. Once they hung up, he went to bed, but sleep didn't come easily.

His thoughts, as well as the dreams he had when he did fall asleep, were of people with no immunity, falling sick and dying from a disease unknown to them. When his alarm went off at six the next morning, he was reluctant to get out of bed even though he knew he had a full day of classes before picking Tarena up from her school. His dreams had been filled with the Native American population being killed by diseases like measles in the nineteenth century. Would the same thing happen to Fragon and his people? In his dreams he also saw the people on the Hawaiian Island when measles overtook the population, driving them into the sea in order to quench the fires of the fever that wracked their bodies.

Reluctantly, he got out of bed and prepared for his day with classes.

He'd just finished his last class when his cell phone rang. Looking down he saw Tarena's number. It was only noon, so he knew she wasn't calling to see where he was.

"Hi Tarena," he answered before the third ring.

"Oh, it's terrible," she greeted him. "Father just called and Mother has become very ill. He called the healer who relocated here with us and he has no idea what to do. Do you think your friend Dr. Gene would know what to do?"

"Oh, my god," Paul exclaimed. "What are her symptoms? Are you with her?"

"She has a terrible headache, her vision is blurry, and she is burning up. Father refused to let me come to be with her."

"He was right. I'll go over to their house. I've been vaccinated against the measles so I can be there safely. I'll keep you updated. In the meantime, I'll leave a key to my apartment at your school office. You will need to go there for your own safety, but it might be too late. I'll call Gene and he should be here within the hour."

Paul called Gene on his way out to his car in the parking lot.

"Paul, I didn't expect to hear from you until Monday."

"I'm afraid Monday will be too late. Dyna has all the symptoms and I'm afraid Fragon, as well as their healer, has been exposed."

"What about Tarena?"

"Her father doesn't want her to come home, but I'm sure she's been exposed. It's possible she was the one who brought the disease home from school. Just to be sure, I'm leaving a key for my apartment at her school. She can go there after school. By that time, you should be here and be able to examine her."

"That was a good decision. Are you going over to be with Fragon and Dyna?"

"What should I do when I get there?"

"Darken the rooms, insist Dyna get into bed to rest and have Fragon use cold compresses until I can get there. It's just after noon now; I should be there no later than one fifteen. Hang tight, I'll be there as soon as I can. Also, try to get their healer over to the house. He's also been exposed. I'll bring enough vaccine to take care of the entire population. From our meeting the other night, I'm certain I will be able to contact all of them."

Paul ended their conversation and hurried to Tarena's school to leave off the key to his apartment, before he made his way to Fragon's home.

His hand hardly left the button of the doorbell than a frantic Fragon opened the door to him.

"Is it safe for you to be here?" Fragon asked.

"It's perfectly safe. I've had the vaccine. I just finished talking to Gene and he is on his way here. I've been told what to do. While I care for

Dyna, I want you to contact the other members of your community who live in Laramie, especially your healer."

"Our healer is here and trying to do what he can for Dyna."

"That's good. I'll go and help him with Dyna. How many other people will be coming to your house?"

Fragon took a moment to mentally count the members of his community who followed him to Wyoming. "Not counting the healer and my family, there are sixteen others. I will begin contacting them and asking everyone to come here."

Immediately, Paul thought about telling Tarena to go to his apartment. As things stood now, he would have to contact her and tell her to come home after school. The thought no more than crossed his mind when the door to the house opened. To his surprise, Tarena entered the house. She was flushed and he could tell she didn't feel well.

"Here is your key," she said handing him back the key to his apartment. "By the time I finished my class I started feeling sick. I went directly to the office to get your key. It was then I decided the best place I could be was with my parents. Did you get a hold of Gene?"

The question hung in the air between them as he watched her start to waver. All he could do was catch Tarena as she collapsed into his arms. He gently lifted Tarena and following Fragon's directions took her to the bedroom Fragon said she occupied.

"Am I needed in here?"

Paul turned to see the healer. The man was dressed in the traditional robes of their people. "Yes, I could use your assistance. It seems Tarena has come down with the same disease as her mother. I have talked to my friend, and he will be here shortly."

"Ah yes, the Earth doctor. Fragon told me of him. I look forward to meeting him. This disease is unknown to our people. I appreciate learning any knowledge he can impart to me."

"I'm glad you feel this way. When I spoke to Gene, he said we should wipe their brows with cool cloths. I will get a basin and a wash cloth to wash Tarena's face if you will do the same for Dyna?"

The healer nodded his head in agreement. Together they went off to find basins and wash cloths.

By the time Paul returned to Tarena's side, Gene arrived along with the other aliens who came to Wyoming with Fragon. He was glad most of the doctoring duties were being taken care of by Gene.

"I feel so horrible," Tarena said when he entered the room.

"I know, honey. Let me bathe your face. Gene is here and is taking care of your mother and the others. He'll be in here to make you feel better soon."

Tarena relaxed and he prayed what little he could do to make her comfortable would be enough. Seeing her so sick and not being able to do anything more than bathe her face made him feel inadequate.

Once she fell asleep, he drew the drapes tightly shut. He hadn't thought to do it earlier. He'd been too concerned with making her comfortable to think about the other things that needed to be done.

At long last Gene came into Tarena's room.

"How many others have come down with the measles?" Paul asked.

"Luckily, only two, and I was able to vaccinate everyone else. I'm here for the duration. You, my friend, look exhausted. Are you sure you were vaccinated when you were a kid?"

"I called my mom just to be sure. She asked if I would need a booster shot or something like that. If so, can you take care of it?"

"You don't need a booster, but what I do want to do is examine you. What you need is a little rest and maybe a good stiff drink. I have a feeling you didn't get much sleep after the bombshell I dropped on you last night. The people who were healthy have been sent home. We have the two who have been diagnosed bedded down in the third bedroom. Fragon has made up a bed for you in his office. Let me worry about Tarena for a while."

Paul did as Gene said and made his way to the office. Once there, he was surprised to see Fragon waiting for him.

"I heard Dr. Gene say you needed a stiff drink. I figured I had just what you needed."

To Paul's surprise, Fragon pulled out a decanter of a clear liquid.

"This is some of the finest spirits from our planet. I was able to bring several decanters of it with me."

"I—I don't drink," Paul protested.

"Sometimes people need to break with tradition. This will help you more than you know."

He poured a small glass that Paul equated with a shot glass and handed it to him. After smelling the sweet aroma of the liquid, Paul took a tentative sip. It had a sweet bite on his tongue but burned the rest of the way down to his stomach.

"Finish it, son," Fragon urged.

Closing his eyes, Paul swallowed the remainder of the liquid. "This stuff makes moonshine look tame."

"What is this moonshine of which you speak?"

Paul tried his best to explain the prohibition of the early twentieth century and the men who were forced to make illegal liquor in hidden stills, but the drink he'd just consumed made him unable to carry on an intelligent conversation.

He barely remembered Fragon helping him to take off his clothes and coax him to lay down on the day bed in the office. He was immediately asleep, or perhaps he passed out from the potent liquor he'd ingested.

Chapter Twenty-Five

Paul awoke to bright sunshine coming through the window of the room where he'd spent the night. His memory of the drink Fragon gave him the previous evening flooded his mind. He took a moment to clear his head of sleep, before realizing he had no headache.

How is this possible? I've gotten drunk before and the reason I stopped drinking was the hangover the day after. I can't believe there's no headache considering how potent that drink was.

"I thought you were going to sleep the day away."

Paul turned toward the door and saw Gene standing in the doorway. "Fragon gave me something to make me sleep."

"He told me. That stuff must have a kick like a Missouri mule. It's almost two in the afternoon."

"How is everyone?"

"That's what I want to talk to you about. I'm afraid things aren't good. There are at least three other patients. They've been moved here so I can treat them all. We caught Tarena before she had a full-blown case, but there are two people who are so far advanced their treatment is going to take a long time. Unfortunately, Dyna is one of them. Their healer and I have been with her around the clock but considering her age and the severity of her condition, it will be touch and go for several days."

Paul could hardly believe what he was hearing. Only days ago, Dyna had shown no signs of the illness. "How can that be? She was all right when we were here to explain about the measles."

"I talked to Fragon about that and he said Dyna, as well as the other patient, both suffered from time warp fever due to the amount of extra time they had to spend in getting to Earth. The healer told me both of them were left with suppressed immune systems. It's the reason the disease hit them so hard. The healer confided in me he doesn't think either of them will survive this. I don't want to give up so quickly, but I'm glad the other people from their party agreed to being vaccinated. Thank goodness the people of their party are clustered here as well as in New Mexico. I have a team down there who are working with many of the people. They also had another healer on their flight. He has been very helpful. It was this healer who told me of the group of people who followed Fragon here."

Paul shook his head. When Gene first mentioned measles, he had no idea of the implications of it. Even when they talked about the impact the disease had on the Hawaiians as well as the Native Americans, he never thought of such implications in the twenty-first century. They weren't talking about people who were without knowledge of modern medicine. True, they were both great civilizations and in no way stupid; they were just not prepared for the terrible disease brought to them by the white men who came to conquer them.

"What do *you* think the chances are for Dyna and the other patient?" Paul finally asked.

"I'd be a fool if I could give you an answer in either way. I'd like to say the healer is wrong and I will be able to pull off a miracle. This is an uncharted territory. It's entirely possible there will be other visitors from outer space in the future. This first contact will give us an idea of what we can do from a medical point of view when new cases of diseases we take for granted are contracted. I called back to the hospital where I work, and they are petitioning the university for a grant for us to study with the healers who came on other ships."

"You should talk to Rand about this. He's been in contact with all the colonies that have been established. He must know all of the healers."

"I'm way ahead of you, Paul. Rand contacted me after you talked to him the other night. He's working with medical personnel all over the world to get these people vaccinated. He was the one who suggested a conference of the healers."

"How—how did he get your number? I didn't...no, wait I did tell him about you and he asked for your number. I guess I forgot that part of the conversation. Things have all been happening so quickly."

Gene chuckled at how flustered Paul became. "The reason I came in here was to tell you Fragon thinks you need to eat and he has breakfast prepared for you."

"What about Tarena?"

"She's sleeping right now. She should be awake and ready for visitors by the time you finish eating."

Now that Paul was completely awake, he agreed with Gene. His stomach was growling, telling him he needed to eat. After glancing at the clock, he realized it was now after three in the afternoon. As he recalled, Fragon gave him the drink at ten the previous evening. He'd slept for over sixteen hours.

"I am hungry. I hope Fragon is a good cook."

"Take it from me, there is a woman who has come in to help us. She's a neighbor, an Earthling, who has been vaccinated. She's a great cook."

"I hope so. All of a sudden I'm so hungry I could eat a horse."

Gene laughed at Paul's statement. "Don't say that around her. She's a Native American and eating a horse is a big mistake."

Paul worked to smooth the wrinkles out of the clothes he'd put on the afternoon before. It was to no avail. He finally gave up and made his way to the kitchen.

It hadn't dawned on him before but as soon as he entered the kitchen, he recognized Emily Whitehorse. He'd met her several times when he'd come to visit Tarena and her parents.

"I've been talking to Professor Fragon and he tells me he gave you some of the fermented beverage he brought from his home planet. He was beginning to think it was too strong for your weak Earthling body to accept. What can I fix you for breakfast?"

"Whatever you're cooking smells great to me."

"I'm fixing some broth and fry bread for the patients who are battling the measles. I think you should have something a little more substantial. You sit down at the table. I make a mean omelet. That's what I made for Dr. Emery and Professor Fragon this morning and they seemed to approve of it."

Paul took a seat at the kitchen table. As he did, he imagined Tarena sitting at this very table eating her meals. He also let his mind wander to what he planned to ask her the night before. In his pocket he had the diamond ring he wanted to give her when he asked her to marry him. Weeks earlier, he'd posed the question to Fragon and received his permission for him to ask his only daughter to marry him.

Thinking of that conversation, he remembered the young man who was to be Tarena's husband and how he'd been lost in the meteor shower. He'd been surprised to learn of Fragon's son, who had also been on one of the ships in their fleet that had been lost.

How could these people accept so many personal losses and still fit into our society so easily? If I lost not only Kathy but also Tarena, I don't know how I would handle it.

Before he could dwell on his dark thoughts, Emily sat a plate with a gigantic omelet and two slices of toast slathered in butter before him.

"I see Emily has prepared a good meal for you."

Paul looked up to see Fragon standing in the doorway. "It looks like a feast fit for a king," he replied.

"I don't know what we would do without Emily and the other neighbors who have come to our aid during this time of tragedy. I just left Tarena and she is anxious to see you. Even with the spots that have come out all over her body, she is still my beautiful daughter."

"I'm anxious to see her too," he managed to say between bites of his midafternoon breakfast.

It didn't take him long to finish his meal and make his way to Tarena's darkened bedroom.

"Your father is right; even with the spots on your face, you're beautiful."

"No, I'm not, but it's nice of you to say."

"If your face was filled with ugly warts you would still be beautiful to me. I know the timing isn't right, but I want to ask you a question. Will you do me the honor of becoming my wife?"

"Wife? Are you sure? Have you asked Father?"

"My answer to all your questions is yes. It will be hard until I get my doctorate and, but once I do, we can talk about starting a family."

"How can I say no to you?" she asked, stifling a yawn. "I'm sorry,

I don't know why I'm so tired."

"I do. Your body is fighting the measles. I think it's time for you to take a nap while I go back to my apartment for a shower and a change of clothes."

Chapter Twenty-Six

Rand exited the jetway and entered the Laramie Airport. It seemed strange to be apart from Nina, but he didn't want to expose her to the measles. Even though she'd been given the vaccine, she was still expecting their first child and he didn't want to take any chances. Instead he'd sent her to Peru before he boarded his flight for Laramie.

His rental car was ready for him when he reached the rental desk. He smiled to see it was a luxury vehicle. With the government making his travel arrangements, he soon learned to expect only the best when he was on these trips.

It was a little after ten when he arrived at the campus where he and Paul spent four years getting their bachelor's degrees. This is where he was supposed to be getting his master's before his world turned upside down and he became an ambassador.

Before he left Washington, Paul gave him directions to his apartment. It was in a much better neighborhood than the apartment they shared for their last three years at the university.

He parked in front of the building and went up to Paul's apartment. To his surprise there was an envelope with his name on it taped to the door.

Rand,
Things aren't going well. Dyna is close to death. Please come over to Fragon's house and we will explain all.
Paul

Rand stuffed the note back into the envelope and put it in his pocket. By the time he reached Fragon's home, the number of cars parked in the driveway as well as at the curb told him something terrible must have happened. He drove around the block and finally found a parking place on the next street over.

The chill of winter brought back memories of the winters he'd spent in Laramie. One particular winter stood out because it was the year his first car decided to die on him. If it hadn't been for Paul he would have had to walk everywhere on campus. He thanked God they took many of the same classes and studied at the library at the same time. It took him almost six months to be able to find a car he could afford to buy.

Thinking back on those times made him marvel at how his life changed. He had a well-paying position with the government, a beautiful wife, and he would be a father in a matter of months. All through his college years, he thought only of becoming an archaeologist.

The arrival of Dragger and his party changed everything. Now the thought of being anything but an ambassador from the United States to these people all over the globe wasn't something he could even fathom.

His ramblings ceased as soon as he reached the door to Fragon's home. He barely raised his hand to knock when the door opened.

~ * ~

Paul saw Rand walking up to the house and hurried to open the door before his friend could knock, as he didn't want to disrupt the quiet of the household now in mourning.

"Is Dyna worse?" Rand asked as soon as Paul closed the door.

"Right now, she's holding her own, but both the healer and Gene don't hold out a lot of hope. One of the others who came down with the measles passed away about an hour ago. I thought I should prepare you before you went in."

"Thanks for thinking of that. I would have gone in without knowing and greeted everyone. Do you know what their funeral practices are?"

Paul nodded. "Fragon and I have been talking about these things for the past few days. It all depends on the region from where they came. These people use cremation but they tell me there are others who believe in mummification.

"I've met with some of the ones who use mummification. They are the ones who came to Egypt and taught the practice to the ancient

Egyptians. They've told me in recent times they have been practicing cremation because of the lack of space for the burial of the bodies."

"Now that you know what you're walking into, let's go in so you can speak with Fragon and the others. They've been waiting for your arrival."

~ * ~

Rand prepared himself to speak with the members of this small contingency of the aliens who had followed Fragon to the colder climate of Wyoming. These were the educators and scholars who worked with or studied under Fragon. On his other visits to the area, he'd been pleased to see how well they had assimilated into and been accepted by the community.

As soon as they entered the house, Fragon started to make introductions.

"That isn't necessary," Rand said. "I remember all the people in your community. I wish the circumstances around this visit were different."

The woman whose husband just died came up to Rand and took his hand in hers. "Do not be sad. My husband didn't tolerate being in the time warp well. He has been weakened ever since we arrived on Earth. Many times, he told me how he wished for death. Today his wish came true. It is for the best."

Rand couldn't believe how easily the woman accepted the things she was saying. He remembered when his foster parents died. He loved them dearly and couldn't accept the fact they were gone.

"Our world has much to learn from you," he said, for lack of any other words of sympathy.

"I have met many people since coming here. The ones who believe in the one god feel the same way. They cry and feel the loss, even though they know their loved one is with their God. You are young, one day, you will feel the same way. Being mated to Nina, you will soon come to see how important the one god is in her life."

Rand could only nod his head and take the woman's hand in his. In an archaic gesture, he brought her hand to his lips and lightly placed a kiss on it.

"I will keep you in my prayers," she said.

He knew she meant every word she spoke and once again marveled at her composure. "You are a strong woman. I pray Dyna is as strong in her fight against this disease that has entered her body."

Rand felt Fragon's hand on his shoulder. Looking up he saw the older man, a grave expression on his face.

"It is time for you to go in and see Dyna. She has willed herself to remain alive until your arrival. I think her moments of life are coming to an end."

"I am so sorry to hear this, Fragon. I feel inadequate to be the one to console you at this time in your life."

"Believe me, you are anything but inadequate. I have conferred with our priests during this time and they have assured me everything that has happened and will happen is the will of the One God. You were sent to our people who landed in Peru just as you were one of the first Earthlings to greet us in New Mexico. We couldn't have asked for a better man to take up our cause and make us feel welcome in this alien world."

Rand couldn't believe how humbled he felt. Never in his wildest imagination had he thought this was the path his life would take.

I told you great things were going to happen to you. Your mother and I are so proud of you. I have also talked directly with God and he tells me everything in your life was orchestrated before you were even born. All is as it should be. This should give you the wisdom you need for everything that is to come in your life.

Rand shook his head after hearing the voice of his 'father.' Ever since he started receiving the messages from beyond the grave, he realized neither of his 'parents' were far from him.

He allowed Fragon to direct him to the semi-darkened room where many of the aliens, including Tarena, sat vigil during Dyna's dying hours.

Even in the darkened room, he was able to make out the telltale spots of measles all over Dyna's face and arms.

"I knew you would come," she greeted Rand, holding out her hand toward him. "Are Nina and the child she carries safe from this disease?"

"Yes, the only outbreak has been in the United States, but everyone from your planet has agreed to be vaccinated. Right now, she is with her parents in Peru. Enough of my family, I am concerned for you."

"I appreciate your concern, but it is unnecessary. I knew before we left Plantas that my health was failing. I told Fragon to leave me behind, but he would hear nothing of it. He said we were a family and he could not envision building a new life without me. My concerns even worsened when I succumbed to time warp fever, not once, but twice. At that time, I prayed to the one god to take my life, but he assured me there were people on Earth I was destined to meet. He also said I needed to meet the man who was going to be mated with my daughter."

Rand smiled at what she just said, even though she knew it drained much of her remaining strength.

"You are a strong woman. I agree, my friend Paul and your daughter Tarena are destined to be together. I pray you will survive this setback and be able to see them married."

"Do not waste your prayers on something that is predestined to happen. Two other times, I have faced death and asked the one god to take my life. In both situations, He denied me the wishes in my heart. He has told me this is my time. I welcome it, as I have lived long enough to raise my daughter, see her happy and have met the man who will become her life mate. I have no regrets."

Rand pulled up a chair and sat next to her bed. Holding her hand in his, he silently prayed for God's will to be done. As he did, he felt Dyna's spirit rise from her body, hover over the room and finally go toward a bright light that seemed to illuminate the entire room.

Unmanly tears ran down his cheeks. Even though he didn't know Dyna as well as he did others of her race, he felt her loss deeply. She wasn't the first of her people to die since coming to Earth, but to him her death was the most significant. Her daughter was Nina's best friend and now his best friend would be making Tarena his wife. It saddened him to think she wouldn't be able to design a wedding robe for her daughter as Moora had for Nina. No matter what her status on her home planet, here he saw her as a leader who would be sorely missed.

"Did you see it?" he asked, when he finally got to his feet.

"What are you talking about?" Paul questioned.

"The light, the bright light that beckoned Dyna's spirit to return to the one god."

Paul shook his head as though he had no understanding of what Rand was saying.

"I think you're losing it, Buddy. I saw nothing."

"Do not despair about it, Paul," Fragon said as he put his hand on Paul's arm. "Rand could see the light of the one god coming to take Dyna's soul home because he is of the Gods. It doesn't mean you are any less pleasing to the one god but you are not descended from our ancient ancestors who once came to Earth as well as Nalo and Seros. Through Dyna, we have learned you were chosen for Tarena by the one god. She was a very spiritual woman both on our home planet of Plantas and here on Earth. In her final words she gave you her blessing."

Rand tended to agree with Fragon. His wife was a special woman and her passing had been orchestrated by a power far superior to any found on Earth or anywhere else in the Galaxy.

Chapter Twenty-Seven

Paul stood at the front of the church where not only his parents belonged, but where he and Kathy had been baptized and confirmed. This was his family's church and to be married elsewhere was something he couldn't imagine. Kathy had been married for several years and given him his precious niece and nephew. Her wedding, as well as the baptism of her children, had taken place in this church. It was only fitting to continue the tradition.

Rand stood beside him. In contrast to the wedding between Rand and Nina, they wore tuxedos. He'd been assured Tarena was wearing a traditional white wedding gown, like the one Kathy wore several years earlier. Rather than an unworldly wedding, this one was steeped in the traditions of his family.

"I sort of miss those wedding robes we wore at your wedding. Why do you think Fragon agreed to this?"

"Fragon is a man of learning. Unlike Dragger, who is a scholar of history, he looks to the future and the assimilation of his people into the societies of Earth. By allowing Tarena to become a high school teacher, he has made it clear he is happy with his surroundings as well as the future of his people."

"I guess you're right. I'm glad Tarena wanted to wait until after Nina had the baby so that she can be the maid of honor. I was also pleased when your birth family were able to come to the wedding. At least I know they will be taking good care of your daughter."

"I think you're too concerned about other things, my friend. Today is your wedding day and the only thing you should be concentrating on is that beautiful woman who is going to be your wife."

Paul laughed. He was looking forward to the moment when he said "I do" and would seal his life to Tarena's for eternity.

~ * ~

Tarena stood at the back of the small church where Paul's family worshipped every Sunday. Surrounded by her bridesmaids, she knew this was a special moment. In a matter of minutes, she would become mated to Paul for the rest of her life.

"Are you nervous?" Nina, asked.

"Nervous, apprehensive, frightened and excited all at the same time."

"At least you've had time to plan for today. As I recall on our wedding day, Rand surprised me. I didn't even know my mother had been working on my wedding robe."

Thinking of the beautiful, traditional robe Nina's mother had fashioned for her brought an unwanted lump to Tarena's throat. Her mother was supposed to be at her side today, fussing over the dress she wore. Even though it was not traditional, her mother would have fussed over her. Only now, that wasn't possible. Since her mother's passing, Tarena had learned much about the 'childhood' diseases of the Earthlings. What should have been a mild infection had taken her mother's life.

I am never far from you, my beloved daughter. On this, the most special day of your life, you are the most beautiful of women. I am pleased you have chosen to wear a dress like those of Paul's people. May you be as happy with Paul as I was with your father.

"Are you all right?" Nina asked.

"My mother's spirit was communicating with me. She has given me her blessing and even approves of the dress I chose to wear today."

Nina's smile was so different than the one she'd usually graced Tarena with, before the baby was born. Bridget Marie had been named for Rand's foster mother. Now Nina's smile was that of a mother and one who loved her daughter more than anyone could have ever imagined. It was as though Tarena's mother was smiling at her from beyond.

"I don't know why she wouldn't be confirming your choice of gown for your wedding. Of all our people, she was one of the first to comfortably adapt to the dress of the Earthlings."

Before either girl could say more, the music of the processional began. Tarena watched as first Paul's mother and father were escorted to the pew at the front of the church. One by one, each of her attendants made the walk down the aisle to where Paul, along with his groomsmen, stood.

She smiled when she saw the minister who had been counseling them on the meaning and responsibility of marriage standing side by side with the priest who accompanied them on the prolonged journey from their home planet to Earth.

"Are you ready, Daughter?" her father whispered in her ear.

"Yes, Father, but are you? I know Paul and I are moving into your house until he finishes his doctorate. Will you be content living in the same house as us?"

"Paul and I meant this for a surprise, but the house will be yours for as long as the two of you will need it. Your mother's spirit and I will be very comfortable in Paul's apartment. I will be close enough to be able to assist you and yet far enough away for you to have your independence. I've even decided to take a cooking class at the vocational school."

Tarena smiled. She knew all about the plans Paul and her father thought were so secret. She'd overheard them talking about it when they thought she was busy in the kitchen preparing them an evening meal several days ago.

The tone of the music changed, and they began the walk that would take her from loving daughter to cherished wife.

~ * ~

Paul watched as two of Tarena's friends, one of her people and one of her fellow teachers at the high school, came down the long aisle. Behind them came his sister, Kathy. As soon as they stood with them at the altar, he knew Nina would come down the aisle followed by Tarena being escorted by her father.

The moment he first saw her, he felt his heart skip a beat. The woman he loved had never looked lovelier. Radiance seemed to stream from her face, even though it was hidden by a lace veil.

"Who gives this woman in marriage to this man?"

Although he expected the words the minister spoke, they came as a surprise and broke the spell woven within his mind by the sight of the woman he loved.

"The spirit of her mother and I do," Fragon replied.

For the first time Fragon turned toward Paul. In a loving gesture, the older man pulled him into a tight embrace before placing Tarena's delicate hand in Paul's larger one.

The remainder of the service passed in a blur until the priest of Tarena's people said, "I now pronounce the two of you mated in the eyes of men as well as the 'One God.' What the one god has sealed, let no one or nothing ever tear apart."

Without further prompting, Paul lifted the veil and for the first time saw Tarena's beautiful face without the lace that had been hiding it from his view. Feeling as smitten as he had when he first saw her at Rand's wedding, he leaned closer and pressed his lips against her eager ones.

From the congregation came applause and comments, but Paul didn't care. He had the woman he loved in his arms and he never wanted to let her go.

Chapter Twenty-Eight

Rand was anxious to return to his home in Peru. He'd been traveling for the last month. Even with being in contact with Nina via video chat, he still missed her. Usually she and the children, Bridget and Ragnar, accompanied them on his trips. Now, the advanced stage of her third pregnancy made her accompanying him an impossibility. He prayed he would be in time to be there for the birth.

As he waited in Buenos Aires for his connecting flight, his cell phone began to ring.

"Jacobson," he answered automatically.

"Hey, Buddy, why so formal?" Paul asked.

"Habit," he replied. "Are you already at the complex?"

"We arrived last night. Thank goodness for that landing strip Dragger and his people put in up here. Tarena was anxious to get here and the kids were getting cranky. I certainly didn't want to have to drive up that mountain in the dark."

"How is your family? You know, this is the first time I'll get to meet your twins."

"You won't find them to be too social. They're at that age where they just want their mother."

"I remember that age all too well. Did Nina tell you we've been able to establish a video link between Earth, Seros, and Nalo?"

"No, when did that happen?"

"From what Nina tells me, her team, as well as teams from the other planets, made contact a couple of weeks ago. If she hasn't told you, I'm sure she wants to keep it as a surprise. She's been in contact with Ragnar for some time, but they just contacted a man named Grato on Nalo."

"Are you sure his name is Grato?"

Paul's question came as a surprise to Rand. "Positive, why?"

"That's the name of the man Tarena was to marry. I don't know how I will feel about her being in contact with him."

"From what I heard, the ship he was on was the only one to make it to Nalo. I'd think you'd be excited for Tarena to contact him. Don't tell me you're jealous?"

"Okay, I won't, but for so long she's thought he was dead. I don't know she'll handle it."

"You're worried for nothing. I felt the same way about Ragnar and Nina, but with him so far away and settled into his new life, I'm just happy she's able to be in contact with him. You'll see, it will be the same way with Tarena. Anyway, take my word for it. I've got to run. They're calling for me to board my plane. I'll see you when I get there."

~ * ~

Paul disconnected his phone and made his way back to the compound where Tarena and Nina were fussing over the twins.

As much as the thought of Tarena contacting her former fiancé bothered him, he put all thoughts of it behind him. Instead he concentrated on his identical twin daughters, Dyna for Tarena's mother, and Janice for his mother. They were only three months old, but already were making their individual personalities known. While Dyna was content to wait for her feedings, Janice was demanding and always ready to be fed before her older more docile sister.

"I just heard the best news," Tarena greeted him. "Nina told me we will be able to video conference with not only Ragnar on Seros, but also Grato on Nalo."

"So I heard."

"How did you hear?" Nina asked.

"I just talked to Rand. He's quite excited about this reunion."

"As we all are," Tarena replied. "If it hadn't been for Ragnar's communication's officer it would have never happened. After he heard about our ship landing on Earth, he was convinced at least one other ship in the group going to Nalo survived. He kept trying and finally found he was right. The ship carrying Grato along with many others made it through the meteor shower with only minimal damage."

"I don't know how I feel about you making contact with Grato," Paul confessed.

"Are you jealous?" Nina asked.

To hear Nina echo the words Rand spoke only minutes earlier came as a shock. "I guess I am. I mean Tarena knew him first and had things been different..."

"Had things been different," Tarena finished his sentence, "I would have never met and married a man who I love more than life itself. Now stop being silly. We're all grateful to the one god to learn that at least some of the party that was sent to Nalo survived."

Paul thought about how foolish he felt for doubting Tarena's love for him. It didn't matter that Grato survived and made a life on Nalo. He and Tarena were living a life he'd never thought would be his to live. In another year he would have his masters and begin his teaching career. His parents were pleased to think he'd be teaching in Laramie where they'd be close to their two newest granddaughters.

"I guess I am being silly. How much do you know about what Grato has been doing with his life?"

He wondered if he only imagined the catch in Tarena's voice. "We'll know more tonight, when we make contact, but from what Nina tells me, they have had a harder time on Nalo than we have had here on Earth and Ragnar has on Seros. We do know he has been mated with one of the women from their party."

"Does that make you sad?"

"How could I be sad to think he has found a mate to share his life? I would hate to think of him going through life alone when I have such a beautiful family."

Paul took her in his arms and kissed her tenderly. "I guess I'm just extremely worried about ever losing you. I can't believe how lucky I am to have found you at my best friend's wedding."

~ * ~

Rand marveled at the beauty of the complex built on the perimeter of the Nazca Lines. His favorite sight in the entire world was seeing the area from the air when his plane was preparing to land at the airstrip the engineers among Dragger's people had constructed.

As the plane taxied to a stop near the terminal, he thought about Paul's reaction to the news that Grato had landed safely on Nalo. While he was excited to speak with and see Ragnar as well as Grato, he was beginning to wonder if he should be as jealous as Paul seemed to be.

As soon as the plane landed, Rand hurried to get off and into the terminal where he knew Nina waited for him. He didn't worry about his luggage. His bags would be delivered to their cottage so there was no need for him to wait for it to be unloaded. Being a diplomat did have its perks.

He was surprised to see Paul waiting for him. "Where is Nina?"

"Don't panic, Buddy. The girls are getting ready for the big reunion."

"I don't think me coming home is such a big reunion. What's there to get ready?"

Paul laughed at Rand's question. "Not you, silly. I mean the video chat with Ragnar and Grato tonight."

"I didn't think I'd hear you being excited about that."

"To be truthful, neither did I, but Tarena made me see this whole thing in an entirely different light. She's pleased to know at least some of their people made it to Nalo. Now, let's get back to your place. I think the girls have a special meal planned for us. You know how they are when it comes to working in the kitchen. They each try to outdo each other."

"Speaking of kitchen skills, how is your father-in-law coming in the cooking department?"

Again, Paul paused to laugh at what Rand said. "To be truthful, I'm glad Tarena is such a good cook, because otherwise, I'm afraid Fragon would starve to death. He's a great mathematician but his skills in the kitchen leave a lot to be desired. Of course, we don't see as much of him as we used to because he's started seeing a great woman. Her name is Judith."

"You don't mean Judith Lowe, do you?'

"One and the same. She was his instructor in the cooking class. I think she took pity on him because of his lack of skills. Anyway, they've become quite the item. Tarena assures me her mother agrees with their friendship. I quit asking how she knows things like this a while ago. She definitely has a link with her mother, even after her death."

"I can understand," Rand commented. "I hear the voices of my foster parents all the time. At first it was frightening, but now I find it very comforting. I'm sure it's the same with Tarena."

The last of the afternoon sun was slipping behind the mountains as they made their way to Rand and Nina's cottage. He could smell the odors of cooking food even before they opened the door.

As soon as they stepped inside, Rand was attacked by his children, each vying for his attention so they could tell him about their adventures while he was gone. He gave each of them their turn before turning his attention to Nina. Her pregnancy was definitely in the final days, but even with her protruding belly, she was the most beautiful woman in the world to him.

~ * ~

"Are you excited about being able to see Nina tonight?" Geni asked.

Ragnar looked up from his supper. "Excited and a little apprehensive. It's one thing to know Nina is married and has children. It will be another to see her with the man she has mated with."

"Do you think she will be worried about seeing you with me?" Geni teased.

"I hope not. I've told her how special you are to me. She's wished me well as I have her."

Together they walked to the communications center that had been set up at the compound. Being winter, they made the compound their home so Ragnar would be close to the University Hospital and Geni would have access to the lab.

"Can we watch too?" six-year-old Audra asked. "I want to see the children."

"I see no harm in it, but the children you are looking forward to seeing might not be there," Geni said. "They are much younger than you.

They might be in bed."

"I thought you said Bridget was only a little younger than me."

"We did, but checking the time between here and Earth, it is night there. That's the time when children, no matter their ages, should be in bed sleeping."

"I don't understand. The suns are shining brightly here."

Ragnar laughed at his daughter's innocent statement. "Times are different in all parts of the galaxy. Even though it is daytime here, I've been told it will be evening on Earth and late night on Nalo."

Audra pretended to pout, but soon decided it would be more fun to be playing outside with her friends than watching the screen in the communication center.

Once Geni and Ragnar were alone, they made their way to the communication center. The officer in charge was working diligently to maintain the connection.

Almost at once, the screen in front of them came to life. The first image on the split screen was that of Grato. The healer in Ragnar was immediately concerned. He recalled his friend as a robust man in his early twenties. The man who dominated the screen looked much older.

"Grato, is that you?"

"It most certainly is. It's good to see you Ragnar. From what the communications officer has told me you have done well. I hear you are not only a healer but also a college professor."

"That's true, and this is my wife, Geni. What do you do on Nalo?"

"You know my expertise was farming. Of course, my parents insisted I study engineering. The farming here is very different from on Plantas. I am glad I have been able to put my engineering degree to use. I have been helping with many building projects but I've been unable to do the heavy lifting I once did. The trip to Nalo was harrowing to say the least. Even before we were trapped in the meteor shower, I suffered from time warp fever. Of all the ships in our contingency, we were the only ones to make it to Nalo. I've recently been told about the ship carrying Tarena and her father's party and how they were able to land on Earth."

"You do know she has taken a husband from among the Earthlings?"

"Yes, and for that I am pleased. I too have found a mate to share my life. She will be joining me soon. Her name is Wasla. She lost the man she was promised to in the meteor shower. He was on the second ship in our party. The storm hit right after we cleared the area, meaning our ship was safe, but the others were lost. At least we thought they were. I can hardly believe in a short amount of time I will once again see Tarena and know she is happy."

The other side of the screen came to life. Ragnar was immediately looking into the faces of both Nina and Tarena along with the men they married. He was a bit concerned about the fact that Nina's face looked a bit puffy, but seeing a full shot of her, made him realize she was in the advanced stages of pregnancy. Nina's husband, Rand, looked every bit the government official, while Tarena's husband, Paul, was dressed more casually.

"I can't believe you actually survived the meteor shower, Grato. I've also been told you have taken Wasla as your mate."

"Yes, she will be here soon. Her man was on one of the ships that was lost. As you know she was trained as a healer and took care of me while I was sick with time warp fever."

For a moment it was as if none of the old friends could find the words to express themselves. Once the awkwardness of the situation wore off, they all seemed to be talking at once.

Ragnar marveled at the different paths their lives had taken. His desire had been to be a healer and married to Nina. It had been given up when she was sent to Earth and he went to Seros. Now he was married to a woman who meant the world and all to him. They also had a beautiful daughter.

Nina, on the other hand, was the wife of a government official and would soon be the mother to three young children.

It was the same with Tarena and Grato. Their lives were so on track until a meteor shower changed everything.

It was as though the one god orchestrated their lives and each of them were happy with their chosen mates. Their futures were bright and their children would be the next generations to mold the worlds into which they had been born. In time there would be no natural inhabitants and aliens. They would all be as one, as the one god desired.

About the Author

Sherry Derr-Wille began her writing career in her sophomore English class in high school. Challenged to get an A on the first test she won the right to sit in the back of the room and write for a year. At the end of the year no one told her to stop the assignment so she didn't at her 40th class reunion, she realized she was the only one who enjoyed the assignment. It was too late because by that time she'd signed seventeen contracts for her work.

Wife to her high school sweetheart of over fifty years, she is the mother of three, grandmother of nine and great-grandmother of five. She is retired and lives in a mid-sized town close to the Illinois border in Southern Wisconsin. Her mantra is READ LOCAL AND BE TRANSPORTED TO ANOTHER WORLD.

Sky Eyes

When Sky Eyes learns she is white, her world is turned upside down. She is no longer welcomed in the Indian village where she was raised. Instead, her white uncle has found her and she must live in the white world as Kathryn Clay. When the facts surrounding her upbringing jeopardize her future in their midst, Kathryn runs away to begin a new life where no one will know of the people who raised her.

Lukas Palmer is intrigued by Kathryn's beauty from the moment he first sees her. Even the journey east to bring friends and relatives to the wild Wisconsin territory didn't quench his desire for her.

CHAPTER ONE

Morning Star's breasts hung heavy with milk. Just six suns ago she'd given birth to twins and her body was now producing enough milk for both babies. In the night, the spirit of death came and took one of the babies to the land of the ancestors leaving only one child to drain her breasts of their heaviness.

Even though she mourned the passing of her daughter, she knew there was still work to be done. Now, with her husband, Running Deer, at her side and her son strapped to her back, she walked toward the river looking for the edible plants to be harvested and dried to be used during the coming winter.

Off to one side, she heard the cries of a child. "Did you hear that?"

"I did, but it is nothing we should concern ourselves with. There is a white settler's cabin close by and it is possible they have a child. It is only calling for its mother."

The wails of the child became louder and Morning Star couldn't help but stray from her husband's side to investigate.

The cabin of the white settlers was constructed of logs and looked very strange to Morning Star. The cries of the infant from inside the cabin grew louder and more demanding. Knowing she shouldn't go any further, Morning Star continued to walk toward the cabin to investigate.

Inside she saw a very young woman lying on a raised bed, her breaths sounding shallow. The babe had been placed beside her and screamed her protests because of an empty belly, at least that was what Morning Star thought.

The white woman opened her eyes, but showed no fear. To Morning Star's surprise, the woman spoke to her in her own tongue.

"My name is Martha and this is my baby. I am dying."

"How is it you speak my language?"

"My husband, Robert, was trained and sent to this area to minister to the tribes. He taught me. Unfortunately, he was killed in an accident several moons ago. He is buried behind the cabin. Now I will be joining him. Will you take my daughter? Her name is Kathryn."

The words Martha spoke seemed to have drained all of her strength. She closed her eyes and almost immediately her breathing stopped.

As though to protest the loss of her mother the baby cried even louder than before.

"What are you doing in here woman?"

Morning Star turned at the sound of her husband's voice.

"The woman, Martha, spoke to me in our language. She said her husband was killed and is buried in the back of the cabin. Now she has joined him in death. She begged me to take her child. I think it is best if we bury her beside her husband. When the task is done, burn this cabin."

"How could she speak in our language?"

"She said she was trained to speak our language because her husband was to minister to our people. I do not understand the meaning of this, but I cannot leave this child to die when I have more than enough milk for two babies."

Running Deer shook his head. "You make sense, but what will the others say about us taking a white child into our midst?"

"I do not care. Don't you think the Great Spirit has sent her to us to replace the daughter the spirit of death took from me in the night? She needs me as much as I need her."

"Of course, you are right. I will bury the woman beside her husband. Once I have finished, I will burn the cabin. If we are going to take this child, what will we call her?"

Morning Star picked up the crying child, giving her comfort. Once the crying stopped, the child looked at her in wonder. "Her mother called her Katheryn. Of course, that is not a name of our people. Just look at her eyes. They are the color of the sky. I will call her Sky Eyes."

With the baby properly named, Morning Star bared her breast and allowed the child to take her engorged nipple into her mouth. While she nursed the baby, Running Deer prepared the woman for burial. He took several of the items from the cabin to put into the grave with her. After wrapping Martha in one of the blankets, he handed another to Morning Star.

She smiled her thanks. Until she could return to her home and retrieve the cradleboard, she had thought would go unused, she could carry the baby in the blanket.

Morning Star sat in the sun and nursed her son while Sky Eyes slept. From behind the cabin, she could hear her husband preparing the grave for the woman and her belongings. She knew he would bury her with the same traditions he had used to bury their daughter earlier in the day. What started as a day of sorrow for Morning Star had turned into one of joy. She would raise the white woman's child as though it was her own. When Sky Eyes was old enough, she would tell her of her white mother who entrusted her daughter to a strange woman in order to spare her life. When she told her of all of this, she would also give her back her white name of Kathryn.

Her eyes were becoming heavy when Running Deer returned to the front of the cabin. "I see both children are contently sleeping. It is almost time for us to return to the village. Have you thought of how you will explain this child when people ask where she has come from?"

"I will tell them the truth. The Great Spirit saw my anguish over losing my daughter to the spirit of death. While the spirit of death waited to claim this child's mother, he sent me to rescue the child and raise it as my own."

"I pray what you are doing is the right thing. I too mourn the loss of our daughter but I am not certain how our people will react to this white child. She is innocent, but I have heard terrible stories of what the whites have done to the tribes to the east of us."

Although Running Deer told her he intended to burn down the cabin, he left it intact when it was time to return to the village.

"Are you not going to burn the cabin?"

"I will do it later. For now, we must return to our home. The sun is going down and I do not want to put you or the children in danger. There are animals in the forest who could hurt you badly. It is best if we return to the village. Besides, this child was present when her mother died. We do not know how much a child remembers, but her day has been hard. It is not proper for her to be present when I burn the house that was meant to be her home."

Morning Star agreed with her husband. She did not want this new daughter to harbor dark memories of, not only the death of her natural mother, but also, the loss of the home her parents worked so hard to build to shelter her from birth to when she became a woman.

~ * ~

Once they returned to their lodge, the woman everyone called Old Grandmother greeted them. "I knew it. I knew the Great Spirit would look kindly upon you this day. When I heard you mourning the loss of your girl child, I prayed to the Great Spirit to give you comfort. Not long after my prayer I had a vision of you finding a cabin of a white settler in the forest. I saw you go into the cabin and rescue this child from the horrors of the death of her mother. Seeing you return to this village as a complete family I know the vision from the Great Spirit was right and true."

"I, too, believe the Great Spirit sent me to the cabin to rescue this child as a replacement for my own daughter. Had I not heard her cries of hunger, I would have never gone into the cabin. With her final breath, her mother begged me to take her child and raise her as my own. She also told me the child's name is Kathryn but I have named her Sky Eyes. I will hold her white name in my heart and when the time is right, I will tell her of her origins and the woman who loved her enough to entrust her care to a stranger."